The WIDOW *and the* HIGHLANDER

PARADIGM
PRESS

MARTHA KEYES

1

West Inverness-shire, Scotland 1762

The only warmth in the library at Dunverlockie Castle emanated from the teacup Christina MacKinnon held in her hand. The room was otherwise dim, the sole window letting in the dreary grays of a sky emptied of its rain only an hour ago. Every now and then, a laugh rang out from the drawing room down the corridor, echoing eerily until it reached Christina.

She stared blankly at the little wisps of steam that curled into the air and disappeared. The tea was almost gone—she had been so eager for its warmth, she hadn't even waited for it to cool fully.

All the formal parts of her husband's funeral were over, but she knew it would likely be some time—days, even—before everyone would depart. That time couldn't come soon enough.

She set the teacup down and put a hand to the long piece of foolscap sitting on the desk beside it. It was gratitude she *should* feel to see the document. But instead, it felt like a weight. She didn't want to inherit Dunverlockie. But she couldn't deny she needed it. Her family needed it. And, whatever her feelings, it belonged to her now, with all its cold, stony corridors and their unwelcome memories.

Her dying father had taken no risks when he'd married her to Gordon MacKinnon. If he was going to sink such a large portion of his money into a fledgling estate like Dunverlockie, he had wanted to ensure that Christina was taken care of in the unlikely event that she was ever widowed.

It had all seemed so distant and improbable when the arrangements had been made, but her father's stipulations in the marriage contract had proven wise. Christina had no doubt the MacKinnons would be turning her out of the castle now, leaving her to her own devices if it weren't for the paper before her.

Footsteps approached—the strong gait of a man—and Christina felt her muscles tighten instinctively. She forced herself to relax. Gordon was gone. She needn't react that way anymore. She hated that she ever had.

The latch lifted, and Angus MacKinnon appeared, his dark hair mussed from having removed his wig. It was he who would have been inheriting Dunverlockie if not for the arrangements Christina's father had made with Gordon. As things stood now, though, he had been shifted back a place in the succession. He couldn't mind so terribly much. He was already laird of Benleith, a grander estate than this one.

Angus smiled at her and closed the door behind him, eyes flitting to the desk. In his hand, he held a folded paper.

"How are you, Christina?" He approached the desk. The smell of whisky hung about him, and she didn't miss the redness of his eyes. They drooped with a hint of laziness born of drink. Had any of the MacKinnon men been sober for more than the time they spent asleep in the past few days?

She rose from her chair, straightening her black petticoats. She never felt entirely at ease with Angus, for all his civility, and she felt even less so with him intoxicated. She should go check on Elizabeth. There were so many men in the castle, and Christina trusted none of them—nor did she trust her sister's ability to control her sharp tongue.

"I am tired," she answered, "but well enough."

He nodded at the various papers scattered over the desk. "It is quite a load to take on, is it not?"

She glanced at them and managed a smile. "Yes, it is. I imagine it will take some time to understand it all."

He unfolded the papers in his hands. "I have a few more things for you to sign. Tallach left them with me after the burial."

Christina suppressed a sigh and sat back down. She must have signed a hundred papers since Gordon's abrupt illness and passing.

He set a few sheets in front of her. "Just a few more formalities associated with the funeral. That is all."

She gave a passing glance at the top of the first paper—yet another document from Gordon's man of business.

He peered over her shoulder at the cup of tea. "Can I get you more tea? There's some in the drawing room I could fetch."

"Thank you, but no," she said, dipping her quill and scratching her signature across the bottom of the sheet.

"Ah," he said with a crooked smile. "I had forgotten. Gordon told me you were particular about your tea."

She gave a perfunctory smile then blew on the ink and moved that page aside.

Angus moved to stand behind her, setting a hand on the back of the chair. Whether it was a possessive stance or merely one to stabilize himself, she couldn't be sure, but it made her uncomfortable.

"I could help you, you know," he said. "With the estate, I mean. As I said, it is a lot to manage—a man's job. All these papers and signatures are only the beginning, I'm afraid. You will be managing tacks, bills with tradesmen, salaries for servants, disputes among the tenants—"

"Yes, I understand," she said, trying to conceal the testiness she felt. She hardly needed the reminder of what she was taking on as the heir of Dunverlockie. Gordon hadn't involved her in any of the estate matters.

In many ways, laying the burden on Angus's shoulders was tempting. But only for a moment. He made her uneasy—the entirety of the MacKinnon clan did, including her late husband —and she hardly wished to surrender any of her power or freedom now that she finally had some.

"You needn't worry yourself on my account," she said. "You have plenty to occupy you with matters at Benleith."

"Oh, things are well enough in hand there—I may have to venture there now and again for short visits, but, I assure you, I shall not leave you here to fend for yourself. I will stay until things are in order."

She glanced up at him. He was smiling, but she couldn't help feeling there had been a hint of threat in his words. Did he worry she would make a bungle of things at Dunverlockie? That she was putting something in jeopardy he had a chance at ownership in? If she died now, Dunverlockie would go to Angus.

She signed the last paper and rubbed her temples, feeling the beginnings of a headache coming on. Angus gathered the papers together, and Christina rose, hoping to end this interaction and go in search of her sister, Elizabeth.

Angus didn't move, though, from his spot behind her chair, and she tried to shift away from him. He stopped fiddling with the papers and looked at her as intently as his unfocused, bloodshot eyes would allow.

"Let me help you, Christina." He came so near she had to blink away his pungent breath. "I could do more than just manage the estate for you, you know."

He put a hand to her waist, and she swallowed down the nausea as she took two steps backward.

"I could take care of you," he said. "Properly. As a wife. You wouldn't need to worry your head over anything."

She took another step back, but it was matched by his own step forward, and panic began to build within her.

"You have been drinking, Angus," she said, trying for a lighter tone than her fear demanded she use. "You know not what you are saying." She turned away from him and put more distance between them, heartbeat pounding in her ears. Angus had a reputation for being determined.

"On the contrary." He followed her slowly but purposefully, his eyes glittering as they took her in. "I never think more clearly than with a few glasses of whisky in me."

The door opened behind Christina, and she startled at the sound.

Elizabeth's dark eyes moved from Christina to Angus, taking in the situation.

"There you are, Christina." Elizabeth's gaze stayed trained on Angus. "I was looking for you. Can I have a word with you?"

"Yes, yes," Christina said. "We were just finishing some matters of business."

Angus's mouth was pulled into a wry, almost mocking, smile, but he nodded.

"You know where to find me if you need me." He ran a hand along the crease in the stack of papers he held and walked to the door, nodding at Elizabeth with a hint of displeasure in his expression.

Christina waited until the door closed behind him then turned from her sister, shutting her eyes in relief. She didn't want Elizabeth to see how Angus affected her. Elizabeth, though younger, had grown protective of Christina in her time at Dunverlockie, and she was impulsive enough that she might well do something rash if she felt Angus was importuning Christina.

Gordon had disliked Elizabeth intensely, calling her all manner of names for her habit of unapologetically contradicting him. Angus seemed to be developing the same animus toward her.

Christina had once had the same fire as Elizabeth within her, but she had learned to guard her tongue more carefully since her marriage. It had become a matter of survival. Gordon had done much more than call her names when he found her unyielding.

Elizabeth came up beside her, putting a hand on her arm. "Was he troubling you?"

Christina swallowed and shook her head, turning toward her sister and mustering a smile. "No. Just having me sign a few more papers. It seems Tallach always has more."

Elizabeth continued to watch Christina, as though she didn't believe her. She was lighter in coloring than Christina, her hair a sturdy brown rather than black. Her tongue could be soft as freshly churned butter or sharp as a tack.

Elizabeth finally sighed and let her hand drop. "He makes my skin crawl. Even more than Gordon did. It must be a MacKinnon trait, for I cannot so much as walk past the drawing room without feeling it. What Father was thinking, marrying you into this family..." She shook her head.

"He knew he was dying. He was merely trying to ensure we were cared for." Christina had said those words to herself a hundred times. He hadn't known what Gordon was like—what the MacKinnons were like. Gordon had been very capable of playing the punctilious gentleman when the occasion required it.

He had fooled them all, in truth. There had been very little of the gentleman in him.

Elizabeth walked over to the desk and brushed her finger

along the feather of the quill. "Ensuring we were cared for and ruining himself in the process. It will be a miracle if we can ever afford to stop renting out Melmuir."

"Well, we hardly have need of it with Alistair off fighting in the Colonies." Their family estate in Kininfar had been rented out ever since their father's death over a year ago, and Alistair had enlisted almost three years ago now. With all of their father's investments poured into Dunverlockie, there had been nothing left for Melmuir and the failed harvest the year of his death.

"Yes," Elizabeth said, "but when the war is over, I imagine he will sell out, and then what?"

Christina shrugged. "He will come here. Or go stay with Aunt Dorothy. I imagine he will wish to see the others after so much time." Christina's younger siblings, including Elizabeth, had gone to stay with their aunt and uncle after their father's death. It was only a few months ago that Elizabeth had made the journey to Dunverlockie, apparently sensing from Christina's letters that all was not well there.

"I suppose so," Elizabeth said. "You intend to keep it, then? Dunverlockie, I mean."

Christina lifted her shoulders. "I have little choice in the matter."

"Surely you have *all* the choice in the matter. That is what it means to own it, does it not? Why not sell it? Be done with this wretched place! You can buy something smaller and more comfortable, far away from here."

Christina said nothing for a moment, setting her hands on the cold stone ledge of the window. Her first emotion on the death of Gordon had been relief, followed by guilt—and then hope. Hope that perhaps she finally had the power to leave it all behind.

But it hadn't been long before the hope was extinguished. "I may be the legal owner of Dunverlockie, Elizabeth, but surely you have come to know the MacKinnons well enough to realize that they would never allow me to sell it."

"How could they possibly stop you? It is yours to do with as you please."

Christina shot Elizabeth a look. "They would prevent the sale. They have the influence for it. Believe me. I have been thinking this through for days now. No one wants to be free of this place more than I."

Elizabeth gave a resigned sigh and sat down in the chair. "I suppose you are right. If nothing else, though, at least the place is free of Gordon."

"Yes," Christina said softly. Dunverlockie was free of Gordon's physical presence, but she doubted it would ever be truly free of his influence and memory.

There was a longer pause, and when Elizabeth spoke, it was with a touch of hesitation in her voice. "Shall you marry again? With an estate like this, you would have plenty of—"

"No." Christina's voice sounded harsh even to her, and Elizabeth looked at her with wide eyes, as though she had been snapped at. "Forgive me, but I have no desire to marry again. None at all."

"Not a marriage like the one you've just endured, of course," Elizabeth replied. "But not every marriage is thus, and not every man is a MacKinnon—thank heaven for that."

Christina only shook her head. Perhaps there *were* men unlike Gordon and Angus and their kinsmen, but Christina had no intention of finding out. She had been mistaken in her judgment of a man once; she would not court the same error again.

2

L achlan Kincaid tossed a clump of hay into one of the stables at Glengour Inn then rested his arm on the pitchfork and watched as the gelding began eating eagerly.

"Aye, eat up," he said with a smile. He loved the smell of fresh hay and the sound of crunching horses made as they ate it. Chomping noises filled the stables just now, crowded to bursting as it was. If he was permitted to spend the majority of his time at Glengour in the stables, he would be content enough.

"Talkin' ta the horses already, are ye?"

Lachlan turned his head to find Glenna Douglas standing in the doorway of the stable, a basket on her hip and her cheek streaked with dirt.

"Ye've no' been here more than a few hours," she said.

Lachlan chuckled and set the pitchfork back in its place. "I canna thank ye enough, Glenna. For convincin' Mr. Gibson ta take me on."

She sent a glance over her shoulder and took a step into the stables, saying in a kind voice. "'Twas the least I could do. After all yer father did for my family. 'Tis only thanks ta him my family is still here, ye ken."

"Aye," he said softly. Before his father's execution, he had ensured a forty-year lease for the Douglases. It had been one of his last acts—and a perfect representation of the sort of laird he had been. "But ye dinna ken *me*. Ye were just a bairn when everythin' happened. Ye've simply trusted my word that I am who I say I am."

She looked at him with a crooked smile. "I assure ye, no one would come *here* and claim to be a Kincaid without verra good reason, sir. 'Twould be foolhardy at best in a place brimmin' with MacKinnons."

"I suppose so," he said with a wry smile. "I didna intend ta tell anyone my real name, but when I heard ye say ye were a Douglas"—he shook his head—"well, I ken how my father felt about yer family, and I could see the goodness in yer eyes."

She gave him a grateful look. "Ye have my word I willna tell anyone yer secret, sir."

He grimaced. "Ye mustn't call me *sir*, Glenna. Unless ye wish my time here ta be short-lived. Besides, ye've no reason ta refer ta me in such a way. I have nothin' ta my name but a few coins and the clothes on my back. I'm no one here."

Glenna shook her head, the smile disappearing from her face. "Ye're wrong about that. The Kincaid name still holds weight here."

"I'm glad ta hear it," he replied with genuine feeling. His father had been a good laird, but it had been more than fifteen years since a Kincaid had inhabited Dunverlockie. "But remember, the name I'm goin' by is Murray."

"Of course. 'Tis best ye remain unknown. Mr. Gibson has always been close with the MacKinnons, and he's sure to pass along anythin' he discovers about ye. Though, they're all too taken up with the funeral ta notice much of anythin' right now."

She rearranged one of the dirty towels in her basket so that it wasn't at risk of falling out.

Lachlan's brows drew together. "The funeral?"

She looked up, tilting her head to the side. "Aye. The laird of Dunverlockie. He died a few days ago. The funeral was on Tuesday. I imagined ye kent already, what with all the MacKinnons stayin' here at the inn."

He shook his head. "I didna realize they were MacKinnons." He looked at her intently. "Ye mean ta say Gordon MacKinnon is dead?"

She nodded. "Sudden-like. Healthy one day and dead three days later. They say 'twas a fever."

Lachlan put a hand to the hair on his chin and pulled at it thoughtfully. He had little sympathy for the death of a MacKinnon, but a change in who was laird would inevitably alter his own plans—whatever those plans turned out to be. He needed time to get his feet under him in order to make any.

He frowned, trying to think back to those hazy memories from his childhood—to remember what he knew about the MacKinnon line. "Who does Dunverlockie go to now? A brother of Gordon? Or did he have children of his own?"

Glenna's mouth pulled into a satisfied smile, one that made Lachlan narrow his eyes in a question.

"Ye've no' been here ta ken all that's happened, I suppose." Her smile grew, as if she took great pleasure in what she was about to tell him. "Gordon has no children, and he has no siblin's—no' anymore, at least. Normally, Dunverlockie would go ta his cousin Angus—he's laird of Benleith, ye ken. *But*"— she raised a brow enigmatically—"when Gordon married, he agreed to settle the property on his wife if he should die before they had an heir."

Lachlan blinked. "Why?"

Glenna shrugged. "Ta tow the estate out of debt with the money from his wife's family. Of course, he only ever signed such a thing thinkin' he would live 'til he was ninety—and have an heir within the first year of marriage."

Lachlan was speechless, but Glenna was happy to fill the silence, still smiling with unconcealed delight. "Gordon must be rollin' over in his grave. Now 'tis my old mistress who's lady of Dunverlockie."

"Yer old mistress?"

"Aye. I was her maid for a year or so—until Gordon cast me off. He didna keep anyone at Dunverlockie whose loyalties were no' with him. And mine were certainly with Mrs. MacKinnon." She sighed and looked at the inn. "But he allowed me ta come here and work. Mrs. MacKinnon made sure of that, bless her kind heart."

Lachlan smiled perfunctorily, his mind taken up with all the information Glenna was giving him, particularly about Mrs. MacKinnon. So the new proprietor of Dunverlockie—of the place Lachlan had been born, of the estate he had been set to inherit—was a woman. A widow. And *not* a MacKinnon. At least not by birth.

"Murray!" The gravelly, peremptory voice of Mr. Gibson sailed from the front of the inn all the way to the stables. "Come!"

Lachlan set the pitchfork against the wall and grimaced. "I'm bein' summoned."

Glenna took a few steps to the side and peered toward the road. "'Tis Angus MacKinnon himself."

Lachlan reached for his cocked hat and set it snugly on his head before hurrying to the front of the inn. It was highly unlikely that anyone would recognize him—he hadn't been in Kildonnan since he was a young boy—but he would take no chance. He clenched his teeth against the pain in his leg. His injury from the war was healing, but it was slow, and he didn't know if his leg would ever be the same.

Mr. Gibson was standing before Angus MacKinnon, who

was clambering back onto his horse, his movements somewhat clumsy. His clothing proclaimed him a man of means, with sturdy but neat riding boots in the stirrups and a coat of fine cut and cloth. Lachlan had only hazy recollections of any MacKinnons, but Angus's Roman nose and angular cheekbones elicited a spark in his memory.

"See ta these bags." Mr. Gibson indicated the leather packs that sat behind the saddle. "And bring Mr. MacKinnon another cup of ale."

"Aye, sir." Lachlan set to the work of detaching the bags, sending a covert look at Angus. He smelled of whisky.

"There's no' much time before the shipment, sir," Mr. Gibson said to Mr. MacKinnon.

"You need not worry." Angus's words tumbled over one another, the beginnings and ends slurring. "I will be taking over everything now. You will send any communications to me."

Lachlan took his time with the second bag, eager to glean any information he could.

"Ta Benleith?" Mr. Gibson asked.

"No, to Dunverlockie. I will be there for the time being. I have a small matter to attend to at Benleith, but I return to the castle this evening."

Mr. Gibson turned toward Lachlan, brows snapping together in annoyance. "Hurry on, now, Murray! Mr. MacKinnon didna intend to stay the night when he stopped here."

Lachlan pulled the second bag from the horse and took brisk strides toward the inn, setting the bags down on Mr. Gibson's desk then hurrying to the tap room. He pulled a metal cup from the shelf and poured ale from the tankard into it. Mr. MacKinnon didn't look to need more drink at the moment, but that was hardly Lachlan's affair.

He stopped just shy of the door, listening to Mr. MacKinnon's voice.

"...I may have one or two more additions to the shipment, depending on a few matters I am attending to."

As Lachlan emerged from the inn door, Mr. MacKinnon's gaze settled on him for a moment, but it left just as quickly. Men like Angus MacKinnon had little attention to spare for servants, and Lachlan was grateful for it. If he could see the marks of a MacKinnon in the face of the man before him, it was possible that Angus could also recognize a Kincaid, given enough time or reason to look at him closely.

Lachlan handed the cup to him, and Angus took it without looking at him. Lachlan paused, unsure whether he was meant to wait for the empty cup.

"We can discuss that more later, when I have a better idea of where things stand," Angus said, draining the cup with ease and handing it to Lachlan.

"Aye, sir," Mr. Gibson replied.

Mr. MacKinnon signaled his horse, and he was soon headed down the lane at a quick pace.

"What are ye waitin' for, Murray?" Mr. Gibson barked, his jowls shaking slightly. "Take that cup inside and get back ta work."

Lachlan nodded and obeyed. He was already tired of the sound of Gibson's voice after a few mere hours, and he would be hearing quite a bit more of it. If he truly wished to see justice served to the MacKinnons, he would be at Glengour Inn for the foreseeable future. Dunverlockie would never be his, but there were other things he could do to seek justice. At the very least, he would make it clear that his father had taken a blame and punishment that should have rightfully fallen to the MacKinnons as well.

It would take patience to find the proper opportunity and to garner the sort of information Lachlan was after, though. He had no doubt the MacKinnons were hiding untoward dealings. A family didn't send a man to be executed like Lachlan's father had been without showing the same cold-bloodedness and greed in other areas of life. If the MacKinnons held power over Dunverlockie—and if Angus was anything like his father or uncle—there were sure to be dark dealings going on there.

The fact that Dunverlockie properly belonged to Gordon MacKinnon's widow now, though...well, it raised many questions, and Lachlan intended on finding the answers to each one.

3

Christina's unease only grew as one day turned into the next without the departure of Angus or his closest kinsmen. With the clamor of drunken men singing and laughing in the castle till the small hours of the morning, Christina had spent some nights in Elizabeth's bedchamber. There was no telling what the MacKinnons might take into their heads while imbibing copious amounts of whisky in each other's company. Angus's advances the day of the burial were a prime example of that—and he hadn't even been particularly drunk.

Additionally, there was an authority and possessiveness in the way he treated Dunverlockie and its servants that made her blood boil and caused an unease for the future to grow within her.

She reined in those emotions as well as she could, though. Elizabeth needed no further reason to treat the MacKinnons with contempt or to flash the teeth of her wit at them. It was a delicate balance for Christina to strike, showing that she understood what was her due and her right as lady of the estate while avoiding any outright contention she might live to regret.

She needed to get away from the castle, even if only briefly.

Angus had left for Benleith an hour ago, and Christina saw an opportunity in his absence. She could be confident that Elizabeth would be on better behavior until his return—particularly if she didn't have Christina to defend.

She left Elizabeth singing softly to herself as she mended the sleeve of one of her shifts. Christina would make her errand a quick one.

The scene outdoors was still subdued and gray, and the damp dirt muted the sound of Apollo's hooves. The clouds that blanketed the sky were more white than gray, and Christina felt a lightening of her burdens as she rode down the lane that led to Glengour Inn. She hadn't had much time alone in the past week, and Dunverlockie couldn't help but feel oppressive no matter who was there. It was a happy change to have two miles of road to herself, with naught but her thoughts to occupy her, even if those thoughts weren't entirely happy ones.

As she came up to the old, stone inn, Glenna Douglas emerged from the doorway, face lit with a smile. Christina slid down from her horse and welcomed her former maid into an embrace.

Before Elizabeth's arrival, Glenna had been Christina's only friend at Dunverlockie, but when Gordon had dismissed the maid for spurious reasons, Christina's interaction with Glenna had become limited to short encounters when circumstances took her and Gordon past the inn. He had almost always insisted upon stopping to speak with Mr. Gibson inside, leaving Christina outside, where Glenna sometimes managed to sneak to for a few minutes.

"My dear Mrs. MacKinnon," Glenna said, pulling back and looking at her tenderly. "How good it does me to see ye!"

"And *you*, Glenna," Christina answered. Glenna had a naturally positive disposition that couldn't help but lift Christina's mood.

She searched Christina's face with sympathy in her gaze.

"How are ye farin'? Since..." She left the sentence unfinished, with a little grimace.

"Well enough. But"—Christina paused. She didn't feel comfortable speaking of it all beside the road, even as empty as it generally was.

"Come," Glenna said, glancing at the inn and taking hold of Apollo's reins. She pulled him in the direction of the stables, and Christina walked beside her.

"I dinna think Mr. Gibson kens ye're here," Glenna said. "'Tis for the best. He'll find somethin' for me ta be about right away if he sees ye."

They turned the corner, and Glenna picked up her pace as they passed by the two small windows on that side of the inn. A man emerged from the stables, and Christina slowed.

Glenna followed Christina's gaze to where the man stood.

He was looking at Christina with an evaluative gaze set under thick, frowning eyebrows. His jaw was covered in a short, dense beard and his brown hair tied in a queue at the nape of his neck.

"Oh, dinna mind Mr. Murray," Glenna said with a smile. "He's new here and aidin' with some of the tasks we've needed help with. Just returned from fightin' in the war."

Though he walked with a slight limp, he certainly looked like a soldier should, broad-shouldered and intimidating. Christina was glad to be meeting him in the courtyard of the inn rather than on the battlefield.

Glenna continued pulling the horse along, and Christina followed, not caring to give Mr. Murray the impression that she was afraid of him. They came to a stop just before him.

"Mrs. MacKinnon," Glenna said. "Let me introduce ye to Mr. Murray. Mr. Murray, this is Mrs. MacKinnon. She's the lady of Dunverlockie I was tellin' ye 'bout."

Christina inclined her head, feeling the man's watchful eyes remain on her even as he bowed.

"Would ye see ta her horse, Mr. Murray?" Glenna leaned toward him and spoke in an undervoice. "I dinna wish for Mr. Gibson ta see her or the horse if we can avoid it. He's go' a loose tongue. Perhaps ye can give the horse's mane a brushin' in the back of the stables?"

Mr. Murray nodded and took the reins without a word, heading back the way he had come.

Christina stared after him for a moment. "Not a man of many words, is he?"

Glenna chuckled. "Nay, he's a kind soul, but like a good soldier, he likes to ken what he's up against afore openin' his mouth." She smiled teasingly. "Or perhaps 'twas yer beauty struck him dumb."

Christina sent her an unamused glance.

"Ye can trust Mr. Murray. But come"—she led Christina into the entry of the barn where two haystacks towered above them —"and tell me how ye've been, mistress."

Christina played with the black lace of her sleeve which hung out of her riding coat. "Uneasy, to be honest," she finally said.

Glenna's lips drew into a thin line. "I had hoped it would be better now."

Christina gave a rueful smile and sighed. "I suppose I should have anticipated that Gordon's kin would be loath to leave. I had hoped they would at least do so once they had drunk the last of the spirits, but Angus has expressed his intention to stay indefinitely."

Glenna frowned. "Oh dear. I did hear him mention ta Gibson that he would be stayin' at Dunverlockie."

Christina grimaced and glanced over her shoulder. Mr. Murray was brushing the horse's mane with a gentleness that kept her gaze there for a moment. "If only that was all. I tell you this in the strictest confidence, Glenna, for I shudder to think what my sister would do if she found out. She is already so sharp-tongued to Angus."

"Found out what?"

Christina hesitated again, but she could trust Glenna. The girl had a wisdom beyond her nineteen years, and Christina desperately needed to talk to *someone*. "He made me an offer of marriage."

Glenna's brows flew up, and she let out a breathy whistle. "I shouldna be surprised, I suppose. What better way for him ta ensure Dunverlockie is his, after all? And he always *has* had an eye for ye."

Christina repressed a shudder. If there was anything that could be worse than being married to Gordon, surely it would be marriage to Angus.

"Do you wish to return to Dunverlockie, Glenna? I was obliged to take on another maid when you left, but you know you have a place at the castle if you wish for it."

Glenna gave a grateful smile, tinged with regret. "Och, I wish I could, mistress, and perhaps I will in time. But my family needs me closer for now, and I dinna think Mr. Gibson could manage without me here."

Christina nodded. Glenna's mother was not in good health, and Glenna was the oldest of a bevy of siblings. As for Mr. Gibson, he should have employed at least one other servant at the inn, but, being the miser he was, he refused to. Without someone as hardworking as Glenna, he could not have managed the slow but steady trickle of visitors Glengour received. He would have been well-served if she left.

"Glenna!" Mr. Gibson's voice rang out, and Glenna shot Christina a significant look then hurried to step away from the haystacks so she could see out from the stable. She squinted then grimaced.

"Aye, sir! I'm comin'!" She looked at Christina significantly. "'Tis Angus. And drunk, from the looks of it."

Christina clenched her teeth. She had been counting on him staying at Benleith for longer. She had no desire for him to see her with Glenna—Gordon had long since poisoned him against the girl—and even less did she wish to see him when he was inebriated again.

The voices of Angus and Mr. Gibson drew nearer, and Christina looked at Glenna in alarm.

"Hide yerself," Glenna hissed. "The horse, Murray!" And with that, she was gone.

Christina looked around frantically for a place to hide, but if the men came into the stables, it was anyone's guess where they would venture. She watched as Mr. Murray and Apollo disappeared through the door that led out of the back of the stables.

She hesitated for the briefest of moments then hurried after them, turning left through the open door and emerging into a small yard that sat right up against the tree-covered hill behind. The smell of manure assailed her, bringing her to a halt.

Her hand was taken up suddenly, and Mr. Murray pulled her away from the doorway just as the voices of Angus and the innkeeper entered the stables. Mr. Murray moved his hand to her upper arm and urged her against the wooden wall, a hand to his lips and his wide, brown eyes alert. They were fixed on her, but it was obvious his mind was elsewhere, focused on the voices in the barn. A scar stretched beneath his right eye toward his ear, getting lost in his whiskers. Perhaps it was that which had made him look somewhat intimidating when she had first seen him.

Apollo nudged her then nipped at the sleeve of her coat, and Mr. Murray put a hand on the beast's cheek, though his eyes never left Christina's. His other hand still held her arm, and even in her fear, she was aware of how little of it was directed toward the man who held her in place. She had never been able to abide Gordon's touch, no matter how fleeting or casual. It had always made her skin crawl.

But Mr. Murray's touch, while firm, felt different.

She pulled her arm away all the same, and he made no move to keep it, the only indication that he noticed a slight flickering of his gaze.

Angus spoke. "She will not be able to manage it all herself —that is for certain. I tried to convince her of that, but she's a stubborn wench."

His words made Christina's muscles tense.

"I dinna doubt she'll come askin' for yer help soon enough."

"I trust so. Gordon kept her admirably ignorant of the state of things at Dunverlockie. He had only one use for her, and I have no doubt he availed himself of that nightly."

Christina's cheeks flamed, and she turned her head to the side, avoiding Mr. Murray's gaze.

"Canna blame him for that, can ye?"

Both of them chuckled.

"She's a rare specimen," Mr. Gibson said.

"That she is," Angus replied as more footsteps sounded.

"A bottle of our best whisky for ye, sir," Glenna said.

"I will take a cup of ale too." The amiability in Angus's voice was suddenly absent.

"Right away, sir," Glenna said, and her footsteps sounded again, this time fading away.

"I thought to find Murray here," Mr. Gibson said. "He's new. And he kens how to care for all manner of horse ailments, I gather."

"No matter," Angus replied. "Send him to Dunverlockie tomorrow."

The men's voices grew softer then faded away entirely as they left the barn.

Mr. Murray's shoulders relaxed, and he took a step back.

Christina hadn't realized how near they had been to one another until the distance grew between them.

He looked at her, and she knew her cheeks were still full of color and heat.

"Are ye well?" he asked, glancing at her arm where he had held it. "I didna mean ta hold ye so tightly."

"I am fine," she said, determined not to appear as humiliated as she felt. She took another step away from him, but her boot resisted. She looked down and shut her eyes. She was standing in a pile of manure. "Lovely."

Mr. Murray's gaze followed hers, and she thought she saw a little twitch at the corner of his mouth. "Och. Ye picked a bad place to stand."

She pulled her boot out, and it made a sucking sound until it broke free with a squelch. "I believe you were the one who selected this particular spot."

His mouth curved up in a half-smile, immediately ridding her of the impression she had first had of a menacing demeanor. "Fair enough," he said, putting out a hand to help her as she pulled her other boot free.

"I trust you have something I can clean this with?"

"Aye." He looped her horse's reins on the sole post in the yard. "I'll make certain Mr. MacKinnon is gone first." He moved toward the door and peered around it.

Christina found her gaze drawn to his form, and she forced it away.

He turned back toward her and nodded, putting out his hand again to help her. "Come. I'll clean them meself. 'Tis only fair."

She accepted his hand. "That will not be necessary. I can see to it if you will bring me a rag and some water."

He helped her into the stables before disappearing into the supply room. Presently, he emerged with a couple of rags in one hand and a chair in the other, and for the first time, Christina noticed the plaid he wore.

He set down the chair against one of the stall doors, and she took a seat in it, though her eyes were still trained on the colors of his kilt. She knew them well. It was unusual to see plaids these days—particularly those with a tartan pattern. It had been over a decade since they had been outlawed. In some places, men turned a blind eye to them, as they knew that such pieces of clothing were all some could afford, but the MacKinnons had not been so generous. They abided by the Dress Act rigorously, and they expected others to do so, as well.

Before Christina well knew what was happening, Mr. Murray had taken up the sole of her boot and began wiping at the manure there.

"Oh," she said, pulling her boot away in embarrassment. "You needn't do that. As I said, I can see to it myself. I should be getting on my way quickly."

"Nay, Mrs. MacKinnon," he said, gently but firmly taking her boot back in hand. "Dinna be stubborn."

Angus had used the same word to describe her, and it nettled her. "It is not stubbornness. It is simply not your responsibility, and I am well able to do it."

He took a rag from the ground beside him. "I'd wager I have more experience gettin' muck off a boot than ye do, Mrs. MacKinnon. Ye'll be gone all the sooner for leavin' it to me. And ye'd no' have stepped there if I hadn't pulled ye into it—ye said so yerself."

She wavered for a moment between a wish to assert her independence and the acknowledgment that he likely *could* do a better job of it than her. In the end, she relented, sitting back in her chair and trying to relax as he wiped the top and sides of her boot in firm, painstaking motions while she held up her petticoats just enough to keep them from becoming dirtied.

She took the opportunity to study him. He was a handsome

man, though certainly more rugged than what she was accustomed to. His sleeves, generously smeared with dirt, were rolled up, showcasing powerful forearms and strong hands she couldn't help but admire.

She cleared her throat. "You are a soldier, then?"

He didn't look up. "Aye. I was."

"With the 42nd?"

He glanced up at her quickly with a question in his eyes. "Aye."

She smiled and indicated his plaid. "It was somewhat obvious."

One side of his mouth pulled up into a crooked smile, and he reapplied himself to his work.

She was silent for a moment, gaze trained on the piece of hair that escaped his loosely tied queue and fell into his face. The 42nd was a particularly large regiment; the odds that Mr. Murray would have encountered someone she knew were very small indeed. But she had to ask.

"My brother is in the 42nd."

He stopped and looked up at her. "Yer brother? And what might his name be?"

"Innes," she said.

His gaze grew intent. "Ye're Alistair Innes's sister?"

She nodded, brows drawing together. "You know him, then?"

He chuckled and relaxed back on the heel of his bent leg. "Aye. Verra well. We were in the same company. Served as lieutenants together."

She stared at him, and a smile grew on her face. "You are in earnest?"

"Aye. I didna think to encounter his family in these parts. I thought he hailed from Kininfar?"

"That is correct." Christina sat forward, the muck on her boots forgotten. "How was he when you last saw him? Safe? In good health?" Alistair was a notoriously bad correspondent, and it took ages for anything he *did* write to make it to Dunverlockie.

Mr. Murray folded the rag, and she found she liked the way he looked with a smile on his face.

"Aye, he was well," he said. "In good spirits, too. One of the best soldiers I ken. Became a close friend of mine when he transferred to my company. I'd trust him with my life."

She breathed a sigh of relief to hear Alistair was not only alive but uninjured. "Trust him with your life, perhaps. But not with the time of a rendezvous."

Mr. Murray's eyes lit up with laughter. "Och, the worst memory of anyone I've ever met." He took her second boot in hand, looking up at her with curiosity in his eyes. "'Tis a pleasure ta make the acquaintance of someone Innes cares so much about. I ken well his love for his family."

Christina managed a smile as she swallowed. She missed all of her siblings, but it had been years since Alistair had joined the army, and after their father's death, Alistair's absence had left her feeling solely responsible for the welfare of the entire family. If not for that burden, she might have been tempted to flee Dunverlockie and let Angus do what he would with it. She wanted no part of it.

But it was hers, all the same, and it put her in a position to meet the needs of her younger siblings.

"Mistress!" Glenna came running into the stables. "I'm that sorry for leavin' ye in such a way, but—" Her brows contracted as she came to a stop. "What happened?"

Christina pulled her boot from Mr. Murray's hands and covered it with her petticoats and riding coat. "Stepped in some dung is all. I should be going now, though. Thank you, Mr. Murray. The rest can be taken care of at Dunverlockie." She had momentarily forgotten her urgency to return to the castle.

She was uneasy at the thought of Elizabeth and Angus encountering one another there without her supervision.

Mr. Murray set down the soiled rags and stood, offering her his hand once again to help her from the chair. He pulled her up with an ease only a broad set of shoulders like his would allow for. "Ye're welcome, Mrs. MacKinnon. I'll get yer horse." He disappeared into the yard, leaving Glenna and Christina alone.

Glenna looked at her with apology written in her eyes. "When I saw that Mr. Gibson and Mr. MacKinnon had come ta the stables while I went for the whisky, I was afeared ye'd be found, mistress."

"I might have been if I had not followed Mr. Murray," Christina replied. "Into the manure." She glanced down at her boots, which looked much improved.

Mr. Murray appeared again, Apollo following behind.

"I'm glad he took care of ye," Glenna said with a grateful look at him.

He certainly looked more than capable of taking care of someone. That was the sort of back made to carry heavy burdens. Christina's, on the other hand, felt weaker than ever, and she hated it.

She had been a strong-willed woman before marrying Gordon, but life at Dunverlockie had slowly worn her down, and she no longer knew what she was capable of. She certainly didn't feel capable of standing up to a man like Angus.

But she had to find that strength. She'd had it once. Surely she could rediscover it.

Mr. Murray interlaced his fingers and bent down, ready to help her into the saddle. Her gaze flitted to the mounting block just a dozen feet away, and she hesitated then took the reins decisively.

"Thank you, but there is no need for that, Mr. Murray."

His brow arched, and in it she saw an implied accusation of stubbornness again.

"I won't force you to dirty your hands with what remains on my boot." She stopped Apollo in front of the block and stepped onto it.

Mr. Murray took the reins while she did so, saying nothing as she clambered—less elegantly than she had hoped—into the saddle.

He handed her the reins. "Mrs. MacKinnon."

She met his gaze, and the sincerity there made her want to squirm in her seat.

"If ye're in need of anything," he said, "ye need only ask. Yer brother canna be here right now, but I'm verra willing ta help in whatever way I can until he returns."

Glenna smiled approvingly.

"Thank you, Mr. Murray," Christina said, more touched by his words than she cared to let on. It was no small thing to have an ally, but the problems she faced were not ones someone like Mr. Murray could help her with.

4

Lachlan's heart thudded as he approached the bend in the road that would bring Dunverlockie into view. It had been many long years since he had seen his childhood home, and he couldn't decide if it was eagerness or nervousness he felt more of at the prospect. The knowledge that MacKinnons had made it their home for the past fifteen years was insult added to the initial injury of the estate being forfeited just before his father's execution. The Crown had wanted Lachlan's father—and all the other rebels—to know that, not only had their bid to put a Stewart back on the throne failed, their choice to support the Young Pretender had cost them everything.

The trees opened, and Dunverlockie Castle appeared, its crenulated towers streaked with black and the warm limestone punctuated with two dozen small windows. He pinpointed the one that looked out from his own former room.

It was there he'd been wakened as more than a dozen British soldiers forced their way inside the castle and took his father. Young Lachlan had thrown off his blankets, grabbed the poker from the fireplace in his room, and run down the spiral staircase, hurtling his slight, eleven-year-old body into the nearest soldier.

He blinked quickly. It had been a long time since he had thought on those events. Everything had changed that morning. He had lost his home and his father in one fell swoop—he had never seen his father again. It was the same day he had been compelled to join the army by the commanding officer who'd come to take his father. And only now was he returning, a full sixteen years later.

But today, he returned not as the heir to Dunverlockie he had been born, but as a lowly inn servant. Mrs. MacKinnon had inherited his home, and while he had nothing against her —in truth, he had liked her more than he cared to admit—the people *she* had inherited it from had gotten it by ill means. Her right to it was built on a rotten foundation, and, if there was any justice in the world, Lachlan would ensure that the part the MacKinnons had played in acquiring it became common knowledge.

He urged his horse toward the stables, pushing aside the unhappy thoughts. As he swung down, he felt the first sense of misgiving, the sound within the stables warning him of someone's approach. But the groom who emerged was a stranger, and Lachlan relaxed. Of course the MacKinnons would not have kept on any Kincaid family servants, and certainly not for this long.

"I've come ta see ta Mr. MacKinnon's horse," Lachlan said, tying his own horse to a post.

"Aye, come in," the man said. He was of middle age and stocky, and he turned back the way he had come.

Lachlan followed, eyes hungrily taking in his surroundings. The stables were both strange and familiar, like a well-known room someone had rearranged the furniture in. He had spent a great deal of time here in his boyhood, seeing to the horses, learning how to treat their ailments, hiding from his tutor.

The stables were full, some stalls containing multiple horses, which meant there were plenty of visitors—undoubtedly the reason why so many MacKinnon men traipsed drunkenly into Glengour Inn in the middle of the night. They were lingering after the funeral as long as Dunverlockie would house them, feed them, and fill their cups with spirits.

A chestnut horse stood in the path between the stalls—the horse Mrs. MacKinnon had brought to the inn yesterday. Lachlan passed it by, letting his gaze run along the stalls, landing on the horse he'd seen Angus riding at the inn.

"That's the one," the groom said as Lachlan approached the stall. "'Tis this hoof which gives him anguish." He indicated one of the front legs which was obviously being favored, only the tip of the hoof touching the ground.

Lachlan stroked the horse in one fluid motion from his neck all the way down his leg. The horse lifted his hoof, affording Lachlan a view of the underside.

He brushed away some of the muck and made a sound of displeasure at the sight. "How long has it been plaguing him?"

"Nigh on a week now," the groom said. "Stepped on a shard of glass."

Lachlan gripped his lips together and let the hoof down so he could reach into his satchel. "Could Mr. MacKinnon no' have ridden a different horse? The hoof needs proper care and rest, no' ta be battered by the sharp stones in the roads here while 'tis in such a state."

The groom shrugged. "He favors this horse above the others."

"He has a strange way of showin' it," Lachlan said under his breath.

"Good day, Kemp."

Lachlan's hand slowed. He recognized the voice of Mrs. MacKinnon.

"Good day, ma'am," the groom replied. "I was nearly

finished with yer horse when the man from the inn arrived." He tightened a strap with a soft grunt.

"Man from the inn?" she asked, and her footsteps drew nearer.

"Aye, ta see ta Mr. MacKinnon's horse."

Mrs. MacKinnon's head appeared at the window of the stall. "Mr. Murray," she said.

He nodded at her and rose out of respect. "Good day, Mrs. MacKinnon."

She presented a striking picture, attired in black from head to toe—with raven hair to match. The effect was to give her creamy skin an almost ghostly, ethereal look. She spoke with the refined speech of someone who had been raised speaking English as much as she had Gaelic—the way Lachlan himself might have spoken if life had turned out differently.

"Something is amiss with Angus's horse?" she asked.

Lachlan glanced at her. She knew something was wrong with the horse. She had been there when they had overheard Mr. Gibson and Angus speaking of it. Why she was so hesitant to have it known that she had been at the inn, he didn't know. But he was intrigued by it.

"Aye," Kemp responded. "Been limpin' since he stepped on somethin'."

She came into the stall where Lachlan was and lifted her petticoats as she bent down beside him, peering at the hoof he held, even as the scent of orange blossom filled the stall—a welcome reprieve, as the stall needed mucking.

"Take care," he said softly enough that Kemp wouldn't hear, and he nodded at her boots.

She glanced down, and an answering smile appeared on her lips as she shifted her feet away from the nearest mess. She could look somewhat grave without a smile, and he enjoyed seeing the difference it made in her appearance to elicit one.

He focused on the hoof again, narrowing his eyes to peer closer at the sad state of it. It was still covered in dirt and dung, though. "I'll need a pick from the harness room."

Mrs. MacKinnon gave him a quizzical look, and he let out an uncomfortable chuckle.

"At least, I imagine 'tis where 'twould be found." He stood up to avoid her gaze and looked at the horse's teeth and eyes as Kemp disappeared and Mrs. MacKinnon stepped out of the stall.

"This horse is in a bad way," Lachlan said with a frown. "'Tis no' just his hoof that needs attention. 'Tis his eye as well."

Mrs. MacKinnon stopped and turned back toward him. "Is it very bad?"

Lachlan grimaced. "He's on his way ta blindness without the proper treatment."

"Good heavens." She glanced toward the door Kemp had disappeared through then stepped back toward the horse and peered at his eye. "I admit, it does not surprise me that Angus would treat his horses poorly. Can you help the beast?"

Lachlan moved the eyelid gently to inspect it. The horse resisted slightly, but Lachlan stroked his neck, and he calmed enough for Lachlan to do what was needed. "I dinna have the proper medicine for it. I think 'twould be best ta have someone called for—someone with more training."

She nodded, and Kemp returned, handing Lachlan a metal pick.

"I can clean the hoof and put a poultice on it," Lachlan said to Mr. Kemp, "but, as I was tellin' Mrs. MacKinnon, this horse needs more care than I can give. Ye'll want ta be callin' for a farrier or a blacksmith who kens his trade well."

Kemp looked hesitant. "I dinna think Mr. MacKinnon wishes for that. He said ta sell the brute if ye couldna mend it."

Mrs. MacKinnon shot Lachlan an aggravated glance. "Sell

the beast to some unsuspecting tenant or cottar?" she said. "I think not. We will call for someone, as Mr. Murray has suggested."

"I dinna wish to go against Mr. MacKinnon," Mr. Kemp said warily.

Lachlan hung back, having plenty to say but knowing that it was not his place to do so.

"Mr. MacKinnon is not your master, Kemp," Mrs. MacKinnon replied, her tone taking on an edge.

"Nay, but 'tis his horse."

"It won't be for long if he refuses to give it treatment—or if he sells it, as you say he intends to. Either way, it is in *my* stables, and I insist that someone be sent for immediately."

Kemp's jaw had a mulish look, but he gave a curt nod.

"If Mr. MacKinnon gives you grief, you may tell him the blame lies with me," she said. "Now, please go."

Frowning, Kemp disappeared from the stables, and Mrs. MacKinnon let out an abrupt breath through her nose, turning toward Lachlan.

Lachlan looked at Mrs. MacKinnon with a hint of admiration. He didn't know much of Angus MacKinnon, but he knew enough to recognize her bravery for what it was. He would hardly have blamed her if she chose not to fight such a battle. No doubt Angus intended to keep as much control over Dunverlockie as he could manage, and it pleased Lachlan to know that Mrs. MacKinnon wouldn't make it easy for him.

"Thank you for caring for the horse, Mr. Murray," she said. "Caring more than its owner, no less."

He looked at the horse's eye again. It was a wonder the beast hadn't hurt both Angus and itself with his vision so obscured. "He'll owe the care he receives as much ta you as ta me, for he would no' have received it without yer insistence."

She sighed resignedly and led her horse to the mounting block. "Undoubtedly there will be a reckoning."

She was probably right. And Lachlan wished he could be there when it happened. Mrs. MacKinnon might be spirited enough to face up to a man like Angus, but he disliked the thought of such an encounter, all the same. It wasn't a fair fight. That was just it, though—the MacKinnons weren't known for fighting fair. Mrs. MacKinnon must realize that. She had been married to one, after all.

How *did* she regard the MacKinnons? And what unfortunate circumstance had brought about her marriage to one of them? She seemed to dislike Angus heartily, but perhaps she had regarded her husband with affection. Lachlan couldn't imagine a MacKinnon deserving the woman before him, though.

She arranged her petticoats once in the saddle. "Good day to you, Mr. Murray. I hope you will feel at liberty to ask Kemp for whatever you need as you tend to that hoof. If he gives you any trouble, please apprise me of it when I next see you."

"Thank ye, ma'am."

She clucked her tongue, the horse moved forward, and she was soon gone.

Lachlan stared after her for a moment. *When I next see you.* He was glad to know she anticipated that.

Kemp gave him no further trouble as he asked for the supplies to poultice the wound, and within an hour, Lachlan was departing. With Kemp sending for someone to see to the horse, Lachlan's services would no longer be needed for the hoof or the eye. It was unfortunate in a way. Lachlan needed *more* opportunities to visit Dunverlockie, not fewer.

As he swung a leg over the saddle of his own horse, he let his eyes rest on the castle for a moment. Sometime, he would manage to venture inside—with or without permission to do so.

But today was not that day. It would be better to wait until the castle was more sparsely populated, when Lachlan would have less cause to worry over being caught as he searched for the papers he intended to get his hands on—if they still existed.

5

It was admittedly far easier to assert herself to Kemp in the stables than it was to face the prospect of explaining her highhandedness to Angus, but Christina couldn't find it in herself to regret what she had done. Neither did she wish to examine whether Mr. Murray's presence had anything to do with her decision.

He had been there when Angus and Mr. Gibson had cast doubt upon her ability to manage Dunverlockie, and the implication by Kemp that it was Angus's instructions which should be obeyed rather than hers had nettled her into setting her foot down. The line she was walking was a delicate one. While the prospect of leaving the management of an estate like Dunverlockie in someone else's hands was appealing, Christina had no desire whatsoever to be ruled over by yet another MacKinnon man.

A knock sounded on the door, simultaneously opening to reveal Elizabeth, who slipped in.

"Ah! You *have* returned, then," she said, closing the door behind her. "How was your ride?"

Christina shrugged. "Good, if only to be away for a bit.

What is that?" Her eyes went to the sealed letter in Elizabeth's hand.

Elizabeth gave it to her. "From Aunt Dorothy. It came while you were out."

Christina broke the seal and unfolded the letter, written in the somewhat uneven script of her aunt. Her eyes glided along the lines, a little smile pulling at the corner of her mouth as she read about her siblings. But it was replaced by a sinking of the stomach as she finished. Aunt Dorothy needed money.

Gordon's reluctance to continue providing for the education and upkeep of Christina's siblings had been a frequent source of conflict. He had always insisted that that burden belonged to Alistair and Aunt Dorothy. Alistair sent money when he could, of course, but they never knew when—or how much—to expect.

Christina's shoulders suddenly relaxed, and the knots in her stomach untied themselves. There was no need to apply to Gordon for the money anymore—or for *anything*. She could send whatever she wished to send, and there was no one to stop her from doing it.

"What does it say?" Elizabeth asked. "How are Ninian and Ross? When I left, they were neglecting their studies abominably."

Christina handed her the letter. "I imagine you will be able to read between the lines better than I. I barely know Aunt Dorothy. I fear she has little affection for me and believes I have been derelict in my duty toward her and the children."

Elizabeth quickly read over the letter, and Christina watched the same hint of a smile play at her sister's lips as she read the lines about their younger siblings. "Little truants," she said, handing the letter back. "I *do* miss them."

"Perhaps we should have them come live here, or visit at least." Christina folded the letter again and looked up at Elizabeth with a smile. "Something to consider."

"If you intend on staying, yes," she replied. "But—but...."

"But what?"

Elizabeth looked around, her expression morphing to one of distaste. "Can you not rent this miserable pile of stone to someone instead?"

Christina had already considered it, and there was no pretending it wasn't appealing. But it wasn't a simple or quick matter to find someone looking for a place like Dunverlockie to rent. It was too remote for most people and too large for others.

"It *is* a possibility," she replied, "but I need to get a better sense for where things stand before pursuing such an option. I know so little about how Dunverlockie is run. In the meantime, though, I can at least send something to Aunt Dorothy."

"Thank goodness for that," Elizabeth replied. "You might go shop for a few things in the toun while you're at it."

Christina stood. "Perhaps I shall." There were a number of things she had been in need of for months now. It hadn't been long after her father's death that Gordon had threatened all the nearest merchants—including those all the way in Fort William—that, if they provided credit to Christina without his express permission, they would lose his patronage and that of all the MacKinnons. He had treated Christina like an extravagant wife rather than the practical one she was. And he hadn't even told her when he had done it. She had learned of it while attempting to buy a handful of ribbons at the haberdasher.

Gordon had humiliated her in every possible way.

"Come," she said, brushing aside the unhappy memories. "I am hungry, and dinner should be ready soon."

They sat down to dinner with seven men, who all seemed to defer to Angus rather than Christina. It was as if they didn't understand that Christina had inherited Dunverlockie—or perhaps they simply didn't care. In their eyes, Angus was the rightful heir.

Christina held her tongue the entirety of the meal, and with the warning in her eyes, she managed to prevent Elizabeth from saying anything too untoward. She could see by her tight-lipped smiles and flared nostrils, though, that it was only a matter of time before Elizabeth lost her ability to hold her tongue any longer.

When the two of them left the dining room to the men at the end of the meal, it was to encounter Malcolm MacKinnon arriving through the front door, a bottle of spirits gripped in each hand.

Christina had had little occasion to encounter Malcolm in the past, but she knew him to be one of Angus's closest kin. She couldn't recall ever having heard him speak. That, in combination with his thick, dark eyebrows and brooding expression had given her a fear of the man.

"Good heavens," Elizabeth said in an exasperated voice, loud enough that Malcolm could hear. "Are we to house every MacKinnon in the country indefinitely?"

Christina stiffened, preparing for the repercussions of her sister's outburst.

Malcolm slowed at her words, his gaze taking in Christina then Elizabeth.

The door to the dining room opened. "Malcolm." Angus closed the door and stepped into the corridor, looking at the spirits his kinsman held. "Your timing is impeccable."

Malcolm brushed past the sisters with another frowning glance at Elizabeth, and she turned to follow his progress. "Impeccable timing, certainly. I am glad to see you've begun to replenish the store of spirits here, Angus, though it will require a great deal more than two bottles, I assure you."

Christina tightened her hold on Elizabeth's arm, partially as a warning, partially to brace herself.

Angus merely sent Elizabeth a scornful glance and looked to Christina. "I was hoping to have a word with you, Christina. I understand you had a farrier sent for to see to my horse."

She nodded, refusing to show any hint of fear to him. "Mr. Murray assured me the ailment—the one affecting the eye rather than the hoof—would require treatment from someone with experience."

Angus smiled, though it was a cold one. "I assure you, I am capable of seeing to my own property."

"Strange that you should be spending so much time *here*, then," Elizabeth said with false sweetness.

Angus's nostrils flared, but he kept a humorless smile on his face. "Ah, but there is so much here at Dunverlockie that needs tending to—and putting in its proper place." His fixed gaze left no doubt as to his meaning.

Christina was torn between the desire to whisk Elizabeth away and the need to fight the battle before her. If she showed any weakness, Angus would take it as an invitation to broaden his influence at Dunverlockie. She settled on refocusing the conversation.

"I had the farrier called for as much on account of your horse as I did on that of mine," she said. "I am sure you understand that I have no desire to see a spread of disease amongst my livestock." Her possessive words both terrified and emboldened her, particularly seeing the effect they were having upon Angus.

His eyes sparkled in the candlelit corridor.

"If you do not wish for your horse to be seen to," she continued, "that is, of course, your affair, but I must insist in that case that you remove it from the stables here—and *not* attempt to sell it to any of my tenants. I am not certain who Kemp sent word to, but I understand there is a skilled farrier recently settled in Craiglinne. I would be glad to inquire with him while I am there tomorrow if you wish it."

Angus frowned. "You are going to Craiglinne?"

She raised her brows at his response. Would he challenge

her on this? "I have a few commissions to fulfill—business to attend to."

"Business?" Angus said, clearly too curious to leave things be.

She nodded disobligingly.

"I would be happy to do that on your behalf," he said. "You have enough on your plate, surely."

The words were thoughtful, but the tone in which they were said was anything but.

"I shall not trouble you," she said. "The merchants in the area must become more familiar with me. And I wish to send the money myself. But thank you, all the same." She turned away to leave, only to be stopped by his voice again.

"Money?"

Quickly gathering her courage, she turned yet again. "Yes. For my siblings."

Angus's jaw worked. "Would it not be wiser to go over the accounts first and see if the estate can sustain such an expense?" He seemed to share Gordon's need to jealously guard what he believed belonged not just to Dunverlockie but to the MacKinnons themselves.

"If the estate can sustain the expense of housing, feeding, and providing ample whisky for all the men here, I rather think it will survive the cost of feeding a few children."

Angus gave a sharp nod. "Good evening, ladies," he said, and he turned with Malcolm toward the dining room.

Christina and Elizabeth walked in silence until the dining room door closed behind them.

"Well done, Christina," Elizabeth said, squeezing her arm. "It is so very satisfying to see Angus put out."

Christina didn't respond, hoping Elizabeth couldn't feel her trembling. She was letting her past fears hold too much sway over her in the present. Angus might intimidate her, but he could never hurt her in the ways his cousin Gordon had—in the ways only a husband could.

The weather cooperated for Christina's planned journey to Craiglinne, and, to Christina's relief, Elizabeth was eager to accompany her. She might have shown confidence to Angus in speaking of her intentions, but the truth was, she hadn't done anything like this since the beginning of her marriage to Gordon, more than a year and a half ago. She and Glenna had come home from Craiglinne with a few items— nothing large or terribly expensive—and Gordon had lost his temper for the first time. And certainly not the last.

Simply put, Christina had grown unused to such freedom, and she was glad for her sister's company as she began to explore it again.

So, it was with a combination of nerves and exhilaration that she handled the reins of the curricle Gordon had used. Before Christina's marriage, her father had taught her to drive, little knowing that she wouldn't be permitted to employ such a skill. Navigating the roads required her to reach into the recesses of her memory.

"What an awful carriage you possess," Elizabeth teased, holding her hat as they rumbled away from Dunverlockie.

"I take neither credit nor responsibility for it," Christina said, focusing on avoiding a particularly deep rut. "Besides, I doubt any equipage could be sprung well enough to counter the roads here. They are atrocious." They dipped and swayed, the creaking of the carriage joints nearly swallowed up in the clatter of the wheels on stone and dirt. "It *does* feel more rickety than I remember, but it has been some time since I went out."

Gordon had made sure of that.

With success, Christina's confidence grew, and Elizabeth's good humor—punctuated by teasing remarks about the curricle and Christina's driving skill—couldn't help but be infectious. By the time they were passing the inn, both of them were laughing as they jostled over the uneven road, Christina feeling full of a freedom she had never thought to experience again.

Mr. Murray and Glenna were in front of the inn, the latter engaged in sweeping while the former was on his hands and knees scrubbing the flagstones. They both looked up as the carriage passed, and Glenna waved an enthusiastic hand while Mr. Murray watched with the barest hint of a smile, the sleeves of his shirt rolled up and a few locks of hair loose from his queue.

Christina and Elizabeth both sent a wave, but Christina hurried to take hold of the reins again as a dip in the road jarred them. She set her focus back where it should be as the road curved around and the inn disappeared from view.

They were just out of sight of the inn when there was a sudden jolt, a loud creak, and then blackness.

6

Lachlan scrubbed roughly at the dirt encrusted in the stone. There had been a few of the MacKinnon kin left at the inn since the funeral a few days ago—those that belonged to the Benleith cadet branch and the Falroch branch as well—but the only two men remaining were preparing for departure, and the inn was in a state.

It was Glenna and Lachlan who were left to clean up after the rowdy bunch—the mud that covered the floors; the empty tankards and bottles, some of them broken; the sloppily eaten food. While they were at it, though, Mr. Gibson wanted the exterior cleaned, as it was what people saw from the road and was in great need of a thorough cleaning.

A muffled clattering sounded somewhere in the distance, and the rhythmic scratching of Glenna's broom stopped as she cocked her ear.

"What was that?" she asked. "In the stables, ye reckon?"

"Nay." Lachlan rose to his feet with an unsettled feeling in his stomach. "It came from that direction." He pointed toward the road, which took a turn fifty yards past the inn and was then obscured by trees.

"Ye dinna think 'twas..." Glenna left the sentence unfinished.

A frantic horse neigh sounded, and Lachlan threw his rag in the bucket of dirty water. "Go tell Mr. Gibson ta ready things in case there's an injury."

He ran in the direction of the sound, not waiting for her to respond.

In battle, Lachlan had learned how impossibly short a distance could feel when the destination was an undesirable one—like the distance between him and an enemy soldier. He now came to understand the reverse: how interminable a distance could feel when the destination was urgent.

He rounded the bend, and the view of a toppled carriage met his gaze. Beside it, the young woman Glenna had identified to him as Miss Innes crawled over to Mrs. MacKinnon, her hair askew and her hat dangling from a nearby bush. The horse drawing the carriage struggled upright and lunged forward, trying to break free. It seemed to have loosed itself from one of the traces and was bleeding from a spot near its ribs.

Lachlan glanced between the horse and the young women. If the horse continued to lunge, it might cause further injury— to itself *and* the women. He let out a curse in Gaelic and hurried over, giving the horse a wide berth at first then reaching a calming hand to its neck, uttering soothing words until he could take the bridle in hand.

The horse calmed under his hold, and he hastened to Mrs. MacKinnon's side, noting the wound on her brow. Just moments ago, her face had been lit up in laughter, an image which had elicited a smile from him. Now, her eyes were clenched shut and her brow wrinkled in pain as she cradled an arm.

"Mrs. MacKinnon," he said, still somewhat breathless from running over. "Ye're injured."

Her lids blinked rapidly, and her body trembled. "Only a bit."

He put a stabilizing hand on her back. "How is yer head?" He gently moved a piece of hair that clung to the wound on the right side of her forehead.

"It stings, but…I am well."

"And yer arm?"

She moved it, wincing slightly.

He looked to Mrs. MacKinnon's sister. "And you, Miss Innes?"

She shook her head rapidly. "I am shaken, that is all. I wasn't thrown as far as Christina was."

He watched Miss Innes for another moment, looking for any sign that she was minimizing her own injury. But she seemed focused only on her sister.

"Can you walk back to the inn?" Miss Innes asked her sister with a glance at the horse. "I am afraid the carriage will be useless. Apollo seems to have broken at least one of the straps."

Mrs. MacKinnon nodded and tried to push off her uninjured arm, but Lachlan stopped her with a firm hand.

"Nay," he said with a frown. "I can carry ye. If ye'll allow me to."

Mrs. MacKinnon looked at him, and he could see the debate in her eyes. Would she truly attempt to walk back to the inn rather than let him carry her? She was stubborn indeed. He couldn't imagine a stubborn wife would have suited a MacKinnon.

Her lips pinched together, and she gave a curt nod.

He picked her up in his arms, careful to let her injured arm face outward.

"Mistress!" Glenna came running, skirts held up, apron covered in dirt, and a fearful look in her eyes as she looked at Mrs. MacKinnon in Lachlan's arms. "We heard a great crash, and I feared…"

"Perhaps ye can help Miss Innes," Lachlan said. Mrs. MacKinnon was petite, but he couldn't hold her indefinitely. "Ye're certain ye can walk?" he asked Miss Innes.

She raised her brows, a glint of amusement in her eyes. "Are you offering to carry us both?"

"Nay, but I can return for ye."

She shook her head. "Thank you, but I can walk."

Miss Innes took the arm Glenna offered, and the four of them made their way back to the inn. Mrs. MacKinnon was rigid in Lachlan's arms at first, but she relaxed somewhat by the time they reached the inn, her eyes shut, whether to manage her pain or because she was displeased with being carried, he didn't know.

Mr. Gibson was waiting in front of the inn, and his eyes were trained on Mrs. MacKinnon.

"Is she...dead?" he asked.

"Nay," Lachlan responded. "She needs a place to lie down. And Miss Innes too."

Mr. Gibson led them inside. The inn was cramped and dark, but compared to the other inns and bothies Lachlan had had occasion to sleep in, it was relatively luxurious. He cringed, suppressing the groans that rose to his lips as he navigated the narrow stairwell with the woman in his arms. It required muscles and strength that he hadn't yet regained since his injury, and he breathed his relief when the corridor opened up at the top of the stairs.

He laid her down on the straw mattress in the first room with aching arms.

"Thank you," she said as Glenna followed them in.

"Nay bother. I'll leave ye ta Glenna for now."

Mrs. MacKinnon looked up at him with a plea in her eyes. "Would you see to—"

He nodded. "Aye. I'm goin' ta see ta the horse."

She relaxed back onto the pillow, and he left the room.

Lachlan knew a fear that the beast would be gone when he returned to the scene of the accident, but it was stretching its neck as far as its body would allow, reaching for the bits of grass accessible on the side of the narrow road. Its side was still bloody, but there seemed to be no active bleeding and, he hoped, nothing fatal, as long as the wound could be tended to properly.

He stroked the horse's neck, allowing it to smell him before he moved to take a closer look at its side. The cut didn't appear very deep—likely torn by a buckle when the trace had broken. He reached for the trace on the ground, though he had little hope it could be reattached.

He stared at it, bringing it closer to his eyes and looking carefully at the broken end of the strap. His brow furrowed. One half of the tear was rugged, while the other half was clean, almost as though it had been cut partially before the rest had torn.

Heart beating a little more quickly, he inspected the rest of the equipment, trying to be swift but thorough. Perhaps he was overly suspicious—too quick to attribute ill motives to the MacKinnons—or whoever might have done this. Surely the groom at Dunverlockie would have noticed a cut in the strap as he had prepared the carriage to be taken out. Ensuring the safety of the equipment that would transport his masters was part of his duties. Either Kemp was a bad groom for not noticing the issue, or he had seen the compromised piece of equipment and allowed Mrs. MacKinnon and Miss Innes to take the carriage out despite it.

And if there *was* ill motive behind this, there was a chance Mrs. MacKinnon and her sister were still in danger.

He inspected the hames and collar, and his frown deepened again. The buckle at the top of the hames was hanging on, but it wasn't latched properly. Whether it had come loose due to the accident or had been that way before, he couldn't be certain, but it was no easy thing for it to come loose on a config-uration such as this. If the hames came loose, it would have fallen down around the horse's legs, causing it to trip, and there was no telling what might happen as a result of *that*.

If someone had indeed meant to injure—or kill—Mrs. MacKinnon and her sister, the combination of a compromised trace *and* an ill-latched hames could easily have accomplished that goal.

It was with misgiving that he unstrapped the horse and led it back to the inn at a brisk pace. The carriage would have to be retrieved later. There was surprisingly little damage to it, all things considered, and it had toppled far enough to the side of the road that any passing carts would manage to squeeze by.

Once he reached the barn, Lachlan put the horse in a stall with a small helping of hay.

"I'll be back ta see ta that injury," he said, then he hurried back to the inn, reassuring himself that the presence of Glenna must have acted as a safeguard for Mrs. MacKinnon and Miss Innes during his absence.

He debated whether he should tell Mrs. MacKinnon what he suspected. She deserved to know, though, didn't she?

And yet, what if he was wrong? Perhaps there was another explanation he hadn't thought of—perhaps he was too intent on finding a reason to blame the MacKinnons. Kemp might have simply been more distracted than usual. And if there *was* another explanation, to tell Mrs. MacKinnon would be to worry her for no reason at all. It was a heavy burden to place on a woman's shoulders, the implication that someone wished her injury or, even worse, death.

And yet, he couldn't deny that it made sense. From what Glenna had told him, with Mrs. MacKinnon having no heir, Angus would inherit Dunverlockie if she died. That was motive enough for a man to orchestrate an accident like the one that had just occurred.

Lachlan picked up his speed. What if there was an alternate plan in case this one failed? The entire situation made Lachlan even more anxious to accomplish the next part of his plan: finding a way into Dunverlockie to search for the letters he hoped to find within.

7

Christina could feel the gash in her forehead, but when she finally had the opportunity to look in a handheld mirror brought by Glenna, she was more surprised by her appearance than the wound. She had left Dunverlockie with a neat, sturdily pinned coiffure. What she saw now was chunks of hair come loose, hanging around her face. A few clung to her wound, which Glenna had spent the last ten minutes cleaning.

"I can make a salve," Glenna said, taking the mirror away, as if she was afraid Christina might be frightened at her own reflection. "It should keep it from scarrin'."

"It is not so terrible," Christina said, pulling back one of the stray locks of hair and sliding a pin over it.

Elizabeth came up and looked at her, tilting her head in an evaluative gesture. "I think it adds a great deal of character."

Christina shot her an amused glance. "No doubt you would like one to match?"

Elizabeth laughed. "I shall make do with the bruises I can feel developing on my arms and legs."

Christina's smile wavered. What might have become of them if the accident had happened farther from the inn—or if

Mr. Murray and Glenna had happened to be indoors at the time—she didn't know. She didn't wish to dwell upon the thought.

She only knew that, even with her head pulsing and her arm aching in the immediate aftermath of the accident, she had been aware of the danger they were in with Apollo so frantically attempting to free himself from the contraptions keeping him hooked to the equipage. Mr. Murray had been wise enough to see to that pressing threat first.

"And what about *yer* arm, mistress?" Glenna nodded at it.

Christina gently bent it. It ached, and a bruise seemed to be forming around her elbow, but nothing seemed to be seriously wrong with it. "A few days should be enough to heal it. I am more worried for Apollo. He cannot have escaped the accident without injury."

As if on cue, a knock sounded on the door. Glenna opened it and moved for Mr. Murray to enter. His gaze went straight to Mrs. MacKinnon, and there was something in his eyes she couldn't pinpoint. Was it relief?

"Was Apollo still there?"

The corner of his mouth pulled up. "Aye. And grazin' peacefully."

Christina relaxed. "I might have known."

"He came with me reluctantly. I put him in the stables until I can tend ta the gash on his side." His eyes fixed on her wound, and he came nearer.

"I was just about to make a salve for it," Glenna said.

Mr. Murray kneeled in front of Christina, his eyes trained on her forehead, his brow furrowed. He put a hand under her chin and gently urged her to tip her head back. Christina's impulse was to draw back from such proximity—it had never been pleasant when Gordon had been so near—but she forced herself to stay put, to betray no fear.

There was no reason to fear Mr. Murray. He had been

nothing but civil and attentive to her. She and Elizabeth were indebted to him.

"Ye've done well, Glenna." He pulled back. "But 'twill be best to get that salve and a bandage on it."

She nodded and hurried from the room.

"Are you a doctor?" Elizabeth asked Mr. Murray curiously.

"Nay." He stood. "But ye learn a thing or two about carin' for wounds when all the *real* doctors are taken up with the most serious injuries durin' a battle."

The image of Mr. Murray on the battlefield came to her unbidden. She found herself fascinated by him—the strength he so obviously possessed and yet the gentleness in his voice and touch.

"Where is Mr. Gibson?" he asked.

Christina lifted her shoulders, and her injured elbow panged with the gesture. "We haven't seen him since first arriving."

Mr. Murray's brow contracted, but he nodded, and there was silence for a time. "Was it Mr. Kemp who prepared the carriage for ye today?"

Christina glanced at Elizabeth. "Yes, I imagine so. Why do you ask?"

There was a pause. "Just that the trace had snapped, and I wondered if he'd perhaps said anythin' to ye about it wearin' thin."

She shook her head. "Is that what happened? Is it what caused the accident?"

"From what I can tell, aye." He put a finger to his dark beard, and his fingers toyed with it. "Was it yer husband who employed him?"

She looked at him with a puzzled brow. Did he think it Kemp's fault? That he was incompetent? Christina had no love for the man, but she didn't doubt he knew his work. Carriage accidents were a common enough occurrence. "I believe so, but he has worked in the stables there for years—well before he became the head groom, from what I understand."

Mr. Murray's jaw worked, and his fingers continued to fiddle with his beard. Christina looked at Elizabeth, who was watching him with curious, narrowed eyes.

"Why do you ask such questions, Mr. Murray?" Elizabeth asked in her frank manner.

His eyes flew to her, as if he had forgotten he was not alone in the room, and he dropped his hand from his beard. "'Twas nothin'. Just a matter of curiosity."

Elizabeth looked unsatisfied with his answer, but Mr. Murray spoke again before she could say more.

"Can I accompany ye back to the castle? Ye can ride with me on the wagon. 'Twill be cozy, but I dinna think it wise for ye ta walk all the way."

Christina considered turning down the offer, but the truth was, she had no desire to walk back to Dunverlockie. The thought of climbing back into another equipage was not terribly appealing, of course, but she trusted Mr. Murray. Perhaps it was silly to do so. She didn't know the man. But he knew Alistair, and for someone who had spent many months disconnected from every member of her family, she found that a comfort.

Glenna soon returned with the promised salve and bandages while Mr. Murray went to speak with Mr. Gibson and ready the wagon. He returned a quarter of an hour later, and an amused smile lit up his face at the sight of Christina. He was unfairly attractive, whether he wore a smile or his more usual somberness.

She pushed aside the feelings of self-consciousness at the realization of what had elicited such a smile from him: the large, white bandage wrapped around her head. "My sister assures me that all of this merely adds character to my appearance."

He gave a little chuckle and offered her his arm. "Ye certainly make it look more bonnie than any wound I've ever seen. And I've seen a fair number of 'em."

Unsure how to respond to such a comment, she looked at his offered arm. "I am certain I can manage the stairs without any assistance." She rose from her seated position on the bed.

One of his brows rose, and he dropped his arm. "I willna force ye ta take it, but" —he grimaced and stabilized her with a hand as she teetered slightly— "a blow ta the head can be unpredictable."

She was half inclined to ask for his arm again, half set on holding her ground. It wasn't her stubbornness speaking, whatever he might think. It was simply that she felt unnerved by his touch. But she would rather he assume it was stubbornness.

He waited a moment then gave a nod, turning to lead the way from the room.

The door led out into a narrow, dark corridor, and Christina blinked quickly, hoping her eyes would adjust to the dimness and prevent her from any potential misstep. She put a hand to the rough, plaster wall to help guide her to the top of the stairs, where she stared down at the steps with a hint of misgiving.

Mr. Murray had carried her up them, and while she had been keenly aware then of just how narrow the stairwell was— his hold on her had tightened considerably during that time— he had somehow managed to shield her from any knowledge of how uneven they were in both width and depth.

He put a hand to the ceiling, tilting his head to prevent it from grazing along the plaster, and stepped down two creaky stairs.

Christina didn't move. She was certain she would need both arms to help her keep her balance, and the injured one complained at the mere thought of having so much required of it.

Mr. Murray paused on the fourth step, looking up at her.

Glenna was behind her, holding some of the remnants of the things she had used to tend to Christina, and Elizabeth behind Glenna. They were all waiting.

Christina looked back down to Mr. Murray, and he smiled sympathetically as he came back up two steps and offered her his assistance again. She gripped the solid mass of his forearm, and it became apparent to Christina how he had managed to insulate her before from the rugged journey that was the inn stairs. The man was all muscle and brawn.

Gordon had been a strong man—Christina had come to know that all too well—but Mr. Murray's strength felt different. It wasn't threatening; it was reassuring. Like restrained, well-controlled power.

At the bottom of the stairs, Glenna bid them farewell, but only with a promise from Christina that she would send word if she needed more of the salve.

Mr. Murray led the way to the wagon and helped both Christina and Elizabeth in. By the time he climbed up, it was clear that he had not been exaggerating when he spoke of a cozy journey. The driver's seat of the wagon was certainly not meant for three people, to say nothing of someone of Mr. Murray's stature, and Christina found herself crowded up against him. So much for trying to minimize her contact with him.

"Are you certain you can drive with so little room for your arms?" she asked.

"Aye, lass," he said. "'Tis but a short ride."

The positive side to such close quarters was that there was little room for jostling, and Christina was grateful for it, as her arm twinged with each rise and smack of the wagon on the rough road.

"You had some of the MacKinnons staying at the inn, did you not?" Elizabeth asked as they bobbed up and down.

"Aye, we did," Mr. Murray responded. "But the last of 'em left today."

"How fortunate you are," Elizabeth replied with a sigh full of ill-bridled resentment.

He glanced over at her and then Christina, who gave a bracing smile.

"They willna leave ye be at the castle, then?"

"No, they will not." Elizabeth didn't mince matters. "Angus seems intent upon settling himself in indefinitely. If I had known we would be trading Gordon for him, I might have been less quick to celebrate the demise of the former."

"Elizabeth!" Christina said in alarm.

"What? Mr. Murray will not betray my shocking sentiments, will you?" She looked at him expectantly.

The corner of his mouth twitched. "Nay. I'll no' betray ye." He was quiet for a moment. "Does Angus no' spend time at his own estate?"

Christina sighed. "Precious little, so far. Though he *has* spent one evening there and stayed the night another time."

Mr. Murray's eyes flicked toward her. "Did he now?"

"Yes," Elizabeth said in a voice full of wistfulness. "We felt particularly fortunate when his cronies accompanied him too. That was a wonderful night, was it not?"

Christina's lips drew into a thin line at Elizabeth's loose tongue—she only hoped Mr. Murray was as trustworthy as he seemed—but she was far too truthful to counter her sister's words. It *had* been a pleasant night with the MacKinnons absent. She had been hopeful that it portended the end of their occupation of Dunverlockie, but she had been wrong.

"You said you were in Alistair's regiment?" she asked.

"Aye."

"He has sometimes mentioned the names of his fellow soldiers in his letters, but I do not recall him mentioning the name Murray." In truth, she would have been hard put to recall any name from Alistair's correspondence, but she hoped her words might encourage Mr. Murray to offer up a little more about himself.

His lip quirked up on one side. "'Tis a forgettable name." He pulled up on the reins, and the wagon slowed to a stop before Dunverlockie. Kemp appeared, and Mr. Murray hopped down from the carriage, putting an end to any possibility he might tell more about himself.

Christina tried to brush aside her curiosity.

"What's this?" Kemp asked, perplexity written on his brow as he came to hold the horse's head.

"We had an accident just past the inn," Elizabeth said as Mr. Murray helped her down.

"An accident?"

"Yes." Christina put out her good hand for Mr. Murray to assist her. He set his hands on her waist, though, and lifted her down like he might lift an empty portmanteau. Not expecting it, she was momentarily breathless, but she quickly composed herself, thanked him, and continued to address the groom. "You may need a few people to retrieve the carriage—it is turned over on the road at the bend past Glengour. One of the traces broke, and Apollo was injured, so you will need to take equipment and another horse."

Kemp uttered an oath under his breath.

"I can help ye," Mr. Murray said, "once I've tended ta the horse. I thought I would come see how Mr. MacKinnon's horse is gettin' along while I'm here."

Kemp nodded, and Mr. Murray turned to Christina and Elizabeth. "If ye need anythin'—anythin' at all—dinna hesitate ta send a message." He held Christina's gaze with an intensity that made his words feel like more than simple civility.

"Yes, thank you, Mr. Murray," she said. "Thank you for everything you have done today."

He frowned. "I'm glad I was there."

She suppressed a shudder at the thought of what might have been had any number of small things gone differently. "As am I."

"Allow me ta walk ye ta the door," he said.

Christina hesitated. She was unused to such chivalry, and she hardly knew how to react to it. But she was spared the necessity.

"Thank you, we would appreciate that," Elizabeth said.

Christina sent her an impatient glance, but the way Elizabeth looked at her was unapologetic and the way she moved to ensure it was Christina's arm rather than hers that Mr. Murray took even less so.

Mr. Murray didn't speak on the path to the castle. He seemed to be focused on admiring the building.

"Where do you come from, Mr. Murray?" Christina asked.

His head turned toward her, and she could swear there was a wryness to his smile. "Och, everywhere and nowhere. My siblin's live with my aunt near Inverness, though. 'Twas there I first went when I returned from the war."

She had more questions she wished to ask—about his siblings and why they lived with his aunt, about what sort of background he came from—but they reached the castle, and his gaze lingered on the door for a moment.

"Can I help ye inside?"

"Thank you," she said, "but you have done more than enough."

There was a hint of regret in his eyes, but he nodded and bid them good day then made his way back to the stables.

Angus showed as much surprise as Kemp at the sight of Christina and Elizabeth inside. His focus rested on the bandage wrapped around Christina's head. He was all solicitous concern —reminding her greatly of how Gordon had been when they had first met—going so far as to ensure the preparation of a cup of her preferred tea, which he subsequently brought into the drawing room himself.

"Perhaps you will allow me to fulfill your errands," he said as he watched her drink. "I cannot think it wise for you to attempt the journey again in your state."

Elizabeth was watching him warily, as though all of his punctiliousness was a reason for suspicion. Christina didn't blame her. Angus could be pleasant when he believed it would get him what he wanted.

"I will not trouble you to do that," she responded. "It will just have to wait until Kemp can ensure the safety of the carriage."

In truth, she had lost a bit of her desire to fulfill the errands Angus spoke of, but she didn't trust *him* to fulfill them for her. Besides, an important purpose of the errands was to develop relationships with the merchants, to ensure they knew she was mistress of Dunverlockie—and that she had every intention of acting the part.

They needed to know it, and Angus needed to know it, but just as importantly, she needed to convince herself that it was what she wanted.

8

After tending to Mrs. MacKinnon's horse and assisting Mr. Kemp and two Dunverlockie servants with the righting of the carriage, Lachlan positioned himself so that he had a view of the road from inside the inn. Something Kemp had said had given Lachlan to think that Angus intended to travel to Benleith that evening.

But there was no sign of Angus MacKinnon or any of his kin all evening long. Kemp had evidently been wrong.

Lachlan was anxious and restless—and for more than one reason. He worried for Mrs. MacKinnon and Miss Innes. To be confined in a place like Dunverlockie with only MacKinnon men for company must have been uncomfortable enough; the knowledge that there might be someone there intending harm intensified the malaise Lachlan felt. The castle was large, with plenty of opportunity and space for ill motives to be concealed and carried out.

Beyond that, he himself was impatient for a chance to venture inside Dunverlockie. He knew it well enough that he was confident he could do so unnoticed, but not if there were half a dozen MacKinnon men roaming about. He needed access to the library—perhaps to the laird's room as well, and he wasn't fool enough to attempt anything while Angus was there.

It was entirely possible, of course, that what he was looking for had been destroyed. If that was the case...well, he would take on that difficulty if and when it was necessary. He wouldn't give up. He knew that, at least. The MacKinnons couldn't be allowed to prosper at his family's expense.

The day after the carriage incident, Lachlan stood in the stall with Apollo, inspecting the wound, when he heard the rumbling of wheels on the road. He set the bandage back in place and hurried from the stables to gain a view of the road.

Two closed carriages passed by.

"Who is that?" he asked Glenna, who was walking toward him.

She glanced over her shoulder, squinting. "'Tis Angus MacKinnon's carriage. And that of his kinsman, I believe. Must be headed for Benleith. A nice respite for the mistress."

Lachlan pulled his eyes away from the second carriage as it disappeared among the trees then looked at Glenna. She still referred to Mrs. MacKinnon as "mistress," despite the fact that she no longer worked for her.

"Ye have a special regard for Mrs. MacKinnon," he said.

"Aye," she responded, and a little nostalgic smile appeared on her lips. "I do now. I was terribly afeared when my father told me the lady of Dunverlockie had asked if I wished to be her maid. I kent the reputation of the MacKinnons, and I reckoned she'd be just like them. I didna wish ta go, but my father encouraged me, and...I'm that glad I did. She was the kindest mistress. Never a sharp word ta me, even when she was out of sorts, as she often was."

He had a dozen questions—and a growing interest in the lady of Dunverlockie. "She was unhappy, then?"

Glenna grimaced. "She had plenty of reason ta be."

Lachlan knew he should stop, but he couldn't. "Because of her husband? Because of Gordon?"

Glenna glanced at the inn behind them, as if she was afraid of Mr. Gibson hearing her, then nodded. "I couldna stop worryin' for her when he turned me away—alone as she would be—but Miss Innes came soon after, and it set my heart more at ease."

Lachlan didn't know Miss Innes, but she seemed to be a confident young woman. That might help with Mrs. MacKinnon's solitude, but it would do little to curtail someone with an aim to hurt one—or both—of them. "She'll have the estate ta herself once Angus MacKinnon returns to Benleith for good, though," he said.

Glenna scoffed. "Aye, *if* he returns for good."

"Ye think he'll stay at Dunverlockie?"

She chewed her lip, hesitation in her eyes.

"Ye can trust me, Glenna," he said. "Though, I dinna wish for ye ta say what ye dinna feel comfortable tellin' me."

She shook her head. "I *do* trust ye, so I'll tell ye what I truly think." She threw another glance over her shoulder. "I've heard the way Angus MacKinnon talks ta Mr. Gibson, and I dinna think he intends ta let the mistress have her way at Dunverlockie." Her eyebrows contracted. "She's a strong woman. But I dinna think she's strong enough ta prevent Angus MacKinnon from doin' what he's determined ta do."

"And what is it ye think he'll do?"

She shrugged. "He believes 'tis rightfully his, and I reckon he'll find a way ta take over the management, even if it means runnin' over the mistress roughshod—or forcin' her ta marry him."

"Ye think he'd force her ta marry him?" For some reason, that possibility had never occurred to Lachlan before now. It was a fairly obvious solution to Angus's predicament, though.

Glenna gave another shrug. "If he's anythin' like Gordon

MacKinnon, there is verra little he wouldna stoop ta do in order ta see prosperity for him and his clan."

Lachlan nodded thoughtfully. If there was one thing he had learned during his many years in the army, it was that men were skilled at creating heroes out of themselves and their causes. Soldiers on opposite ends of a battlefield from one another were inspired by the belief that they each fought for right. No doubt, Angus labored under the same assumption.

"Will ye help me keep her safe?" Glenna asked.

"Aye," he said softly. "I will."

Glenna's shoulders relaxed a bit, and she smiled at him. "I'm glad ye came, Mr. Ki"—she laughed nervously—"Mr. Murray. 'Twas a dark day for Kildonnan when Dunverlockie was taken from the Kincaids."

He let out a sigh. "I hope the future will be brighter." He looked at the road, thinking. "Tell me, Glenna. Do ye think Mr. Gibson will mind if I take the evening off? After I've tended ta the horses, of course. I've some matters ta attend to, but I get the feeling he hasna taken ta me terribly well."

She smiled. "Mr. Gibson takes ta no one. But aye. Go do what ye need ta. Now that the MacKinnons are gone, 'twill be fair quiet. I'll tell Mr. Gibson for ye."

"Thank ye, Glenna. Ye're a kind lass."

He finished his tasks quickly then changed his clothing—the last thing he needed was to bring attention to himself with the stink of stables—and took a piece of bread from the kitchen, hurrying from the grounds of the inn and into the trees just as the sky began to darken for the night.

It had been over fifteen years since Lachlan had explored the trees in the area surrounding Dunverlockie. In some ways, the area he had once known was vastly different. The trees were taller and fuller, and there were bushes in places that had once been bare. But there was still enough familiar about it that he never lost his way for more than a minute or two, and within half an hour, he saw the familiar outline of Dunverlockie rising up in the twilight. Only two of the windows were lit, the majority of the castle resting in obscurity, like the darkness gathering around it.

Lachlan paused for a moment, identifying which of the rooms were lit: the dining room and the study. He could only hope that whoever was in the study would have left it by the time he reached it.

He kept in the trees, making his way around the east end of the house and heading for the door that led to the servant quarters. There were other doors leading out from the castle, but Lachlan was convinced they would be locked. The servant entrance, though, was generally left open until the last one went to bed.

Muscles taut, he tugged on the rusty pull, wincing as the hinges creaked. But the door opened, and he waited a moment, listening for any indication that someone was near.

Two voices speaking in Gaelic met his ears, and he waited as they faded away. He opened the door in a swift movement—creaking was less likely the more quickly it was done—and stepped inside.

It was dark, the only light a tallow candle far down the corridor. It barely illuminated the area directly around it: narrow stone walls and a couple of doors leading to bedrooms used by the servants.

As lightfooted as he could manage, he made his way down the corridor. His heart pounded against his chest, and he felt more alive than he had since his last battle, just before he'd taken the edge of a sword to the leg. The thought made his injury ache dully, but he ignored it and pressed on, taking note of every door he could escape through if someone appeared.

The winding stairs that led up to the next floor were cramped, and he scaled them rapidly, knowing well that, the longer he took upon them, the more likely he was to encounter someone. And, if he did, there would be many questions and few answers. His *sgian-dubh* provided little comfort—he had no intention of using the knife, no matter whom he came upon.

Coming to the top of the staircase, he peeked around the corner. Muffled voices sounded somewhere in the vicinity. If they were servants heading for the staircase he stood on, he would be trapped. He hurried across the corridor and into the library, shutting the door with care.

With his back against the closed door, he let his breathing calm. There were a few embers left in the fire grate, as though a servant had been in not long ago to extinguish the fire. He hoped the dim light would be sufficient for his needs.

He let his eyes rove over the room—it was only moderate in size, but what it did contain was of high quality. Mahogany bookcases fanned out from two corners of the room, ending just shy of the mantel. The desk had been made to match—purchased by Lachlan's own grandfather—and he felt a flash of anger. This might have been his. He might have sat in the same seat as his father and grandfather, read the same books, slept in the same bedchambers.

Instead, it was the MacKinnons who did so. And with no right at all to any of it.

He walked over to the desk and opened the drawers one-by-one, eyes straining to see the contents. He shuffled quietly through a few papers, but he had little hope he would find what he was looking for here. Such documents would be kept in a less conspicuous place, likely in some sort of trunk, which might well be locked. There was no trunk in the library, though.

He spent a few more minutes there, but the last of the embers were fading, and there was no light left in the sky but the stars and the crescent of a half-moon. It must be nigh on nine o'clock. The house felt strangely quiet. He could only imagine it would be vastly different if the MacKinnon men hadn't been gone.

He slowly opened the door, looking out into the corridor with the space the small gap afforded. There was no one there, though there was light coming from the drawing room. It was likely that Mrs. MacKinnon and her sister were there, enjoying their time free of the MacKinnons.

Lachlan hesitated for a moment. If Gordon MacKinnon had kept his father's papers, it was probable that they and the other important documents with them would be in the laird's bedchamber.

From what Glenna had said, Lachlan sincerely doubted Mrs. MacKinnon would have shared a bedchamber with her husband, but perhaps she had moved her things there since his death. There was only one way to find out, and he had better use his time inside Dunverlockie well. His intimate knowledge of the second-floor bedchambers would serve him well, at least, but it would be best to do his investigating while Mrs. MacKinnon and Miss Innes were still in the drawing room. He slipped across the corridor and to the stairwell, taking the stairs two at a time. They were stone, at least, and didn't creak.

The corridor was well-lit, and Lachlan made directly for the laird's bedchamber. He closed the door softly behind him and stared at the room. He had come in his father's room many times as a child, always with a great deal of curiosity. The large carpet that covered the floor was unchanged, but the bed hangings and covers were unfamiliar. The smell, too, was different.

The fire was lit, and it elicited a spark of surprise in him—there had been no light in this window when he had looked on from outside. Mrs. MacKinnon *had* evidently taken over the laird's room. It was much better than Angus having done so. He applauded anything she did that might prevent a MacKinnon from having his way with Dunverlockie.

He walked over to the bed and sat upon it. It was soft, and it yielded easily to the weight of his body. He had spent the last sixteen years sleeping in tents—on the ground for the majority of that time as he'd made his way up the ranks and onto a cot. The bed he slept in now at the inn was better than a cot, but only marginally so. It had a mattress, at least, but it was one of straw—and unevenly packed, at that.

This was the bed he might have been sleeping in had life gone differently. Or perhaps not. Perhaps his father would still be alive if not for the MacKinnons.

He knew an impulse to stretch out—to lay on the bed and reimagine his life. But he couldn't forget his purpose. His visit to the castle might be for naught, but nothing was more certain to guarantee that than if he was apprehended.

He strode over to the trunk at the foot of the bed and opened it softly. He had expected to see Mrs. MacKinnon's belongings inside—petticoats, shifts, and such—but it was men's clothing he found. Apparently she hadn't moved Gordon's things yet. In any other situation, he would have assumed it to be out of a sense of respect or nostalgia, but, given what he knew of the marriage between Gordon and Mrs. MacKinnon, it didn't ring true.

He stilled as footsteps sounded in the corridor. What if she entered to find him rifling through her dead husband's belongings? What could he possibly say to justify his presence here?

But the footsteps passed, and he breathed a sigh of relief, increasing his speed as he sorted through the trunk's contents. There were no papers there, though, and he shut the lid with a frown. Where *did* the MacKinnons keep their most important and secret documents?

There was a sudden muffled thud—Lachlan had no trouble recognizing it as the closing of the castle's main door—followed by the distant sound of men's voices.

He swore. Had Angus and his men returned, then? At such an hour?

He rushed to the door on the tips of his toes and peaked out. The voices were growing louder, sailing up the stairwell toward him. It might be best to stay in Mrs. MacKinnon's room. Surely Angus wouldn't have the gall to come inside. But there was no telling when Lachlan would have the opportunity to escape.

No, it was better to go now.

He slipped out through the door and shut it, trusting the men's talking would mask the noise it made. The gap below one of the doors farther down the corridor showed a glimmer of light—Miss Innes's bedchamber, he assumed—but the others were dark. There were two ways down to the ground floor from here, and there sounded to be at least three men upon one set of those stairs. The other stairs—used exclusively by the servants in Lachlan's childhood—were at the far end of the corridor. His only option was to hope he could get there before Angus and his kinsmen reached the top of the main stairs.

Halfway there, he realized it was a futile endeavor. He wouldn't reach them by the time the men turned the corner. So he did the only other thing he *could* do, pushing open the door of the nearest dark room and slipping inside.

His heart thundered so violently, he had to strain to hear the voices in the corridor. But a sound much nearer made him whip around, eyes searching the dark of his own childhood room.

Mrs. MacKinnon stood beside her bed in her shift, hair tumbling over her shoulders and a candlestick threateningly raised above her head.

9

Christina stared wide-eyed at the outline of the tall, dark man in her bedchamber. Her arm was raised and ready to strike with every ounce of strength she possessed if he took a single step toward her. She had only just been freed from the aggressive attentions of her husband. She had no intention of submitting to those of one of his kinsmen without all the fight she had within her.

But it was not one of Gordon's kinsmen staring back at her in the dark. It was Mr. Murray. Her surprise made her upraised arm waver for a moment, but she cocked it back even farther.

He looked just as alarmed as she did, though, and the finger he put in front of his lips was pleading rather than menacing. He wanted her silence, and her first inclination was to scream. But for whom? Angus had just returned with at least two or three of his men, and she had no desire to make them think they were welcome in her room—no matter how extraordinary the circumstances. She didn't even want to plant the thought in their heads.

Mr. Murray stayed by the door, allowing his finger to drop from his mouth when she made no cry. His chest heaved, and his wide gaze remained fixed on her, reminding her of a hunted fox.

The voices of Angus and his men lingered in the corridor—they sounded to be discussing something—and Christina took the time to plan what she would do if Mr. Murray made any attempt to approach her once the threat of the men was gone. Could she truly have been so misled about a man—again?

She refused to give in to the panic inside her, but her arm was too tired to maintain its position for much longer, and she lowered it, holding the candlestick between her and Mr. Murray to make it clear that she would use it if he gave her reason to.

He gave a nod as she did it, as if he understood, and she felt more confused than ever. What on earth was this man doing in her bedchamber? Or in the castle at all?

Finally, the voices faded—the men seemed to be returning down the stairs. It was far earlier than they generally went to sleep, and Christina was unsurprised at the knowledge that they likely meant to imbibe more before bidding one another good night. There had been more than one morning when she had gone down to partake of breakfast, only to find one or two of them unconscious on the floor.

She watched Mr. Murray warily as the voices disappeared altogether, knowing this was the moment her safety hinged upon.

He put his hands out in front of him, palms facing her. "Please. I can explain, Mrs. MacKinnon."

Relief flooded her as he stayed in place. Perhaps this was all a mistake. Perhaps he *didn't* intend her any harm. She wouldn't show any weakness, though. He was far stronger than she, and she knew how quickly a seeming gentleman could change into a brute if the opportunity for it presented.

"I certainly hope so," she said in a stony voice.

He looked at her evaluatively, and she suddenly felt uncomfortably aware of her state of undress. But only once did his eyes flick away from her face, returning swiftly from the expanse of skin her shift revealed around her neck. She instinctively reached for her wrapper with the arm not holding the candlestick and winced. It was still painful from the accident.

Mr. Murray stepped toward her, teeth clenched in a sympathetic expression.

She hurried to raise the candlestick up, and he immediately backtracked, his hands coming up again in defense.

"I mean ye no harm, Mrs. MacKinnon. I swear it."

Her nostrils flared, and she felt a sudden and inexplicable urge to cry. She swatted it away hurriedly, ascribing it to the pain in her arm. "You expect me to believe that when you have invaded my room? At this time of night?"

"I ken how it must look," he replied. "Will ye allow me ta explain it?"

She didn't know whether she wanted an explanation. Part of her simply wanted him gone. She could threaten him with the wrath of the MacKinnon clan if he ever stepped foot in Dunverlockie again, but the truth was that, if MacKinnons chose to pursue him, it would be because he had come into their territory unbidden, not because they were avenging a wrong against her. She had outlived her use to them once the money from her father had moved to their hands, and they wouldn't endanger their kin on her account.

"I can sit down on the floor if 'twould put ye more at ease," he said.

She nodded, jaw clenched tightly.

"Can I get that for ye first?" With his head, he indicated the wrapper she had reached for.

She didn't want his help. But the only other options were to remain in her thin shift or struggle into the wrapper on her own with a fair amount of pain and the possibility that she wouldn't manage it in the end.

She chose the former, feeling it would be too harmful to the image of strength she wished to maintain if she couldn't manage the latter.

"No," she said.

He nodded and slowly lowered himself to the floor, letting one leg rest on the wooden planks while the other was bent at the knee. His back rested against the door.

She remained standing for another moment then sat on the edge of the bed, keeping the candlestick in hand and her eyes on Mr. Murray, looking at him expectantly.

He didn't speak right away. His fingers fiddled with his beard, and his gaze was trained on the rug that covered most of the floor in the bedchamber. Was he creating a story he thought would satisfy her?

"Well?" she said.

Hooded under a frown, his gaze flicked up to her face. "Mrs. MacKinnon," he said gravely. "Can I trust ye?"

She blinked at him. "Trust me?"

He met her gaze squarely, but there was wariness in his brow, and it puzzled her as much as his words.

"I rather think *I* should be the one asking that of *you*," she said. "And I admit, I had hoped I could trust you, given your friendship with my brother, but I am sure you can understand how your appearance here has thrown great doubt upon that."

He nodded. "Aye. Of course. What I mean ta say is"—he let out a sigh—"well, if I tell ye the truth, 'twill be puttin' my life in yer hands."

"It is already in my hands, Mr. Murray," she said coldly. "I could call to Angus now, and he should likely kill you on the spot." She declined to point out that Mr. Murray would have little trouble silencing her before she could accomplish such a thing. She imagined he realized that himself. But he didn't say so. Nor was she entirely certain that Angus would win in a battle with Mr. Murray. In stature, Mr. Murray had the advantage.

"'Tis true," he said. "Well, then." His hand dropped from his beard, and he set it on his knee, where his kilt draped. "If ye're ta understand, I suppose the first thing ta tell ye is that I grew up here."

Her eyebrows knit. "In Kildonnan?"

He shook his head, holding her gaze. "At Dunverlockie."

"You were a servant here?"

He shook his head again, saying nothing, as if he expected her to understand everything with that simple gesture.

"I do not...I do not understand."

He grimaced. "Ye said ye didna recognize my name from any of yer brother's letters. Well, there's a reason for that." He hesitated a moment. "My name is Kincaid, no' Murray."

She stared. She knew of the Kincaids. It was a name she knew well, for it was the one most loathed by the MacKinnons.

"*You* are a Kincaid of Dunverlockie?"

He nodded once, and she could see the wariness in his eyes, watching to see how she would react—what she would do with the information he was giving her.

She narrowed her eyes, casting her mind back to a letter she had received months ago. "Alistair *did* mention you."

A little smile—one full of reminiscence and affection—tugged at the corner of Mr. Murray—of Mr. Kincaid's mouth.

Not for more than a moment did she consider asking why he would conceal his identity. It was clear why he wouldn't wish it to be known in MacKinnon territory—or what was *now* MacKinnon territory. But she certainly had other questions. "What are you doing here?"

The smile faded. "I was lookin' for somethin'. Some letters."

Her brows knit together.

"They belonged to my father," he explained.

Understanding dawned on her. "He was the one who..." She

stopped, realizing how unfeeling her next words might seem. She should have kept the thought in her mind.

"Aye. He was executed."

There was silence.

"I am sorry," she said softly. She knew what it was to lose a father, but to lose one in such a way....

"Thank ye." He said it in a voice every bit as soft as hers—as soft and tender as his appearance was rough and sturdy. The small glimmer of vulnerability brought on another strange desire to cry within her. It had been a very long time since she had seen any display of gentleness in a man. She felt a sudden and strange kinship with Mr. Kincaid—he was unwelcome in this place, just as she was. And yet, something was keeping him here.

A number of things connected in her mind as she looked at him. He, the son of a known and reviled Jacobite, had served with Alistair in the Highland Regiment. The sentiment among many of the soldiers there was distinctly anti-Jacobite from what she understood. Had this man *ever* heard someone lament his father's death? How must it feel to return to this place and see it occupied by the MacKinnons? She didn't know the history behind the hate between the families, but she knew it was real and potent.

She looked at the candlestick in her hands and set it on the table beside the bed. Mr. Kincaid's eyes watched her, and she could swear there was a glint of gratitude in them as she did it. A shaft of moonlight seeping through a gap in the curtains fell across his face, highlighting the scar under his eye, evidence of a brush with death. The limp he walked with, too, was an indication of how he had fought for the country that had executed his father.

"These letters you refer to," she said. "What precisely are they?"

"Proof."

"Proof of what?"

He held her gaze with a slight grimace. "That yer husband's father should have been executed on the same scaffold as my father."

She said nothing. She had never met her father-in-law, but she had heard plenty of stories.

"Ye dinna believe it?"

She gave a little laugh. "On the contrary. I have no trouble at all believing such a thing. I would believe anything you told me of the MacKinnons."

"What, then?"

She lifted her shoulders, hesitant to give voice to her true thoughts. "It is just...I cannot help but wonder what the purpose is. Even if you found these letters you speak of, what good would it do now? The time has long passed since anyone could be punished for involvement in the rebellion."

He nodded. "I ken. But the truth matters. Does it no'?"

"Yes," she said. "It does. But is it worth risking your life over? For, make no mistake, that is what you are doing, being here at Dunverlockie tonight."

"My life has been at risk for as long as I can remember, Mrs. MacKinnon. If I can risk it for the crown and country that killed my father and took my home, I can certainly risk it ta clear my father's name."

She had no argument against his words. There *was* none. Indeed, she admired the sentiment and strength Mr. Kincaid demonstrated to pursue such a quest.

He put a hand to his leg and, with a slight wince, shifted his position.

"You needn't sit on the floor any longer," she said.

He searched her face then, seeming satisfied with what he saw, gave a grateful smile, pushing himself up from the floor and using the mantel as support. His gaze settled on the small wooden figures there, and he put a hand to one—a squirrel.

"What are these?" he asked, a small but curious smile on his lips.

"My siblings," she said.

He shot a quizzical glance at her and picked up the squirrel.

"That is Ninian," she said. "I made one for each of them before coming here."

"Ye made them yerself?"

She nodded. She hadn't indulged her love of carving since then.

Mr. Kincaid turned the figurine in his hand, letting the light of the fire illuminate it. "And why is Ninian a squirrel?"

She rose from the bed and went over to the hearth with an affectionate smile on her lips. She put out a hand, and Mr. Kincaid gave her the figurine.

"He climbs trees as well as one, and he is forever sneaking food from the kitchen."

Mr. Kincaid's finger reached to touch the squirrel's cheeks, which were full. It held a nut to its mouth despite that.

"Ye've a talent for it," he said as she set the squirrel back on the mantel. He looked around the room. "This was my bedchamber when I was a lad. I suppose 'tis why I chose this door when I realized I couldna reach the stairs in time—habit."

Christina raised her brows and watched him as his eyes took in the room. The revelation was another small but strange connection between them, and she wasn't certain what to do with the way it made her feel.

"These letters you spoke of," she said, "where do you suspect them to be?"

He lifted his shoulders. "If they havna been destroyed, I'd wager they'd be kept with the other valuable documents belongin' to the MacKinnons. My father kept his own correspondence in a separate place from his other documents. 'Twas a secret he kept from everyone, includin' my mother. But I had assumed Mr. MacKinnon—yer husband's father, I mean—

would no' have stopped lookin' 'till he found them and destroyed them. Perhaps I'm wrong, though." His brow furrowed. "Perhaps they're still somewhere in the castle."

Christina looked at him warily. "You mean to return, then? To keep looking?"

He waited then nodded once. "I canna give up. No' when I've come so far."

She smiled wryly. "And I am to turn a blind eye to these violations of the law? And of my own home?"

"Only you can make that choice." He turned to reach for the door. "But I give ye my word that I willna take anythin' that doesna belong ta me or prove the part the MacKinnons played in my father's fate."

She stared at him for a moment, her lips pressed together. Allowing him to breach the walls of the property that now belonged to her went against everything she was attempting to prove—that she was mistress of Dunverlockie and would brook no interference.

But the alternative was to make Mr. Kincaid a hunted man and provoke a conflict she had no desire to watch unfold or feel responsible for. Mr. Kincaid was alone; Angus had a host of men at his disposal. It was hardly a fair fight.

"Very well," she said reluctantly.

"Thank ye, Mrs. MacKinnon," he said, turning toward the door again. But he paused. "I meant what I said about comin' ta me if ye ever stand in need of help."

"You have helped me more than enough already with the accident."

He turned again to face her, his expression troubled.

"What?" she asked, perplexed.

His hand dropped from the door latch, and his jaw worked for a moment. Even beneath the thick beard, she could see its strength. The light of the orange flames in the grate nearby gave the hair on his chin and cheeks a reddish hue.

"Ye believe 'twas naught but bad luck, then?" he asked.

Her smile faded completely. "What do you mean?"

He hesitated again, and she thought on the questions he had asked about Kemp.

"Ye seem a capable woman, Mrs. MacKinnon, and no' one ta take fright easily."

She resisted the urge to squirm. She had thought those same things of herself once, but if he only knew how weak she had become under the thumb of Gordon, Mr. Kincaid would never say such a thing.

"I debated tellin' ye, but"—he shook his head—"I canna put it from my mind."

She stared at him, feeling her pulse begin to pick up speed.

"The trace on the carriage," he said. "It looked as though it had been cut. No' clean through, but halfway—enough ta compromise it."

Her eyelids fluttered. "You think someone intended to harm us."

He held her gaze intently, not saying a word, and she put a hand to her stomach as chills cascaded over her neck, back, and arms, making her skin prickle. She could see his meaning in his eyes. "You think someone meant to *kill* us."

His apologetic grimace was answer enough.

She shook her head, taking a step back. "No. I cannot believe that."

"Did ye no' just say ye would believe anythin' of the MacKinnons?"

She *had* said that. And it wasn't that she couldn't believe what Mr. Kincaid was saying. She didn't *want* to. She didn't want to believe she was living in a house with people who wished her harm. How could they think to get away with such a thing?

"I have no doubt Angus is anything but pleased with my

inheriting Dunverlockie," she said, "but to—to—to *murder* me? And my sister too? Surely he would not be so callous."

"Ye know him better than I," Mr. Kincaid said, but he sounded unconvinced.

She felt nausea roil in her stomach, and she shut her eyes. She *did* know Angus. He had the same determination her husband had—an eye single to the welfare of the clan.

When she opened her eyes, Mr. Kincaid was watching her carefully, his brow creased in a deep frown—worried. "I could be wrong. 'Tis why I hesitated ta say anythin'. Mrs. MacKinnon"—he reached for her uninjured arm, and she pulled it away.

He retracted his hand immediately, gaze fixed on her wrist, which she hurried to cover with her other hand, ignoring how her elbow panged with the movement. But she hadn't been quick enough. She saw it in his eyes—he had noticed the bruises there.

His gaze flashed back up to her face, suddenly alert.

"It is just a bit painful from the accident."

He nodded, but she knew he didn't believe her. He had been well aware of which arm she had injured in the accident, and the bruises on the other arm were fading rather than fresh. They looked a sickly color in the light of the fire, and still vaguely in the shape of fingerprints—Gordon's fingerprints. They had lingered for two weeks now, as if to spite Christina— to force more reminders on her.

"You should go," she said, suddenly eager for Mr. Kincaid to be gone. She hated the look in his eyes, knowing he saw her as weak now.

"Aye," he said. "Thank ye, Mrs. MacKinnon. Ye ken where ta find me."

She didn't acknowledge his words, merely standing in place as he pulled the door open. He peered out then disappeared into the corridor.

The door shut behind him, and Christina glanced down at her arm, rubbing the bruises, as if she could erase them. When she had first entered this room after Gordon's death, she had been so profoundly grateful to know that it was a place she could now truly call her own. She could fall asleep free of the worry that Gordon might come in, breath stinking of drink, demanding his due.

But with the knowledge she had just gained from Mr. Kincaid, it suddenly felt lonely and unsafe.

10

Lachlan managed his escape from Dunverlockie without any complications. He could easily hear the merry-making and raucous laughter of the men, coming from the dining room, as he made his way down to the ground floor.

He paused at the head of the servant staircase, nostrils flaring as he thought on what he had seen in Mrs. MacKinnon's bedchamber—the bruising on her arm. He could guess it wasn't Angus or the other men in the dining room who were responsible for it, but all the same, he knew a desire to unsheathe his *sgian dubh* and issue them a warning they couldn't ignore. If a man would cause such harm to his wife, there was no limit to what his kin might do once her husband was gone and his estate had fallen to her.

Lachlan took in a deep breath, reminding himself that this was a war, not a battle. His strategy was important, and barreling into a dining room full of drunken MacKinnons was the move of a man with a temper and no real plan.

He continued down the steps, light of foot, making his way down the corridor and through the door he had entered over an hour ago.

He was woken early the following morning by the unwelcome, burly voice of Mr. Gibson, demanding Lachlan see to the passengers who had apparently arrived while he had been at Dunverlockie the night before. The innkeeper seemed intent on making known his displeasure with Lachlan, grumbling between orders. Lachlan helped a frenzied Glenna to prepare some bannocks and ale for the two men, who were eager to get on their way again.

"Were ye able ta attend ta the things ye spoke of yesterday?" she asked as she brought back the preserves on a wooden tray.

"Nearly," he said. "'Twill take more time."

She shot him a significant look. "No' if Mr. Gibson has any say in the matter. 'Twas ill luck for those men ta come while ye were out."

He sighed. "I'll be sure ta make up for it today."

True to his word, Lachlan spent the day mucking the stalls and cleaning the inn. He spent a great deal more time on the mucking than he normally did, for it allowed him to keep an eye on Mr. Gibson, who had been tasked with repairing a few minor issues with Mrs. MacKinnon's carriage.

"I'll return it ta Dunverlockie," Lachlan offered as Mr. Gibson finished his work.

Mr. Gibson shot him a sidelong glance, as though he was suspicious of such an offer, but he was a lazy man, and he assented after a moment, leaving the carriage to Lachlan.

Lachlan retrieved one of the inn's horses—Mrs. MacKinnon's needed more time to heal before being put to use again—and readied the carriage. His eyes ran along every piece of equipment, looking for any sign or indication of tampering. But there was none. Now, if only Kemp could ensure it remained that way.

Perhaps he had been too quick to tell Mrs. MacKinnon his suspicions, but when he'd seen her in her bedchamber, candlestick raised in readiness to attack, he had realized how difficult he would find it to ever forgive himself if she came to harm because he had failed to warn her.

He had meant what he'd said: she was a strong woman. But a woman with the kind eyes he'd seen that night—no matter her strength—was simply unequipped to confront a depraved and determined man.

He felt the weight of her safety on his shoulders, much as he might try to shrug it off. It wasn't just that he owed it to her brother, though that was certainly part of it. She had been hurt, her life controlled by the MacKinnons. In that way, they were the same, and it entangled her in his goal. His success meant her success; his failure meant her suffering.

It was true that Mrs. MacKinnon was also the most beautiful woman he had ever seen—a beauty that had struck him momentarily dumb when his eyes had adjusted enough to see that it was her bedchamber he'd stumbled into. But, more than her beauty, it was the impossible mixture of kindness, strength, and fear in her eyes that drew him to her. It was a haunting, ethereal beauty, full of unspeakable stories he needed to hear —and dreaded hearing.

When Lachlan arrived at Dunverlockie with the carriage half an hour later, Mr. Kemp met him at the stables. He knew a feeling of disappointment not to see Mrs. MacKinnon there as he had the last time, but as he led the inn's horse away and on the path back to the main road, she appeared up ahead.

"I saw your arrival through the window," she said. Her breath came somewhat quickly, as though she had hurried there and was still trying to catch it. The wound on her head had scabbed and seemed to be healing quickly—thanks, no doubt, to Glenna's ministrations.

He tried not to betray the pleasure he felt at seeing her. She was only recently widowed, after all, and it was unlikely she held him in very high regard after the events of last night.

"I thought of coming out to the stables," she continued, and he was surprised to see a little twinkle in her dark eyes, "but I admit I was curious to see if you would make another attempt to come inside."

He laughed, running a hand along the horse's neck. It seemed to sense they wouldn't be leaving quickly and reached its neck to the ground, searching for food. "Or ye could simply let me in yerself and save me the trouble of hidin'."

She raised a brow but still smiled. "I may have agreed not to inform Angus about your doings, but I hope you did not take that to mean I would go out of my way to assist you."

He shrugged playfully. "'Twas worth askin'."

She looked toward the stables. "I see you brought the carriage but not the horse. How is Apollo?"

"Restin'. But he should be well enough ta return ta ye in a day or two."

She nodded. "Thank you for taking care of him."

"Nay bother," he said. "I also inspected the carriage before returnin' it. It looks ta be safe, but"—he grimaced and shook his head"—that doesna mean 'twill remain that way. I encourage ye ta give everything a look if ye intend ta go out as ye did before."

"What, and offend Kemp by showing such blatant distrust of his work?"

Lachlan let out a sigh. "Aye, 'tis a mite awkward. Well, ye can always call upon me if ye wish for me ta drive ye somewhere."

Her mouth turned up at the corner. "With the understanding that I return the favor by welcoming you into Dunverlockie?"

He smiled but gave a shake of the head. "No need ta return the favor."

She held his gaze for a moment, as if trying to puzzle him out.

He shrugged a shoulder. "Or if ye prefer his escort, Angus could accompany."

She scoffed. "Hardly. Though at least I could trust the safety of the carriage in such a scenario, for Angus would never make an attempt on my life if it also put his own in danger."

"Ye make light of it," he said. "Do ye still doubt, then?"

She reached out to pet the horse. "I don't know, to be honest. I suppose I simply don't wish to entertain the notion, but I cannot deny that it is possible. The MacKinnon lairds have never shied away from what would bring more prosperity to the clan. The irony of it all is not lost upon me, though."

"Irony?" Lachlan asked.

She turned her head to stare at Dunverlockie. "My father believed himself to be ensuring my well-being and that of my siblings when he insisted on the clause in Gordon's will—that Dunverlockie fall to me if Gordon were to die without any children. I only mean that it is ironic that it should be that very decision which put my life at real risk."

Lachlan said nothing, searching her face for an indication of how she felt. Was her nonchalance as she spoke of the danger simply disbelief? Was she trying to seem stronger to keep him from worrying? Or did she hold her life so cheaply? She had no men in her life to provide protection, and Lachlan was limited in what he could do.

She turned back to him. "Thank you again. Perhaps I shall come visit Apollo tomorrow. I can bring him back with me, then, if he is ready. It will save you the trouble."

"'Tis no trouble, but I ken Glenna would be happy ta see ye."

"Good day to you, Mr."—she paused—"Murray."

He nodded and pulled on the reins, feeling impatient already for the visit she had suggested.

11

C hristina sat down for breakfast with Elizabeth in the dining room, feeling more tired than usual. Morning was the only time of day they could hope to have the room to themselves, as the MacKinnon men remained abed until much later—assuming they had made it back to their beds after staying awake into the night drinking and singing and laughing, often so loudly that it woke Christina with a start.

"How divine is a bit of silence," Elizabeth said contentedly, accepting a cup of tea from Christina. She looked inside it and paused, an expression of distaste on her face. "This is not *your* tea, is it?"

Christina shot her a look. "No, it is not. I know you well enough not to commit such an egregious error of judgment as *that*. I had Janet bring a second pot of water for me." She reached for the smaller pot she always used for her own tea— just big enough to fill her cup twice.

Elizabeth sighed her relief and sat back, stirring her tea. "Does *anyone* enjoy that blend aside from you?"

Christina shook her head. "And that suits me very well."

"How did you manage to find—to say nothing of *preferring* —such a...well, such an *atrocious* blend of leaves?"

Christina shrugged. "I admit I didn't particularly like it at first. But it grew on me steadily." She didn't care to delve into the history with Elizabeth. There were few things Christina had been able to call her own at Dunverlockie, and her particular blend of tea was one of them. It had become a way to assert what little power she had in her marriage—to set herself apart from her husband, even if it was in a way that Elizabeth or others might find trivial or silly.

The door opened, and Angus appeared. Christina glanced at Elizabeth, whose lips pursed in displeasure.

"You are up early," Elizabeth said in a falsely sweet voice.

Angus gave no sign of hearing this besides a quick glance.

"Were you aware, Christina, that Angus has taken up residence in the laird's bedchamber?" Elizabeth asked as if conveying a mildly interesting bit of news.

Christina tensed, but in truth, she was glad for Elizabeth's forthrightness. She *had* noticed Angus's silent act, and she had been waiting for the time—and the courage—to address it when he was not surrounded by his entourage.

Angus seemed unperturbed by Elizabeth mentioning it, though, and he took a seat at the table, reaching for the larger teapot. "I thought it would be easier to sort through some of Gordon's things that way—there is an entire trunk to go through."

Christina and Elizabeth shared an incredulous look at the impossibly flimsy excuse for such a blatant and aggressive show of authority at Dunverlockie.

"Surely you might have had the trunk moved into your own bedchamber," Elizabeth said.

"Even that would be unnecessary," Christina said, feeling her pride flaring up. "I am perfectly capable of sorting through Gordon's things, Angus."

He reached a hand toward hers, and she retracted it. He stared at her for a moment, then pulled his own hand back. "I told you, did I not, that I would not allow the burden of Gordon's death to fall entirely on your shoulders? Besides," he said, taking a sip of tea, "there are documents and other things that belong to the clan, and I'm certain you can appreciate that I am the best one to take charge of those things."

"And just how long *do* you intend to stay here, Angus?" Elizabeth asked, her tone of polite curiosity beginning to fracture.

He shot her an unpleasant smile. "As long as I can be of assistance. Speaking of which, I took the liberty of bringing you another bag of tea when I passed through Craiglinne."

Christina stared at him, blinking. She felt Elizabeth's eyes on her, but she continued looking at Angus.

He shrugged. "I noticed your supply running short and imagined it was something you had intended to do the other day when you had the accident on the road. I thought I might save you the trouble. I see your arm is still giving you pain."

She realized she had been holding her elbow, and she dropped her hand. She hated showing weakness to Angus, and she wasn't certain what to make of his errand on her behalf. Was he truly being considerate? Or was it a desire to disarm her, perhaps? There was *always* an ulterior motive. She could only be grateful he hadn't broached the subject of marrying her again.

"That is kind of you," she said, "but I assure you that you needn't put yourself out on my behalf. I enjoy getting out."

He gave a conciliatory nod. "Certainly. I had not realized it would give offense. I can certainly attempt to return the tea if you wish."

"No, of course not." She knew how petty it would seem if she insisted on such a thing.

Living under the same roof as Angus and his men was not agreeing with her. She felt exhausted by it, and her stomach increasingly swarmed with disquiet to the point that she felt ill.

She soon excused herself, and Elizabeth followed suit.

"I think it is time for you to say goodbye to your special blend of tea, Christina," Elizabeth said as they made their way up the stairs. "If you have acquired a taste for *that*, certainly you can acquire a taste for another strange mixture."

Christina looked at her, frowning. "But why?"

"I trust nothing that has passed through that man's hands."

Christina didn't respond for a moment, but her stomach roiled even more. "It is not as though he made it himself."

"No, but that does not mean he had no opportunity to do something to it."

Christina stopped at the top of the staircase, turning toward her sister. "Are you being serious, Elizabeth?" She spoke in a whisper, aware that MacKinnon men slept in the nearby bedchambers. "Do you think I am in such danger?"

Elizabeth held her gaze, a frown creasing her brow. "Truthfully? I hardly know. You know I have no love for Angus—or *any* MacKinnon."

"*I* am a MacKinnon, Elizabeth," she replied.

"In name only." She paused, looking down the staircase they had just come up. "I haven't wished to worry you, and perhaps it is simply an exaggerated distrust of MacKinnon men which makes me feel this way, but"—she took Christina's hand in hers, and the lace on Christina's sleeve fell back, revealing the same fading bruises Mr. Kincaid had glimpsed in the light of the fire and moon.

Elizabeth's eyes closed, and her nostrils flared. "If a man tasked with protecting you could do this, what would his kin not do when they undoubtedly see you as a threat to their clan?"

Christina pulled her arm away from Elizabeth's hold and arranged the sleeve so that it covered the marks. They were evidence of the final battle of wills between her and Gordon, before he had fallen suddenly ill.

"Can you not insist they leave?" Elizabeth asked pleadingly. "They have no business being here now that the funeral is over."

Christina sighed. "If I thought it would do any good to insist on such a thing, I assure you I would have done it. But I know firsthand how volatile are the tempers of the MacKinnon men, and an outright demand like the one you suggest will be taken by them as provocation. The situation requires more strategy and subtlety than that. I merely need the time to reflect on how to go about it."

Elizabeth gave her a sympathetic grimace. "And all the while, Angus is digging his claws deeper and deeper into Dunverlockie."

"We need to get out," Christina said. It was difficult for her to think clearly surrounded by her husband's kinsmen. "I thought to walk to the inn today to see how Apollo is getting along. Would you like to join me?"

Elizabeth nodded.

Grim and confining as Dunverlockie often felt, Christina could never deny how well she loved the area surrounding it, particularly at this milder time of year. She could lose herself in the thick forest, walk along the rushing river, or admire the stormy sea, all within minutes of each other.

The winter before Elizabeth's arrival had been long, dark, and the loneliest days Christina could remember. Going out for a walk to the toun—or even the inn—had been impossible most of the time, not only due to weather but because of how little daylight there was. She had been forced to content herself with short walks on the grounds immediately surrounding the castle and returning inside for a cup of tea afterward.

To walk the path to the inn on a relatively warm May day in the company of her sister—and without the prospect of returning home to Gordon—was more happiness than she had believed possible a few months ago. Her problems had certainly not disappeared, but fresh air and sunlight had a way of making even the gloomiest ones seem more surmountable.

The image of Glenna and Mr. Kincaid emerging from the inn door, too, lifted her spirits, nearly managing to rid her of the weight in her stomach. Little reason though there might be for it, she felt safer in Mr. Kincaid's presence. Whether it was a function of his stature or the fact that he felt like a proxy for Alistair, she didn't know.

"Come to see Apollo?" Mr. Kincaid asked.

"Yes," she said. "Do you think he's able to return to Dunver-lockie today?"

Glenna came up beside Christina as they followed Mr. Kincaid toward the stables. "I've a mind ta keep him here if it means ye'll return every day," Glenna said.

"*I* am certainly not opposed to that," Elizabeth said. "I begin to think it might be preferable to Dunverlockie, if only because the company is better. And safer, no doubt."

Christina met Mr. Kincaid's curious glance, but it was Glenna who spoke. "Are the men givin' ye trouble?"

"I think that is all they are capable of giving," Elizabeth said dryly.

"But truly, mistress," Glenna said, her clear gaze directed at Christina. "Do ye feel unsafe?"

"Everyone else seems to think I should," Christina said. "You would know better than any of us, though. You have had the most prolonged acquaintance with the MacKinnons, Glenna. What is your opinion?"

They reached the stables, and Glenna stopped at the entrance, a thoughtful expression on her dirt-stained face. "I dinna ken most of the Benleith MacKinnons by much more than their reputation, mistress. But Angus MacKinnon and his men inspire fear and obedience by that reputation. The toun here is uneasy ta ken he's remained at Dunverlockie this long. They worry 'twill be *him* actin' as laird and that he'll raise the rents, pushin' everyone out."

Mr. Gibson's voice rang out from inside the inn, calling for Glenna.

"I must go," she said, "but yer sister's right, mistress. The furnishin' here is no' what ye're accustomed ta, but ye can come stay at the inn if 'twill keep ye safe. Mr. Murray and I will ensure it."

"I don't think that will be necessary," Christina replied. "But thank you, Glenna."

She nodded and hurried toward the back door of the inn.

Christina debated whether to introduce Elizabeth to Mr. Kincaid by his proper name—and status—but she didn't wish to do so without ensuring that he had no objections to Elizabeth knowing the truth. She hadn't yet told Elizabeth of the late-night encounter with Mr. Kincaid in her own bedchamber. Christina wasn't entirely certain how to feel about it herself.

He showed them to Apollo. A bandage was wrapped around the horse just behind his withers.

"He's healin' well, but I think 'twill be better ta keep him here another day if it doesna put ye out ta do so. He's no' ready for a saddle yet." He adjusted the bandage slightly and turned toward Christina and Elizabeth. "Would the two of ye like ta come inside for a cup of ale and some bannocks? There are still a few left over from when the MacKinnon men were here—they're no' fresh, of course, but..." He shrugged.

Christina looked at her sister.

"I am happy for any excuse to delay our return," Elizabeth said.

They sat down in the dim coffee room of the inn as Glenna brought a small tray of bannocks and Mr. Kincaid poured them each a cup of ale. Christina had been inside the inn but a few times and Elizabeth only the day of the carriage accident. It was better than many of the inns on the Highland roads, but if one had experience of the inns nearer to Edinburgh—or of most Lowland inns—it left much to be desired. With few windows, low ceilings, and sparse furnishings likely accumulated from the sale of old, unwanted furniture from nearby estates, it relied for its business on being the only inn for miles and a necessary stop between Skye and Fort William.

Their coze in the coffee room was short-lived, though, as Mr. Gibson put a quick stop to it once he realized what his workers were about. Christina and Elizabeth stood along with Glenna and Mr. Kincaid, taking their leave.

"Ye'll be back soon, then?" Glenna asked as she cleared away the empty cups.

Christina nodded. "I am sorry we've made Mr. Gibson upset with you."

Glenna waved a hand. "He enjoys bein' upset. Good day to ye, mistress. Miss Innes." She curtsied and left toward the kitchen with the trays.

"She's tellin' the truth," Mr. Kincaid said, coming up beside Christina as she walked toward the door. He had to stoop under the doorway. "'Tis for the best if he has a few opportunities ta shout and grumble on any given day. Otherwise, it builds up, and the result isna pretty." They emerged from the inn. "I'll send ye word if I think the horse needs more time. Or perhaps I'll bring the message personally." His smile teased her.

"Perhaps you will consider knocking if you do," she replied significantly.

Elizabeth shot Christina a puzzled look, as though she wished to understand what the cause for amusement was.

Christina avoided her eye, and they were soon on their way back to Dunverlockie.

The dinner hour was approaching when they reached the castle, and the two of them parted ways to clean up and prepare for the meal. But Christina only remained in her bedchamber for a few minutes. She had something else she wished to do first.

She pretended to fumble with the latch of her door for a moment, paying attention to the sounds around her. Angus rarely spent time in his bedchamber during the day, and she was almost certain he and his men had gone out hunting. They had often done so when Gordon had been alive, returning late into the afternoon, just after sunset—and expecting dinner to be awaiting them, despite the fact that it had been served long before.

Christina went to the door of the bedchamber which she had always known as Gordon's and pushed it open. The curtains of both windows had been pulled aside, and the afternoon light poured onto the floor and bed in large rectangles. Her eyes lingered on the trunk at the base of the bed for a moment, but she was certain Mr. Kincaid had already looked there, and her gaze moved around the room, settling on the tapestry hanging on the wall opposite the bed, old and worn from the sunlight.

She had never paid much attention to it until she had walked in one day and seen Gordon come out from behind it. He had been angry with her for coming in unannounced, but then, he had often been angry at her. But when Mr. Kincaid had spoken of his father having a place where he concealed important documents, the memory had come to mind again and made her wonder if there was perhaps something behind the tapestry.

She walked over to the edge by the window and pulled back on it. It was much heavier than she had anticipated, and her arm objected at its use. She narrowed her eyes, peering at the stone wall behind the tapestry. It was bathed in shadow, most of it still insulated from the light shining through the window behind her. Her eyes searched for any reason Gordon might have had to venture there.

She could see nothing but limestone. She tilted her head to the side, looking carefully at one particular stone which seemed to jut out more than its fellows. She slipped behind the tapestry and let it hang against her back, pushing her nearer to the wall as if it wished to envelop her and hide all its secrets. She kept her eyes on the single stone, though, and put a hand to it. The top had a groove, as if meant precisely for fingers. She pulled, and the stone yielded.

Though it had protruded from the wall, the stone was surprisingly light, as though the back had been cut away so that it was little more than a veneer. She set it gently at her feet. A dark hole gaped where it had been, and with the little light that managed to find its way behind the tapestry, Christina saw what appeared to be a leather folio and, beside it, a scroll of paper, tied with string at both ends.

Her heart pattered against her chest, and she hesitated. She had no idea whether Angus was aware of this or, if so, how often he accessed it. If she removed something, would he notice? She reached for the scroll and removed the ties, setting them at the edge of the hole. The papers didn't move—they had apparently been rolled for a significant amount of time. She unrolled the edge, her eyes straining to see what was contained on the sheets.

They were certainly letters, but it was too dark to make out anything clearly. She hesitated briefly then scooted closer to the edge of the tapestry for more light.

It was addressed to Harold, her father-in-law. Her eyes flitted to the bottom, where the edges curled in, trying to roll back into the cylindrical shape they were used to. The signature had only a letter "k."

Kincaid.

She removed the top paper from the rest, letting it roll up and slipping it into the hole to take with her, then slid the tied string around the remaining papers. If Angus *did* know of this hole, he would be unlikely to miss a lone sheet from the roll. Her eyes rested on the folio for a moment. Angus and his men wouldn't return for hours yet, and this bedchamber was not his, no matter what he seemed to think.

She pulled out the folio, unwrapping the leather string which kept the top flap shut, and reached inside. The documents within bore official seals and looked to relate to Dunverlockie. These, at least, belonged to *her* now.

There was a *thud*—the closing of the front door—followed by the echoing but muffled sound of voices belowstairs. Christina hurriedly dropped the papers back into the folio, wrapping the string to close the flap again and setting it into the hole. She took the lone, rolled paper and gripped it under her chin, using both hands to put the stone back in place, then hurried out from behind the tapestry as the sound of men's voices approached.

Panic built inside her, and she grasped the paper tightly then hurried to fold it in half and slip it into the front of her stays. Footsteps reached the door, and, wide-eyed, she tiptoed toward the chest at the foot of the bed, kneeling beside it and opening the lid as the latch lifted.

The door opened, and she glanced over, feigning surprise, even though she thought she might faint from fear.

Angus stopped short in the doorway, eyebrows contracting.

12

"What are you doing?" There was a steely edge to Angus's voice.

Christina attempted a smile, hoping it looked innocent—or perhaps challenging, if she was fortunate. "Sorting through Gordon's things. You had mentioned there being a few items in here that belong to the MacKinnons, and I thought I would ensure that nothing belonging to me is mistakenly removed."

He strode over to her and grabbed her by the arm, pulling her up from the ground so that their faces were mere inches from each other. "How dare you come into this room unbidden?"

Anger flashed within her even as her arm throbbed in his hold. "How dare I? This castle belongs to *me*. The only bidding that matters here is mine."

His eyebrow went up, and his top lip pulled up in contempt. "Is that right?"

She tugged on her arm to remove it from his grasp, and he tightened his grip for a moment then released it.

"Yes, it is." She suppressed the impulse to rub her arm where he had held it.

"And who will defend your claim? Hm?"

"The law." She wanted to take a step back, to draw away from him, but she knew he would see it as weakness, so she held her ground.

He gave a soft laugh, and he seemed to relax slightly. "Have you thought no better of your refusal, Christina? If you married me, you would have the might of the MacKinnons behind you. They would give their lives for you at my command." With two gentle fingers, he touched the large curl that hung from her neck, and the brush of his skin against hers made goosebumps shoot across her skin. She took two hurried steps backwards, searching the room for anything she might use as a weapon.

"You needn't marry me to make such a command," she said. "And that you would hang such a thing over my head says quite enough about you to make me refuse the offer."

His mouth pulled into a sneer. "Get out."

She debated pressing the fact that he had no right at all to tell her to leave a bedchamber—even less so *this* particular one, which rightly belonged to her—but she held his gaze for another moment and turned away, forcing herself to take steady and confident steps toward the door.

She yanked it closed behind her and walked to her own bedchamber. Once inside, her legs wavered beneath her, and she put a hand to her chest where the letter sat concealed, as she stumbled to the bed to support her trembling limbs.

C hristina was half-tempted to take dinner in her room and invite Elizabeth to join her. She never wanted to see Angus again after the encounter in the bedchamber.

But that was not within her power. All she could do was choose not to show him any hint of fear or give any indication that she had been in the wrong by entering the laird's bedchamber. It was only her dislike of the room—the unpleasant memories it housed—that kept her from claiming it as her own. A few minutes in the bedchamber alone shortly after Gordon's death had convinced her she wasn't ready for the mental and emotional assault such a gesture would require, much as it might appeal to her pride.

So she walked with Elizabeth down to the dining room when the time came, and she told her sister nothing of what had happened nor of the letter hidden in her stays. It was safest to keep it on her person.

The secrets seemed to be piling up, and Christina hated keeping things from Elizabeth. But now was not the time to rectify that.

There were even more MacKinnon men than usual at dinner—eight all told—and Christina felt her blood run hot at the sight of them. She had hoped that their numbers would dissipate over time, but that was not what was occurring. She knew a few of them by name and reputation, but there were also some unknown to her. There was no pretending she had any control at all over who entered the estate that belonged to her. There were even two dogs laying on the floor beside the table.

As Christina and Elizabeth approached, Angus motioned to Malcom beside him to rise, and together they came to help the women into their chairs. To all appearances, it was a gesture of politeness, and yet to Christina, it felt like another demonstration by Angus of his control.

"I am pleased you could join us so soon," Angus said as he helped scoot the chair in. "After seeing you in my bedchamber, I thought you might be late coming down to dinner."

Christina felt heat seep into her cheeks and sent a sidelong glance at Elizabeth, who had refused Malcolm's help and was pulling her chair toward the table herself as she stared in wide-eyed confusion at Christina.

Christina sent her a warning glance.

Talk was sparing as people served themselves from the dishes on the table, and Elizabeth nudged Christina, a question in her eyes.

"Later," Christina said softly.

One of Angus's men said something crass in Gaelic to the man sitting beside him, and snickering ensued.

"Must we have animals with us at the table?" Elizabeth asked.

"Och, Malcolm won't hear aught against the dogs," one of the men said.

Elizabeth looked him in the eye. "You mistake me. I wasn't referring to them. I am quite fond of dogs."

The men's smiles faded as they took her meaning, and their lips curled up in anger.

Christina forced herself to take a deep breath. How would they survive at Dunverlockie with Elizabeth's sharp tongue and the MacKinnon men's quickness to anger?

"A spirited lass," one of the two men said, still in Gaelic. "Perhaps she'd do for *you*, Malcolm. Ye could tame her. Or perhaps she'd tame *you!*" More laughter ensued, this time coming from a few of the men. The hint of a derisive smile played at the corner of Angus's mouth.

Elizabeth reached for her napkin. "Such entertaining conjecture. But I assure you, I wouldn't marry a MacKinnon if he were the last man on earth."

Malcolm's hard eyes bored into Elizabeth, and Christina reached a hand over to her sister, setting it atop her leg, hoping she would receive the intended message. But Christina could hardly blame her for her response to the provocation being offered. If Elizabeth hadn't been there and those had been spoken in reference to Christina, she would have been tempted to respond the same way. But one sharp tongue was more than enough kindling at this table.

"Who said anythin' about marriage?" said one of the men. His rejoinder was met with even more laughter.

Elizabeth stared at them, hands holding her utensils suspended in the air. "I believe even pigs have a more refined sense of humor. Allow me to rephrase what I said to cater to your understanding. I wouldn't let a MacKinnon—and certainly not such a one as *that*"—she gave a toss of her head to indicate Malcolm— "*touch* me if he was the last man on earth."

A rumbling of whispered reactions coursed around the table, and Malcolm's jaw hardened, his nostrils flaring.

"Assumin' ye were given a choice in the matter," said the man beside Malcolm.

"Sounds like a challenge ta me," said another, gaze fixed on Elizabeth. "Let's test her mettle, then. These Innes women dinna ken what's best for them. They need ta be broken ta bridle."

"Gordon made a start of it with the prettier one," the first man replied. "Perhaps I'll have a go at it now. Finish the job, ye ken."

"Enough," Christina said, her voice cutting through the chuckles. She could feel the red heat coming off her cheeks like steam from a fresh cup of tea. "Shall we, Elizabeth?" Christina pushed her chair out, and Elizabeth hesitated for a moment. She still had a fair amount of uneaten food on her plate, but Christina didn't care. She couldn't allow the trajectory the night was on.

Elizabeth pinched her lips together and set her napkin down on the table with more force than was necessary, pushing her chair out. She looked around the table once more and followed Christina out of the room.

She shut the door behind them, and Elizabeth let out something akin to a growl. "I know you were right to have us leave, but...." She shook her head, her hands flexing and clenching. "*What* was Angus speaking of, Christina? You were in his bedchamber?"

Christina let out a scoffing laugh. "*His* bedchamber? No. The one he has usurped under the guise of helping me? Yes."

"But why?"

Christina grimaced. "There are some things I need to tell you."

When Elizabeth finally left Christina's bedchamber, it was only with the assurance that Christina would keep nothing more from her. She promised to hold her tongue on a much tighter rein in return, apologizing profusely for the turmoil she had been causing Christina.

"I have such a wicked tongue," she lamented, taking up Christina's hand and placing a remorseful kiss atop it.

Christina laughed off her sister's regretful gesture, but she was relieved that Elizabeth had promised to mind her words more. She only hoped it wasn't too late. Glenna's suggestion that they come stay at the inn was looking more and more enticing to Christina.

While the conversation at the dining table had resulted in a strengthened understanding between the sisters and a sobering of Elizabeth's attitude, it seemed to have a very different effect upon the MacKinnon men. Their raucous laughter and yelling sailed easily up the stairs to the bedchambers above, providing a continual reminder to Christina as she settled into bed of how stifled she was in the castle. She called for a kettle of hot water to be brought up and made herself a cup of tea, sipping it slowly as she considered her situation.

Whether sleep overtook her gradually or the volume of the voices downstairs lessened, she didn't know. But she awoke with a start some time later and quickly clutched at her stomach. The portion of dinner she had eaten had not agreed with her.

A clattering somewhere outside her bedchamber jolted her, and she blinked for more clarity of vision in the firelight. The sound had come from across the corridor—the direction of Elizabeth's room.

Christina threw the bedcovers from her and hurried to put on her wrapper, grateful that her injured arm was healing quickly. She lifted the latch and opened the door, looking out into the dark corridor. The door to Elizabeth's room was ajar.

Christina reached for the nearest candlestick—the same one she had threatened Mr. Kincaid with—and ran toward her sister's room, heart thudding.

There was a struggle occurring in the room, and Christina spent only a moment taking in the large form Elizabeth was grappling with before rushing over and striking him on the head with all the force she could muster.

He was momentarily stunned, whether from the force or from the surprise, Christina didn't know, but it was enough to free Elizabeth from his grasp.

"Come!" Christina grabbed her sister's arm and pulled her along with her out of the room and toward her own, where she latched the door behind them and helped Elizabeth to the bed.

Elizabeth's chest was heaving, her body trembling, and she let out something between a laugh and a sob. Christina wrapped her arms around her, and Elizabeth returned the embrace willingly.

"We are going to the inn," Christina said, anger and fear mixing inside her so that she felt she might be ill.

Elizabeth shook her head against Christina's shoulder. "We cannot let them win, Christina." But her words trembled as much as her body.

"They *won't* win," Christina said. "But we need time—and

space—to consider our options." The law was on her side, but she had little confidence in its power to help her. The MacKinnons had been a law unto themselves for so long, and they had the support of many of the officials in the area.

They sat on the bed, waiting for any indication that the man in Elizabeth's room would attempt to follow after them, but none came.

"No doubt he is lying upon my bed now, fast asleep," Elizabeth said. "He was very drunk—if not for that and your intervention, I should never have been able to escape him." She shuddered slightly and stood.

"Let us gather a few things to take to the inn," Christina said. "You can make do with my clothing for now. I daren't go in your room."

"You mean to go to the inn *now*?" Elizabeth asked.

Christina nodded. "What if one of the other men comes?"

Elizabeth's eyes went to the windows. The curtains were drawn for the night, but both of them well knew that beyond, it was utterly dark outside.

"The moon is nearly full," Christina said, taking two shifts from her trunk. "We can leave from the servants' entrance."

Elizabeth looked at her for a moment, her hand clasping her upper arm where the man had gripped her. Christina swallowed down her emotion at the sight. She had never wished for her sister to know such treatment at the hands of a man. And she would do anything to prevent it.

Elizabeth finally nodded.

They helped one another dress then set a few essentials in the portmanteau stored beneath Christina's bed, cocking their ears at different points to listen for any sign of life in the castle. But it was quiet at last. Christina set her purse in the portmanteau last—Mr. Gibson would certainly expect to be compensated for the lodging he would be providing—and slipped the letter beneath her pillow back into her stays.

As Christina peered out into the corridor toward the servant stairs, she was reminded of Mr. Kincaid doing the same thing just two short days ago.

She hoped their escape would be as uneventful as his had been.

13

L achlan turned over in his bed, away from whatever sound had woken him so soon after he had managed to find refuge in sleep. His thoughts were slow to give way to slumber these days, and the light sleeping he had learned during his time as a soldier had not yet given way to the relative safety of his new life.

He kept his eyes shut, frowning as his ears caught the sound of crunching footsteps, let in through the broken pane in the window next to his bed. There were no guests at the inn tonight; it was likely an animal. Or several. He sat up as muffled whispers were added to the footsteps, and he peered through the window into the dark surrounding the inn, blinking as his eyes attempted to adjust.

Two figures huddled together below—both women, given the shape of their forms.

He sprang up from his bed and reached for his breeches, pulling them on and stuffing his shirt into them. He had been reluctant to give up the wearing of his plaid, but it drew too much unwanted attention.

He slipped out of his room and down both sets of narrow

stairs—he didn't need a candle to light the way anymore, so well did he know the inn by now. He took care to open the door so that it creaked as little as possible. He wore no shoes, and the cold stone in the courtyard in front of the inn provided another means of ensuring he was fully awake.

Coming around the side of the inn the window of his room looked down on, he stopped short. Mrs. MacKinnon and Miss Innes stood there, the former approaching the small window to Glenna's small bedroom and reaching out a hand to tap on it.

"Wait!" he said in a shouted whisper, and both women's heads snapped around to look at him, fear in their wide eyes. It was replaced with relief, though, and he walked toward them, his thoughts racing to understand what in the world could bring these two women to the inn in the middle of the night—and evidently on foot.

As he strode over to them, Mrs. MacKinnon put out a hand toward him. The gesture did nothing to allay his concerns, and he took her hand in his. It was ungloved and cold, and he set his second hand over it, chafing the soft skin. Early summer nights in Kildonnan were colder than those in the Colonies.

"What is it?" he asked. "What is wrong?"

She made a small move to retrieve her hand from his grasp —as if she had reached for him without thinking and was now embarrassed by it—and he allowed her to take it back, despite his own desire to keep it. It touched him to know that her impulse had been to reach out to him.

"It is only Angus and his men," Mrs. MacKinnon responded. "They've become..." she trailed off.

"Unbearable," Miss Innes supplied.

Mrs. MacKinnon met his gaze, and even in the dark night, he could see how troubled they were. "One of them attacked Elizabeth tonight."

Lachlan stilled, his gaze darting to Miss Innes. "*What?*"

Miss Innes attempted a smile. "He was no match for my sister and her candlestick, I fear."

Lachlan looked at Mrs. MacKinnon, whose expression was anything but amused.

"Are ye hurt?" he asked urgently, his eyes searching both of them from head to foot. These were Alistair Innes's sisters, and they'd just been attacked. All his fears and suspicions had been borne out.

"Nothing worth mentioning," Miss Innes said, gripping her right arm.

Lachlan resisted the urge to curse and glanced in the direction of Dunverlockie. "Stay here," he said. All his intentions for carrying out justice in secret fled. He couldn't wait for the opportune time to teach the MacKinnons their lesson; they needed to be challenged *now*.

Mrs. MacKinnon reached for his fist, which was balled tightly. The gesture jarred him, and he blinked, relaxing his hand and looking at her.

"Please do not," she said in a pleading voice. "It would be folly. There are eight of them there tonight. The only one certain to come away injured—or worse—would be you."

Lachlan stared at her, trying to force his breath to come evenly despite the fact that he could feel the blood pulsing in his veins. The first time he had felt this sort of anger had been when his father had been taken. It came on from time to time, disturbing the customary hold he had on his temper and emotions.

"We didn't come to involve you or ask for your intervention," Mrs. MacKinnon said. "We only hoped you might have room for us here. Just temporarily."

Lachlan nodded, letting out a breath, reminding himself that what mattered most was that the women were taken care of. "Of course, of course. Come inside, out of the cold. There's naught but meself, Glenna, and Mr. Gibson here tonight, and they're fast asleep." He took the leather bag Mrs. MacKinnon held and led the way to the door, opening it for them to pass through. He used the flintbox to light the candle next to it and guided them up the stairs.

"I'm afraid we dinna have a room ta fit the two of ye in a bed together," he said as they entered one of the rooms. "The MacKinnons broke both of the larger beds. But perhaps tomorrow we could move one of the other beds into this room if ye wish ta be together." He lit the candle on the dilapidated bedside table with the one in his hand.

"Whatever is less trouble," Mrs. MacKinnon said. "We do not wish to put anyone out, but we will pay for the rooms as usual, of course."

"Nay, Mrs. MacKinnon," he replied. "'Twill no' be necessary. As ye can see, we have plenty of vacancy."

"All the more reason for us to pay," she said. "I insist."

Lachlan contemplated pressing the issue.

"I wouldn't argue with my sister if I were you," Miss Innes said. "She is terribly stubborn sometimes."

Mrs. MacKinnon met Lachlan's eye with a slight smile, raising a brow as if to challenge him.

He chuckled softly. "We can discuss it tomorrow after ye've had the chance ta rest."

"Is there a room right next to this one?" Mrs. MacKinnon asked.

Lachlan nodded. "Aye, come wi' me."

Mrs. MacKinnon hesitated, looking at her sister with concern. "Are you certain, Elizabeth? Certain that..."

Miss Innes put a hand on her sister's arm and smiled reassuringly. "I am well. You needn't worry. Sleep, and we can talk things over in the morning."

Mrs. MacKinnon was frowning, but she nodded and followed Lachlan from the room.

He showed her to the next door and set the candlestick

down once they were inside. The inn's rooms were sparsely furnished, with a small bed, a short bedside table with a basin upon it, and an armoire with one of its doors missing. The ceiling was short enough that Mr. Kincaid's head nearly grazed it in the lower areas.

"Mrs. MacKinnon," he said as he set down the portmanteau beside the bed. "I'm sorry I reacted the way I did outside. 'Twas foolish."

"It was." She laughed softly, and he couldn't help but smile in response.

"But there is nothing to forgive," she said. "If there had only been four of them, I would have been tempted to let you go. But I think eight is too many even for someone as threatening as you."

His eyebrows drew together. "Do ye find me threatenin'?"

She turned to him, tilting her head to the side. He was suddenly aware of the fact that, beyond pulling on his breeches, he had spent no thought at all on his appearance before going outside. He was barefoot and in nothing but his shirtsleeves, which gaped open at the neck, and he didn't dare imagine what the state of his hair was. He ran a hand through it, probably only aggravating the mess.

"No," she said. "But when I first saw you here, I was certainly intimidated."

He breathed a sigh of relief at her reassurance. He didn't want Mrs. MacKinnon to be afraid of him.

"And when you appeared in my bedchamber the other night, I was forced to reexamine my assumptions about you for a moment."

"I didna mean ta frighten ye," he said. For a woman with Mrs. MacKinnon's history, it must have been a terrifying experience.

"I know," she said.

"I promise I would never harm ye."

She held his gaze, and there was a sadness in her eyes as she nodded.

"I'll leave ye ta rest now. I sleep upstairs, right above this room, so ye need only bang on the ceilin' if ye need somethin'."

"Thank you, Mr. Kincaid," she said, and the sincerity in her voice stirred something inside him. "I couldn't bear if anything were to happen to Elizabeth."

She looked less strong and capable in that moment—more like a woman shouldering a load too heavy for her. He contemplated taking her hand to reassure her, just as she had done to calm him outside. But to do so would be to cross over a line in their relationship which he was fairly certain she didn't wish to cross.

Instead he merely nodded. "Dinna fash, lass. I willna let anythin' befall ye. Ye're safe here."

She gave a little smile of acknowledgement, and he wished her good night, stepping out into the dark corridor where only the sliver of light from the two rooms dispelled the deep darkness.

There was one more room beside Mrs. MacKinnon's, and he stared at its door for a moment. Perhaps it would be better to sleep closer. But he had specifically told Mrs. MacKinnon he would be sleeping on the floor above. He turned toward the stairs, and Mrs. MacKinnon's door opened.

"Mr. Kincaid," she said in a whisper. "I forgot..." She extended a hand toward him, within it a creased and folded paper.

"What's this?"

"I found it," she said. "It was hidden, along with more like it, I can only imagine, in the laird's bedchamber at Dunverlockie."

His gaze flew to hers.

"I'm afraid it isn't precisely what you were looking for, as it is addressed *to* my father-in-law rather, but perhaps it will be helpful. I believe it was written by your father. I didn't have time to inspect it all, as Angus returned while I was in the room."

His eyes widened even more. "He found ye lookin'?"

"He found me in the bedchamber, but I don't think he suspects what I was there for. Though that didn't stop him from being angry and suspicious."

"What did he do?" Lachlan pushed down the anger rising again within him.

"An implied threat or two." She hesitated. "And a promise of protection if I would marry him."

Lachlan shut his eyes. She had risked herself for this letter —been importuned by Angus over it. "Lass, I never meant for ye ta endanger yerself on my account. I was only teasin' when I said ye could save me the trouble—"

She put a hand up to stop him. "It was my own curiosity that took me there. But I thought you should know. I am not certain whether Angus knows of the location of the papers. I suspect not. But Gordon certainly knew, for it was when I recalled seeing him behind the tapestry in the bedchamber once that I wondered if there was perhaps something there."

Lachlan thumbed the letter in his hand, looking down at it. He didn't want her putting herself in danger out of curiosity. But it was certainly not his place to say any such thing.

She was right about the letter, though. It wasn't exactly what he had been hoping for, but it still might have what he needed. And at least now he knew where to look the next time he was inside Dunverlockie.

"Thank ye, Mrs. MacKinnon," he said.

"You are welcome," she said. "I hope it is helpful in some way. Good night, Mr. Kincaid."

Lachlan didn't sleep when he returned to his own room. First, he read the letter. It was full of incriminating information about his father. Unfortunately, the obviously implied collabo- ration of Mr. MacKinnon wouldn't be strong enough to accomplish what Lachlan needed it to accomplish. He wanted there to be no doubt in anyone's mind that the man had supported Bonnie Prince Charlie on his landing in Scotland, only to turn on the prince and his fellows—Lachlan's dad first and foremost —when it became clear the uprising was doomed to fail.

He would have to keep searching, but until he could do that, there was little purpose to spending his energy on the subject.

The situation of Mrs. MacKinnon and Miss Innes, however, was enough to keep him awake once he lay in bed, his hand supporting his head on the thin pillow as he stared at the vaguely discernible texture of the ceiling.

He was glad they had come to the inn. It *was* safer. But what would it mean for Dunverlockie? It had the appearance of a retreat, and that was exactly what Angus wished for. It was an urgent situation with no obvious solution.

Mrs. MacKinnon must seem easy prey to Angus—she had no connections, familial or businesswise, to bolster her claim to Dunverlockie Castle. And, even if she had, Lachlan was torn about his own wishes. Surely he would rather his childhood home be in the hands of her than Angus MacKinnon, but what he truly wished he could do was to regain it for the Kincaids. The MacKinnons had no reasonable claim to it, whatever the law might say.

What Mrs. MacKinnon needed was a male family member who could make the MacKinnons think twice about taking their claim to Dunverlockie for granted. Alistair wasn't here to do that, and from what Lachlan had garnered, the younger brothers of Mrs. MacKinnon and Miss Innes were simply too young to be of any use.

Lachlan tapped the finger of his free hand on the bedspread then stopped. The MacKinnons didn't *know* Alistair Innes. What if Lachlan simply pretended to *be* him? He could claim every right to protect the sisters, then.

He grimaced. It was a good idea, perhaps, but its execution would be messy. What would Mr. Gibson have to say to the revelation that his servant Mr. Murray was suddenly claiming to be a Mr. Innes? Besides, it would be easy enough for Angus, once alerted to any suspicion on Gibson's part, to look into Innes's whereabouts.

It wouldn't pass muster, this idea of his. He would have to come up with something else. Soon. Once Angus had his claws firmly in Dunverlockie, it would become less and less easy to extract them.

He continued tapping his finger, his gaze following the uneven plaster lines above. One of them trailed on longer than the others, ending in a pattern that brought to mind Mrs. MacKinnon's hair the night he had found himself in her bedchamber, the way it had fallen over her shoulders, curled at the ends.

His finger stopped tapping again, his eyes fixed on the plaster line as his heart began to pulse against his chest and his breathing came faster.

Perhaps there *was* another way. It was bold, certainly. The thought of it set his blood on fire with an eagerness and a hope he hadn't felt in years. But the emotions were quickly overtaken by the nerve-wracking prospect of explaining the idea to Mrs. MacKinnon.

14

U nable to sleep, Lachlan rose early to see to the horses. They had a way of setting his mind more at ease, but today, memories of his first meeting with Mrs. MacKinnon filled his mind. When he finished brushing and feeding them, the sun was just peeking over the horizon, illuminating the edges of the sky with a warm, pink glow. Glenna would be awake soon, and Mr. Gibson within the hour after that.

Lachlan changed from his clothes, saturated as they were with the smell of stables, and headed for the kitchen. It wasn't that he thought a cup of coffee and warm bannocks would change Mrs. MacKinnon's mind or make her more open to his idea. He merely needed to do something with his hands, to occupy his mind while he waited for the opportunity to speak to her.

"What's all this about, then?" Glenna came into the kitchen with a bemused expression.

"I couldna sleep," Lachlan replied, setting the bannocks over the flame below. "Thought I would put meself ta work."

She took a seat in the only chair in the kitchen—a spindly

wooden one with a broom propped against it. "A girl could get used ta this, ye ken."

"Och aye," he replied with a chuckle. "In return for seein' ta my duties in the stables, no doubt?"

She lifted a shoulder and stretched out her legs, leaning back in the chair. "Ye seem ta have it all in hand without any aid from me."

"And all it took was no sleep at all," he said.

She stood and came to look at the bannocks. "Ye've made a fair amount. I hope we have enough customers ta finish 'em, or else Mr. Gibson will threaten ta ring my neck."

"Most of 'em will be eaten for breakfast by Mrs. MacKinnon and Miss Innes."

She shot him a funny look, and he left watching the boiling kettle and the bannocks to come nearer. He doubted Mr. Gibson was awake yet, but he didn't wish to take any chances. He didn't trust the man.

"I woke in the middle of the night to the two of 'em comin' ta yer window," Lachlan said. "I hurried down to speak with 'em, and they told me of the troubles they've been havin' with Angus and his men. It's no' safe at Dunverlockie for two women."

Glenna shut her eyes in consternation. "The brutes," she said in a harsh whisper. "And now he'll think the castle is his for the takin' no doubt."

Lachlan said nothing.

"We canna let 'im have it," Glenna said, wringing her hands in her lap. "He'll ruin everythin'. I talked to Maggie recently—she's a tenant on Benleith land—and she says Angus has been raisin' the rents there, pushin' out the farmers to make way for sheep. I know he'll do the same here."

"I ken, Glenna. And I have a plan for it."

"Ye do?" The hope in her eyes reminded Lachlan how much

more than his own future rested on Mrs. MacKinnon's response. All the tenants of Dunverlockie would benefit from it.

"Aye, but 'tis only that—the beginnin' of a plan. It may no' work. I'll tell ye when I've had more time ta develop it."

"Of course. Only tell me how I can help, and ye ken I'll do it."

Footsteps sounded above in Miss Innes's room.

"I'll go see ta the ladies," Glenna said.

By the time Mrs. MacKinnon and her sister came down, Lachlan had cleaned the entire coffee room. Miss Innes appeared first, and Lachlan found himself eager for the view of Mrs. MacKinnon, as though he could no longer recall her appearance.

Perhaps it was simply that he was looking at her through different eyes now, though—the eyes of a man about to suggest something so outrageous, it would be a miracle if she didn't leave the inn on the spot.

Suddenly, with the striking and strong woman before him, his idea seemed the height of audacity. Never had he been more terrified to do something—or more eager. It was strange. The idea had at once appealed to him, for it was the route he hadn't seen to achieving his own goals. But as Mrs. MacKinnon approached him, smiling and looking so kind and beautiful, he wondered if there might be plenty of other reasons to wish for her agreement to his plan.

"Mr. Murray made it all," Glenna said as the sisters came to one of the tables in the coffee room.

Lachlan helped Mrs. MacKinnon into her chair with a quizzical look at Glenna. "A disavowal in case I've made 'em poorly."

Glenna smiled, but it fell as Mr. Gibson entered the room. His brows drew together at the sight of the Innes sisters, and Glenna caught eyes with Lachlan before hurrying over to speak with the innkeeper.

Lachlan wished he could sit down with the two women, but Mr. Gibson would hardly appreciate such a decision.

"Mrs. MacKinnon," he said, gathering up the tray he'd brought everything on. "Once ye've had the chance ta breakfast, could I have a word with ye?"

Her brows went up. "Of course."

"There's no need ta rush," he said. "I'll be at the stables when ye're ready." He gave a little bow and left. The stables were perhaps the only place he could rely on the ability to be private with her.

She didn't keep him waiting long. No doubt she was curious what he could possibly need to speak with her about—perhaps she assumed it was regarding the letter she had brought him.

She looked somewhat pale this morning, but her gaze was clear and direct, and Lachlan found it harder than usual to speak as she approached.

"Forgive me for keeping you waiting." She smiled as she said it, but there was curiosity in her gaze.

"Nay," he said. "I didna mean ta rush ye. Perhaps I shoulda waited 'til ye were done eatin'."

She shook her head, and he glanced around for any sign of Mr. Gibson. "Would ye mind comin' in the stables with me? We can look in on Apollo while we talk."

He led the way into the dimmer light of the stables, and the familiar scents and sounds calmed him a bit. He was keenly aware of the irony of the situation. He had faced the barrels of enemy muskets and frigid winters in the French colonies, but never had he felt less sure of himself, less prepared for what was required of him than he did now. The outcome of this conversation could change everything for him.

"What was it you wished to speak about with me?" Mrs. MacKinnon asked as she looked at the fading injury on her mare's side.

Lachlan took in a deep breath, setting a hand on the mare's

flank. "'Tis regardin' a thought I had early this mornin' while considerin' yer plight."

She looked at him with interest, and he hoped he looked more calm than he felt.

"Ye own Dunverlockie," he said, starting with something less difficult. "At least in the eyes of the law, ye do. But Angus doesna care for the law when it doesna serve him. He is more interested in power. It is the only language the MacKinnons speak."

She nodded, moving her hand from the horse's withers and along its back until her hand neared his. Her gaze was on him, and he wondered if she would allow her hand to reach his. But she pulled it away at the last second.

"In Angus's view, ye dinna have any power. Ye're naught but a woman."

She scoffed, and he held up his hand. "'Tis no' my view, but ye agree 'tis Angus's, do ye no'?"

"Unarguably."

He nodded. "What ye need is a way ta change that. Ta be certain he understands that ye have someone on yer side ta fight for ye." His heart was beating faster by the second, and he was grateful for the shifting and munching of the horses in the others stalls to mask the sound.

Mrs. MacKinnon's eyes were slightly narrowed, her brow furrowed as she thought on his words.

If Lachlan didn't speak now, he might lose his nerve, and he couldn't allow that. He had promised himself he would do what was necessary to achieve his goal. He wouldn't balk here.

"What I am suggestin' may be a shock ta ye," he said. "But I hope ye'll consider it, all the same, Mrs. MacKinnon. I told ye I'd do what I could ta protect ye, and I meant it."

She looked confused. "What *do* you propose?"

He smiled wryly at her word choice. "I propose...well, I

propose ta propose, I suppose." He gave an awkward laugh that sounded strange even to his ears.

Her brows snapped together, and wariness entered her eyes.

"I ken," he said. "'Tis no' what ye expected. But I ask ye ta listen for a moment. Ye've no male kin ta protect ye, do ye? No' with Alistair gone."

She shook her head, but the guarded look on her face only settled deeper.

"As yer husband"—he resisted the urge to swallow—"I'd have every right ta protect ye. And yer sister, too, of course. Ye dinna have Alistair here ta do so, and I ken this is what he'd wish for. 'Tis more than just that, though. I ken ye dinna think the accident in the carriage was intended ta harm ye. But ye must consider, Mrs. MacKinnon, how much Angus stands ta gain with ye gone. He can bully ye and fight the law to get what he wants, but with ye gone, he wouldna have ta. Dunverlockie would fall ta him if ye died now, would it no'?"

She didn't give any answer, but nor did she refute his words.

"A marriage is an opportunity for ye ta push him a step—or perhaps many steps—further back in the line of inheritance, for the estate falls ta him only if ye dinna have children of yer own ta inherit."

She blushed, but she kept her eyes on him.

"Unless I've misunderstood the situation?" he said.

She shook her head, and her brows drew together as she searched his face. "You fail to mention one result of such a plan —what *you* get out of it. For if I were to do as you say—to marry you"—she shifted her weight—"then Dunverlockie would not be mine. It would be yours."

"Aye," he said slowly. "'Tis true that, in the eyes of the law, Dunverlockie would belong ta me." He thought he detected a hint of anger in her eyes. "But"—he pressed his lips together and sighed—"I swear to ye, Mrs. MacKinnon. I wouldna treat it as only mine. 'Tis home ta me, I admit. And I canna deny that I stand ta gain from what I propose. But is that no' what the best compromises result in? Something ta gain for both parties involved?"

She turned to the mare and put a gentle finger to the healing wound, maintaining her silence until Lachlan thought he might burst. But he wouldn't pressure her to respond.

He watched as she shut her eyes and her brow wrinkled, as if in pain.

"I cannot," she said. "I am very sorry to disappoint you, Mr. Kincaid. But I cannot." She turned and, without meeting his eyes, slipped through the stall door and out of the stables.

15

Christina hurried from the stables, a hand on her stomach, which swirled and writhed.

Mr. Kincaid had proposed that they *marry*. Of all the things she had expected him to say to her, that had certainly never even entered the realm of her thoughts. She had been expecting him to question her about the habits of Angus and his men, perhaps, so that he could find a way to the laird's bedchamber where the papers were hidden.

She stopped before turning the corner to the front of the inn, setting a hand on the wall and taking deep, steady breaths. She shouldn't be so overset by a conversation, even if it *was* a complete and utter surprise.

It wasn't as though she didn't see the wisdom in what Mr. Kincaid had suggested. It was precisely *because* she had seen it that she had so quickly refused him and left the stables. There *had* to be another way—one that didn't involve irreversibly joining herself to another man who needed something from her. Angus proposing marriage to her had disgusted her; for some reason, Mr. Kincaid's proposal filled her with sadness.

Had she come to think him above such a selfish arrangement? That his interest in her was genuine attachment?

If that was the cause for her reaction, she could blame no one but herself.

Either way, she had to believe an alternative to his proposal —and Angus's—existed.

Elizabeth was coming down the stairs when Christina reentered the inn. She took one look at Christina and said, "You are unwell."

Christina shook her head, frustrated that the minutes she had spent preparing herself to appear unfazed had apparently been ill-spent.

Elizabeth looked at her critically. "You *are*. You have been drinking that tea, haven't you? It will be good for us to spend some time here without that wretched stuff. Then we will know for certain whether Angus did something to it."

Christina shushed her sister as Mr. Gibson appeared in the stairway. But she thought back on the tea she'd had before bed last night as her stomach roiled with nausea. She had been attributing her increasingly frequent stomach pains to the stress of her situation, but perhaps she was wrong. She kept her bag of tea leaves in her bedchamber, but she often neglected to lock the cupboard it was in.

She had managed to find something hidden in the bedchamber Angus occupied, had she not? It would be quite simple for him to have contaminated something in *her* bedchamber, and what better than her tea? She took it more than once daily, and he could be certain that only she would be affected by whatever was in it.

She suppressed a shudder as they entered the coffee room. When Elizabeth had first suggested the idea, Christina had thought it unnecessarily morbid. Now she wasn't nearly as certain.

Well, if her symptoms lessened here at the inn, she would know with more surety.

Glenna was seeing to the request of the sole other person in the room: a man who looked to be a traveling merchant. Christina sat down with Elizabeth at the table farthest from him, and Glenna came over to them a few minutes later, having served the man a cup of ale.

"What can I get for ye, ladies?" Glenna's voice was raised to a higher volume than usual, as if she was asking for someone else's benefit. She lowered it, eyes watching the room for signs of Mr. Gibson, no doubt. "Is everythin' well, mistress? What did Mr. Murray want from ye?"

"Nothing," she said quickly. "Just to show me how Apollo is getting along."

As if on cue, Mr. Kincaid appeared in the doorway to the room. His gaze met Christina's, and her heart stuttered. Why did she feel guilty for rejecting his idea? Of course it was natural to feel sympathy for his plight, to want him to achieve his aims. But those broad shoulders and that determined jaw must certainly be able to find a way that didn't require such a sacrifice from her.

On the other hand, it was that very strength he had been offering her—he had invited her to lay her burdens on his back. And, in truth, as he looked at her just now, she wanted to do just that. She couldn't imagine regretting it. But she had never imagined Gordon would turn into the sort of man he had become, either. She was evidently not a capable judge of character.

But there was no censure or resentment in Mr. Kincaid's eyes, only the usual somber kindness. She wished she could make him understand her thoughts and feelings, but how could she possibly convey it all?

The merchant called to Glenna, and she scurried away to take his cup and coin. He rose and left the inn.

"Can I get the two of ye somethin' ta drink?" Mr. Kincaid asked the sisters.

"I could do with a cup of tea if you have any," Elizabeth said.

Glenna came over, tray balanced on her hip with the merchant's dishes atop. "Mrs. MacKinnon prefers her own tea, which I'm afraid we dinna have here. Do ye wish for me ta fetch it from Dunverlockie?" Her eyes twinkled. "Perhaps Mr. Murray will accompany me and show Mr. MacKinnon what we all think of 'im."

Christina smiled weakly and shook her head.

"I don't want her drinking any more of the tea for now," Elizabeth said. "You can see how ill she looks, and I, for one, suspect Angus has had a hand in it."

Mr. Kincaid frowned, his eyes focused on Christina with a measure of worry in them. "Ye think he's poisoned it?"

Elizabeth gave them all a significant look. "He went out of his way to procure another bag of her tea for her the other day—the first time in his life he has put himself to trouble on someone else's account, I imagine. It is common knowledge at Dunverlockie that she only takes her own particular mixture."

"Aye," Glenna said. Her gaze, too, was on Christina. "'Tis suspicious, as ye say. And ye *do* look unwell, mistress. I can assure ye, it wouldna be the first time a MacKinnon was suspected of scheming. There are plenty of people who believe 'tis they who bear the responsibility for the disappearances in the area over the last two or three years."

"What disappearances?" Mr. Kincaid asked.

Glenna shrugged. "A few people—cottars' children and servants. No one the MacKinnons care enough about ta mind. The lass, Rachel, who worked here afore me was one as left without a word. There were whispers in the toun that"—she looked over her shoulder—"that Mr. Gibson was the one responsible."

"Good heavens," Elizabeth said. "And you were not afraid to replace her?"

"She had little choice," Christina said. "Gordon dismissed her, and it took all my powers of persuasion to convince him to allow her to work here."

"I'm not afeared," Glenna said. "I could handle Mr. Gibson with a whack o' the teapot if he tried aught. Besides, I've got Mr. Murray here now, and I'm fair certain Mr. Gibson's afeared of *him,* and he kens we're friends, the two of us." She nudged Mr. Kincaid with her elbow, looking up at him playfully, and Christina felt a flicker of jealousy.

"Nay," Mr. Kincaid said. "He doesna care for me, though I dinna ken why. I've done naught but make things easier for him since I came."

"He takes his lead from the MacKinnons," Glenna said. "'Tis why he dislikes me."

"Well," said Elizabeth, "while I would be the last person to argue against someone teaching Angus MacKinnon a lesson— or Mr. Gibson either—I think we need not trouble you to do anything just yet, Mr. Murray. It will be safest if my sister drinks what all of us are having." She looked at Christina with a puckered brow. "I haven't any idea how long it takes for the effects of poisoning to wear off—we must hope the symptoms won't become *worse* before they get better."

All eyes were on Christina now, and she felt the need to allay everyone's evident worries, even though she herself was secretly troubled at the thought that perhaps she had been unknowingly ingesting poison. What *would* Elizabeth do if Christina were to die? And what of their other siblings?

"There is no need to look at me as though I were about to expire," she said. "It is only a stomach ache."

"A *few* of them," Elizabeth said dryly, "starting, I might add, shortly after Angus's arrival at Dunverlockie."

"The important thing is that she doesna keep drinkin' the

tea," Mr. Kincaid said. "But ye must be honest with us, Mrs. MacKinnon, about how ye're feelin'. Perhaps we should call for the surgeon."

"No." She stood, but he was in her way, and he looked at her with as much stubbornness as she was often accused of. "I *will* tell you if I feel unwell enough to merit sending for the surgeon. But I rather think I will feel better if I simply rest upstairs for a bit."

He gave a reluctant nod and let her pass.

Why he cared so much for her well-being, she didn't know. Did he have hope she would change her mind about the arrangement he had suggested? She wouldn't. She couldn't.

But if it wasn't that, where did this consideration come from? Things might well be easier for him, just as they would be for Angus, if she was gone. He would have no qualms fighting against Angus for Dunverlockie, but while Christina was the owner, he was in a difficult position. She was an obstacle on the route to his goal, and unlike Angus, she was not one he had any justification for removing from his path.

She could only be grateful that was the case. The last thing she needed was another man anxious to be rid of her.

16

Lachlan's mind worked as fast as his body for the remainder of the day. He had known a disappointment after Mrs. MacKinnon had fled the stables that felt as though it might crush him—to have victory so close he could taste it—but he had forced himself not to show it when he had encountered her inside a few minutes later.

He wouldn't punish her for rejecting what he acknowledged was an enormous request. He could only guess that she had strong reasons for rejecting the proposal out of hand. Just before she had left the stables, he had glimpsed fear in her eyes —the same fear he had noticed there before—and it dismayed him to think it might be directed toward him.

He would give her no reason to fear him.

But without a marriage to her, his path to seeing justice served would be a rocky one at best—and the possibility of re-obtaining Dunverlockie had fled as quickly as she had.

He needed to see the rest of the papers she had mentioned. That was the first step—the *only* step at this point.

He was mucking out the stalls in the afternoon when Mrs.

MacKinnon emerged into the stables, unaccompanied by her sister.

"Mrs. MacKinnon," he said in surprise, setting the shovel against the wall and stepping out into the pathway between the stalls. "What can I do for ye?" He tried valiantly not to hope that she had reconsidered his offer.

"I have been thinking...." Her hands were clasped together, but her fiddling thumbs let him know that she was nervous, and the light in her eyes that she was eager.

Against his will, he felt another sliver of hope lodge in his heart.

"I have no love for Dunverlockie," she said. "I know it holds great meaning for you, and I respect that, even if my own experience there has not been a happy one. The truth is, I have no desire to live there, no desire to own it. It has brought me nothing but trouble." She swallowed and met his gaze squarely. "I would like to sell it to you."

Lachlan blinked.

The fumbling of her hands quickened, and an eager look entered her eyes. "For a very reasonable price, of course. All I require is the means to purchase an estate—much smaller than Dunverlockie—one which could provide enough for me and my siblings to live on. Enough to provide an education and a few opportunities for them. I do not have any great aspirations, I assure you. To be my own mistress again is more than I ever hoped for, and I would gladly exchange Dunverlockie for a life and an estate which requires me to work."

The words she was speaking, the hope in her eyes brought a lump of emotion into Lachlan's throat. She was willing to leave being lady of Dunverlockie Castle—and all its land and tenants —for an estate that required her to labor with her own hands for its upkeep, if only she could be free.

And he couldn't give that to her, much as he wanted to. In

this moment, he thought he might give up his own aspirations, if only he could make hers possible. But it wasn't within his power.

"Mrs. MacKinnon." He frowned deeply, his voice brimming with apology. "I'd buy the estate from ye in a heartbeat if I had the money. But...but...I have nothin'—only what I could get when I sold out of the army."

Disappointment crept into her eyes, and he suppressed the urge to reach out a hand and comfort her.

"Dunverlockie *was* my inheritance, ye see. When they took it from us, they left my family with nothin'. I joined the army ta survive, and I sent what I could back ta my brothers and sisters." It had been when he had seen them—the life that they were living—that he had made the decision to return to Dunverlockie and see justice done.

Mrs. MacKinnon shook her head with a soft laugh that mocked herself and took a step back. "Of course. I quite understand. It was a silly notion. I should have thought it through more before suggesting it. Forgive me." She gave a quick attempt at a smile and turned away.

Lachlan reached for her hand. He couldn't let her leave like that—his heart twinged at her embarrassment and at his inability to give her the answer she wanted. "Forgive ye for what, Mrs. MacKinnon? Ye offered me a chance at what I want, and I wish more than anythin' I was in a position to accept it. I see how 'tis a burden to ye."

She gave a wry smile, and her gaze rested on their hands. "A cruel irony, is it not? My burden is your dearest wish."

He bit his tongue. He wanted to remind her that he had offered a way to relieve her of it without depriving her of its financial benefit. But there was no need. It had only been a few hours since their conversation. He allowed her hand to drop softly.

The clopping of horse hooves on the road grew louder, and Lachlan craned his neck to see who it might be and whether they intended to stop at the inn.

He swore in Gaelic. "'Tis Angus and his men."

Mrs. MacKinnon's eyes widened. "I cannot see him after what happened. Not yet."

"Dinna fash yerself," Lachlan said. "I'll see ta him. Ye can stay here while I go."

She moved to stand behind one of the haystacks, and he strode out of the barn.

"Mr. MacKinnon," Lachlan said as he approached. Angus and his men had all stopped in the road in front of the inn. "How can I help ye?"

Angus's eyes roved over the inn as if he was searching for something. The Innes sisters, Lachlan could only suppose.

"We are on our way to Benleith," he said, "but I wanted to stop and check in on Mrs. MacKinnon and Miss Innes. I woke to find them absent from the castle this morning. I understand they came here."

Lachlan considered lying, but there were few places the two women could possibly have gone in such a short time and on foot. Besides, Angus could easily have the truth from Mr. Gibson.

"Aye," Lachlan said. "They're here."

"I should like to speak with Mrs. MacKinnon," Angus said.

"I'm afraid that's no' possible." There was no way on God's green earth Lachlan would give Mrs. MacKinnon up to the coward in front of him, whatever Angus meant to say to her.

Angus's eyebrows went up.

"She's in her room," Lachlan explained. "She gave firm instructions that she no' be disturbed for any reason."

The edge of Angus's mouth curled up in a smile, and his eyes flickered toward the second story of the inn where the rooms were. "No matter. I shall stop here on the return journey from Benleith instead. I trust by then she will no longer be feeling...indisposed." He said the last word with a slight mocking inflection that made it clear he didn't believe the excuse he had been given. Lachlan itched to teach the man a lesson about just how indisposed one could become.

But he only nodded in deference, and the party of MacKinnons continued onward. Lachlan waited until they disappeared behind the trees at the bend in the road before returning to Mrs. MacKinnon in the stables.

She was still behind the haystack when he entered, a wary expression on her face as if she wasn't certain it was Lachlan's footsteps approaching. She breathed a sigh of relief when she realized it was him.

"Thank you," she said, and he offered his hand to help her out from the small space between the two stacks of hay. "You must think me the greatest coward on earth." She brushed a few pieces of straw from her black dress, and Lachlan wondered what she might look like once she put off her mourning. Perhaps it was that which made her look so somber.

He chuckled. "Nay, Mrs. MacKinnon. If I had to choose which is the coward between ye and Angus, 'twould certainly no' be you."

She shot him an amused but disbelieving look. "You flatter me, Mr. Kincaid. But a woman who takes shelter behind a mound of straw cannot, I'm afraid, be considered anything but a coward."

"And what of the man who intimidates a woman by invading her property with a court of brutes? Is that the measure of true bravery?" He pulled a bit of straw from her hair, forcing himself to do it quickly without sacrificing gentleness.

She met his gaze. "No, I suppose you are right."

He let the piece of straw go, watching it flutter to the

ground. "Cowardice masquerades as bravery while it can—while it is certain of victory. When failure looms, though; when a person's power begins to slip away—*that* is the true test. And when Angus faces such failure, he will no longer be able to hide what he truly is."

Their gazes held for a moment, her eyes searching his.

"I should return," she said, breaking the contact.

He nodded and let her go. He had no other choice.

L achlan could feel his body begging for rest, but the absence of Angus and his men from Dunverlockie was not an opportunity he could waste. They hadn't returned since their stop at the inn yesterday, and Lachlan didn't know when the opportunity would present itself again.

So, he slipped the strap of a leather satchel over his head so that it sat diagonally across his chest. He hoped it would be large enough to carry back whatever he found. He intended to make a thorough search of the laird's bedchamber while Angus was gone.

He glanced through the window, judging whether he would need a torch. The moon was beginning to wane, but there was plenty of light for his needs—he knew the way. He would go through the woods. It was a much quicker route than taking the actual road, and he was still hoping to return in time for a few hours of much-needed sleep.

He stilled, frowning at the sound of a thud coming from somewhere below, as if something had fallen. He had waited until the inn was quiet, not wanting anyone to know of his errand, but perhaps Mrs. MacKinnon or her sister was still awake.

But there was no further sound, and he left his room, closing the door softly and tiptoeing down the set of stairs that led from the top level of the inn to the second story. He glanced down the corridor, noting the glow of firelight beneath the crooked gap between the door and the floorboards. It *had* been Mrs. MacKinnon, then. Hopefully not worrying over her situation.

He sighed and turned back toward the second set of stairs then stilled at the sound of a door latch closing—it was soft, but it had unmistakably come from the door to the inn below-stairs. It seemed strange that Mr. Gibson would be up and about—the only time he was found doing anything but sleeping at such an hour was if the needs of a late-night arrival forced him from his bed. And that was certainly not the case.

Lachlan hurried the rest of the way down the stairs then out the door to investigate. From the corner of his eye, movement caught his attention, and he whipped his head toward it just as a dark figure disappeared around the side of the inn. He followed, only to catch the same short-lived glimpse as the hooded person turned the corner that led to the back of the inn —and the woods.

Lachlan picked up his pace. Whoever it was, they had no business sneaking out of—or into—the inn at such an hour. Cracking twigs and rustling leaves let him know that his quarry had vanished into the woods. He could catch him if he ran quickly.

An orange glimmer on the leaves of the forest made him frown—it reminded him of the colors of some sunsets he had seen since returning. He turned to see where the light was coming from. In Mrs. MacKinnon's window, a few small flames licked up at it, illuminating the stone on the inn's exterior.

Lachlan cursed and ran back the way he had come.

He didn't bother opening the door quietly or trying to hush his footsteps up the stairs. No one seemed to be awake, though, despite the smell of smoke which strengthened as he neared

Mrs. MacKinnon's room. The smoke escaping through the gap under the door dulled the hue of the fire within.

He lifted the latch, but it resisted, and panic surged inside him as the sound of crackling grew in volume. Someone had locked her in.

He stepped back, taking stock of the door, then hurtled his shoulder into it with all his strength, once, twice, three times.

Finally, it gave way with a great splintering, and he emerged into the room.

Fire crept along some of the floorboards and toward the bed where Mrs. MacKinnon lay. The area it covered was still minimal—no doubt the person responsible hadn't counted on Lachlan being awake and about.

The sound of Lachlan breaking the door down seemed to rouse Mrs. MacKinnon, though, for she stirred, turning over in bed then blinking and coughing.

Lachlan rushed over and, without a word, flipped the bedcovers back and scooped Mrs. MacKinnon into his arms, striding past the flames that would soon have separated them from the path out to the corridor.

He pulled the door to behind him, hoping it would contain the fire a bit longer. "Fire!" He called out as loudly as he could, kicking a foot against the wall to rouse the inn then carrying Mrs. MacKinnon downstairs.

"Can ye stand?" he asked when they reached the landing at the bottom.

She nodded hurriedly but didn't move.

"Mrs. MacKinnon," he said gently, still holding her in his arms. He could feel her trembling through the thin fabric of her shift.

She looked at him, and he could see the alarm in her eyes, as though she wasn't entirely sure what was happening.

"I need ye ta let me go," he said gently. He didn't *want* her to let him go—not when she was holding him so tightly, like she needed him. He wanted to hold her closer and assure her that everything was all right. But there was no time for that.

The iron grip around his neck eased, and he set her feet on the floor.

"Can ye go ta the kitchen and get some water?" he asked. "And get Glenna."

"Yes, of course." Her eyes darted up the stairway, though. "But...Elizabeth."

He put a hand on her shoulder. "Dinna fash. I'm goin' ta her right now." He didn't wait for a response before running up the stairs and to Miss Innes's room.

Miss Innes was in the corridor, wearing only her shift, but she faced away from Lachlan, toward the door to her sister's room.

"Christina!" she called out, running toward it in her bare feet.

"Miss Innes!" He ran after her, grabbing hold of her wrist just shy of Mrs. MacKinnon's door and pulling her away. She resisted.

"She's downstairs." Lachlan said with a cough. "She's safe downstairs."

Miss Innes stared at him then nodded blankly, and he hastened to lead her to the stairs.

Glenna and Mrs. MacKinnon were at the bottom, holding pots of water. Lachlan reached for the one Mrs. MacKinnon was holding, and Glenna followed him upstairs.

"Go get more!" he said just as Mr. Gibson appeared in his nightshirt and cap.

For twenty minutes, the five of them refilled pots, ran up and down stairs, and doused flames. When the final flare sizzled and sent up smoke, the room was filled with heaving chests and sporadic coughing.

Lachlan had removed his coat and cravat shortly after they began fighting the flames, and he wiped at the sweat on his brow with his shirtsleeve. It came away sooty. He glanced at the others—they all looked the same. Mrs. MacKinnon's face was streaked with dirt, and bunches of her hair had come loose from the plait that hung down her back.

But she was safe. She was alive.

17

Christina stared dazedly at the charred streaks that showed the path of the fire in her room. One leg at the bottom of the wooden bed frame had begun burning, and a few embers still glowed at its base.

Mr. Kincaid must have noticed the same thing, for he stepped toward the bed and poured what water remained in the pot he held onto the ashes.

Christina's gaze flickered as she watched a bit of smoke trail up from the floor. She had only woken when Mr. Kincaid had entered her room. If not for that....

"What happened?" Glenna asked in an incredulous voice. Her shift hung loosely about her, covered in dirt and soot, particularly at the bottom hem. She was barefoot, just as all of them were, with the exception of Mr. Kincaid, standing on the portions of the floor that hadn't burned.

"Mrs. MacKinnon must no' have snuffed out her candle," Mr. Gibson said.

Christina pulled her eyes away from the bed to look at him. She had *not* forgotten. She distinctly remembered snuffing out the candle because the thought she'd had as she was doing so had been what an ill weapon the inn candlestick should have made. It was made of a splintering wood at the bottom—only the base for the candle was metal.

"No," Elizabeth said in a decided voice. "That cannot be what happened, for the candle is intact." She pointed to the one on the short table next to the bed. It stood erect, if at a slight angle, only half-burned.

"What, then?" said Mr. Gibson in a skeptical voice. "The fire jumped from the grate?"

Elizabeth shrugged. "It only takes a spark."

Mr. Gibson gave a little huff, but he was prevented from saying whatever was on his lips.

"'Twas neither thing," Mr. Kincaid said. "'Twas no accident. I saw the person responsible."

Christina's gaze flew to him, but his gaze was already on her, watching for her reaction, no doubt.

"Who?" Elizabeth said, and Christina could see in her sister's eyes that she already believed she knew the answer.

Mr. Kincaid shook his head. "I went after 'im before I realized what he'd done, but 'twas dark, and I stopped chasin' 'im when I noticed the flames in the window. There's no way ta ken who he is now."

"Will ye call for the justice of the peace, Mrs. MacKinnon?" Mr. Gibson asked.

She glanced at Mr. Kincaid, whose eyes were still on her. She didn't know what to do, in truth. She wanted his counsel. "I am not certain yet. It is something I need to think on."

"Could I have a word with ye, Mrs. MacKinnon?" asked Mr. Kincaid.

She nodded, and the others turned to leave.

"I'll go prepare the other room for ye, mistress," Glenna said as she left.

Elizabeth was the last to leave, and she closed the door

behind her, though the intent in her eyes was clear: she would be waiting for the chance to speak with Christina.

There was silence for a moment, then Mr. Kincaid approached her with gentle footsteps for a man so large. "Ye're no' hurt, are ye?" His eyes were full of concern.

She shook her head and was embarrassed to find her eyes stinging and her hands shaking. She looked down, clasping them together to stop the trembling, and Mr. Kincaid took another step toward her, covering her hands with his.

"Are ye certain?" He stooped his head so he could see her eyes.

They were filled with tears, and she tried to hurriedly blink them away. She succeeded only in freeing some, which spilled onto her cheeks. His hands held hers firmly, but the impulse to tremble only seemed to gravitate out, affecting her arms and legs.

"Och," he said softly, and he pulled her into his arms.

Her impulse to draw back was weak and meager, and she surrendered to the strength of his hold, letting her head rest against him. He smelled of fire and soot, just as she did.

"Ye're safe now." His arms were around her, and her head rested against his chest, but for some reason, the breath that ruffled her hair with those faint words felt more intimate than anything else. The pleasure she took from it rattled her from her momentary peace, and she took a step back.

"I'm just a bit jarred."

His arms fell slowly to his sides, and she could see the question her sudden movement had elicited in his eyes.

"I owe you a debt of gratitude," she said. "Yet again. You saved my life—all of our lives."

He grimaced. "'Twas only chance that put me in the right place at the right time."

She looked at the boots he wore. "What *were* you doing?"

He smiled wryly. It was dark in the room, but she could

easily see the sweat on his forehead, neck, and chest, and the elbow of one of his shirtsleeves was singed.

"A visit to Dunverlockie?" she asked as understanding dawned. "While Angus is still away."

He gave a nod.

"I cannot blame you, I suppose," she said. After all, she had refused him perhaps the only means of entering Dunverlockie legitimately—as its owner. "Do you think it was Angus?"

He shook his head. "The man was too short. And Angus is too much of a coward ta do such a thing himself. But I'm certain 'twas one of his men who did it."

"Should I call for someone to investigate?" she asked.

"If 'twould set yer mind at rest," he responded with a shrug of the shoulders. "But in truth, I dinna think aught would come of it."

She took in a breath only to cough as the smoke in her lungs tried to escape. He was right. With no real description of the culprit and with the MacKinnons exerting so much control in the area, little was likely to happen.

"Come," he said. "I'll walk ye ta yer new room. I reckon Glenna's finished preparin' it." He opened the door for them to leave.

Christina hesitated before walking to the door and stopping there. "I think I might sleep on the floor in Elizabeth's room instead." She looked up at him with a smile that mocked herself. "I told you I was a coward. Are you not convinced?"

"Nay, lass, ye'll never convince me of that," he said quietly as they walked to Elizabeth's door. He faced her when they reached it. "I'll no' let ye come ta harm while I'm here, Mrs. MacKinnon."

Her eyebrows knitted together. What was it that made this man so decided upon protecting her? "Even when I have denied you what you most want? When I stand in the way of your obtaining it? Your purposes would have been better served leaving the fire to burn."

He blinked, and the lines on his forehead deepened. He looked almost angry.

"You cannot deny it is true." She had to force herself not to squirm under his censuring gaze.

"I'm no' Angus, Mrs. MacKinnon. I care for yer well-being."

"But why? You have no obligation toward me."

Even beneath his beard, she could see his jaw working. "I dinna care ta see my friends in danger."

His friends. The words touched her more than she expected.

"Well, I am grateful for it," she said. "Thank you."

He reached a hand to her forehead and brushed at it, pulling his thumb away and rubbing the ash between his fingers. Somehow his every touch was gentle.

"Sleep well, Mrs. MacKinnon," he said, and he turned away.

Christina stared after him for a moment then put her hand on the door latch, took a deep breath, and immediately coughed. The smell of smoke still permeated the inn, and there was a tickle in her throat that wouldn't be dispelled.

Elizabeth was lying in her bed, but the covers had been pushed to the side, and she was staring at the ceiling, the light of a single tallow candle casting shadows on the uneven walls. She seemed to have shed her dirty shift for a new one, and her hair had been replaited. She hurried to sit up as Christina entered then motioned for her to come sit beside her.

Christina obliged, and Elizabeth wrapped her arms around her without saying a word. They stayed that way for a time, and Christina didn't try to stop the few tears that came. She was overwhelmed—with the threats on her safety, with her responsibilities, with life in general. She had hoped things would improve after Gordon's death, but so far, the reality was proving to be otherwise.

"What did Mr. Kincaid want?" Elizabeth finally asked.

Christina sighed. She hadn't yet told Elizabeth about his proposal, and she had promised not to keep anything from her. "He was worried for me, I think, and he doesn't trust Mr. Gibson." She paused then looked at Elizabeth. "He offered to marry me."

Elizabeth reared back slightly. "*What?*"

"Yesterday. In the stables after breakfast. He thought it the best way to protect me—us—from Angus. He thinks Angus's boldness at Dunverlockie is a result of my not having anyone to stand up for me."

"And he is right, of course," Elizabeth said. "What, then? Did you accept his offer?"

Christina grabbed at her messy plait, not meeting her sister's eye. "I couldn't."

Elizabeth said nothing, but from the way her shoulders sank, Christina had the impression that she was disappointed, and she felt the need to defend her decision.

"How could I chain myself to another man after I've just been freed of Gordon?" No one despised Gordon as Elizabeth did. Surely she would comprehend.

A little smile trembled at the corner of Elizabeth's mouth. "I cannot think it would be so very terrible to be chained to a man like Mr. Kincaid. You cannot persuade me that you find him unpleasant to look at."

Christina elbowed her sister in the ribs and was grateful the room was too poorly lit to betray the blush that crept into her cheeks. She had enjoyed the feeling of being in his arms more than she cared to admit to Elizabeth—or herself.

"I am teasing, of course," Elizabeth continued. "No one could blame you for never wishing to be married again. *I* certainly don't. But, well, Mr. Kincaid is nothing like Gordon, Christina."

"Neither was the Gordon Father promised me to anything

like the man I lived with. What is that?" She indicated a little scrap of fabric beside Elizabeth on the bed.

Elizabeth took it up, and a tartan pattern became visible in the dim light. "I found it in your room when we were putting out the fire. I think the culprit left it behind."

Christina frowned and took it, bringing it closer to her eyes. The tartan was a black and gray pattern.

"Do you recognize it?" Elizabeth asked.

Christina shook her head. "It is not at all familiar to me—not one of the patterns that was made in this area. Certainly not what the MacKinnons were wont to wear."

Elizabeth put out a hand to invite the fabric's return, and Christina looked up at her as she gave it back.

"I intend to discover exactly who it belongs to," Elizabeth said.

Before Christina could respond, there was a little tap on the door, and the sisters' gazes met. Elizabeth rose and went to the door, opening it only slightly then swinging it wider. It was Mr. Kincaid, arms full of blankets and pillows.

"If ye wish ta sleep in here," he said with a glance at Christina, "ye'll need these."

Christina rose from the bed and hurried to help Elizabeth relieve him of his burden, after which he bid them goodnight.

Elizabeth closed the door, but she cocked a brow at Christina. "Would Gordon ever have done such a thing?"

Christina gave a little laugh and set to making herself a bed on the floor.

"Let me do that," Elizabeth said. "I can make my own bed."

"It is not *your* bed," Christina said. "It is mine."

Elizabeth narrowed her eyes as if she might press the issue, but she decided against it and continued to help arranging the blankets and pillows. Where Mr. Kincaid had found so many, Christina didn't know, but she was glad for the comfort their weight brought.

Elizabeth climbed back into her bed and snuffed out the candle. "Do not trouble yourself, Christina." She stretched a hand toward her, setting it on Christina's arm. "Not for the world would I wish you to marry unhappily again. We will find another way to set everything right."

Christina didn't respond, but Elizabeth seemed not to have been expecting one, for she shut her eyes and let out a sigh as she sank into her pillow.

Christina let her gaze settle on her sister's peaceful face, obscured by the dark of the room. She couldn't see a way out of her troubles, and staring at Elizabeth, it was more keenly driven home to her than ever that her own life was not the only one at stake. Angus seemed not to care whether Elizabeth's life was forfeit along with Christina's, so long as he achieved his goal.

She tossed and turned on her makeshift bed, her thoughts and worries preventing her from the rest and oblivion she so desperately wanted. The one time she managed to nearly fall asleep, her eyes flew open, the image of fire flashing across her mind, followed by the form of Mr. Kincaid bursting through the door, lit by the trail of orange flames creeping across her floor.

He had rescued her twice. And what had she done to repay him? Did she not owe him something? She was certain she did. And yet, she couldn't stomach the prospect of marrying out of such obligation, nor of being a pawn in someone's game. Her father's good intentions notwithstanding, she had been traded into marriage with Gordon, and he had treated her like an object to be used and disposed of at will.

But perhaps Elizabeth was right. Mr. Kincaid had never treated her as an object. He had been nothing but kind and respectful toward her—toward everyone she had seen him interact with. He had sworn he wouldn't treat Dunverlockie as only his, despite the fact that it *would* be, according to the law of the land.

After what felt like hours of rolling from side to side, Christina admitted defeat and, as quietly as she could, crept out of her blankets. She couldn't lie down and do nothing any longer. Elizabeth was sound asleep—she had always been a deep sleeper—and Christina watched her for a moment. She wanted so badly to protect her sister, and the weeks since Gordon's death had shown her how incapable she was of doing so.

She sighed, reached for Elizabeth's wrapper, and went to the door, lifting the latch carefully. Elizabeth didn't even stir at the sound.

As Christina reached the door to the room where the fire had occurred, she paused. She was hesitant to look at it—to remember what had happened, but perhaps even more hesitant to be reminded of what *might* have happened.

But ignoring those things did not make them go away. Whether she acknowledged it or not, someone seemed determined to kill her. They had compromised the safety of her carriage, they had tried to poison her, and they had attempted to burn her in her sleep.

She needed to face that reality. Perhaps it would give her the courage to do what she needed to do.

She lifted the latch, opened the door, and stilled.

Mr. Kincaid lay in the bed, the covers pulled up around him, his eyes closed. The bed was far too short for a man of his height, and his legs were curled up, his knees hanging over the edge of the bed, reminding Christina of her younger brothers.

She hurried to close the door, cringing as the hinge squeaked and Mr. Kincaid's eyes opened.

He threw the bedcovers off and stood. "What happened?" He blinked quickly, as if to clear away the sleep.

"Nothing at all," she said in a reassuring voice. "I did not know you were in here. That is all."

His body relaxed. The strings at the top of his shirt were untied, and Christina averted her eyes from the view it afforded.

"I only thought I would be more likely ta hear if...." He left the sentence unfinished.

"If the person came back to finish what they started," she supplied.

"Aye," he said.

She looked around the room again. It had never been a cheerful room by any stretch of the imagination, but now there was an eeriness about it that gave her the chills, and she wrapped her arms around herself to stop them.

"Ye couldna sleep, I take it?" He ran a hand through his hair. Most of it had come loose from the queue, and, combined with his open shirt and bare feet, it gave him a very unkempt appearance. Elizabeth's words echoed for a moment in her mind: *I cannot think it would be so very terrible to be chained to a man like Mr. Kincaid.*

She pushed the thought away hurriedly. "No, I am afraid not. But I did not intend to keep *you* from sleep as well."

"Nay bother," he said with a smile made all the more charming for its sleepiness. "I ken what it's like no' ta be able ta sleep." He glanced down at the bed. "Besides, I'd rather keep ye company than lie down in *that* again."

Christina laughed. "I think it is meant for someone a bit... smaller than you."

"Aye, like a bairn." He stretched his back, wincing.

Her heart began to hammer, and she knew the time had come. "If you truly do not intend to sleep again...I wanted to speak with you." She said the last words quickly, forcing them out before she could lose her nerve.

He raised his brows and nodded. "Aye, of course. What is it?"

She swallowed, and the words stuck in her throat. How could she say what needed saying?

He noticed her hesitation and took a step toward her. "Mrs. MacKinnon, ye ken ye can ask me for anythin'."

She smiled ruefully. "Do you mean that?"

His eyes narrowed slightly before he responded. "Aye."

She took a deep breath and released it slowly. "Will you marry me?"

18

Lachlan often chose silence over words, but for once, silence was thrust upon him. He was speechless. Perhaps he was dreaming; perhaps this entire scene was a creation of his mind.

But he could feel the aching in his injured leg from having run up and down the stairs so many times earlier, and the smell of burnt wood still hung oppressively in the room.

"I have shocked you," Mrs. MacKinnon said. "Forgive me. I am nervous, I think. But, to be fair, you shocked me with talk of it the other day."

"Mrs. MacKinnon," he said, frowning. "Ye've no' slept. Ye're still agitated from the fire."

"No," she said as she wrung her hands. "Well, yes, but I do know what I am saying. It is highly unusual, I know. But I have been thinking about it a great deal, and I am convinced that a marriage between us is the only way forward."

He said nothing. Words escaped him tonight.

A sudden change passed over her face, and her eyes took on an arrested look. "You have changed your mind."

"Nay," he said. "It's no' that." He rubbed at his beard, unable to identify exactly what it was that was giving him pause. "My offer stands."

She put up a hand. "Before you say that, I think you should know that there are a number of...stipulations that would need to be agreed to before discussing the possibility any further."

His brows went up, and suddenly he had the strangest desire to laugh. This situation was ludicrous.

"Perhaps we should sit down," she said.

He chuckled, and they took the only seats available—beside one other on the bed. "Och. Perhaps I should be takin' notes. I dinna have the best memory." For some reason, he felt the need to diffuse the strangeness of the situation—and what he was feeling inside—with humor.

"There are not *that* many stipulations to discuss," she said, scooting away from him a bit more. It wasn't done with unkindness. It occurred to him that Mrs. MacKinnon was careful about how close she allowed herself to others.

"Verra well," he said. "Tell me, then. What stipulations do ye have?"

She straightened herself as though she was preparing to give a formal speech, and the gesture brought a little smile to his lips, given that she was wearing nothing but her shift and a thin wrapper. Her face still showed a few faint streaks from the ash.

"These are my terms, Mr. Kincaid, and I assure you that I am not opposed to hearing whatever terms *you* deem necessary in order for such an arrangement to be acceptable to you. If both of us are in agreement, I think it best that we put it in writing."

He gave a nod, secretly wondering what terms she could possibly think he would demand in order for him to agree to marry her.

"When we talked in the stables," she continued, "we

discussed the fact that, if we were to marry, Dunverlockie would legally be yours. I assure you, I have little desire to interfere with things, but I hope you can see that the arrangement effectively deprives me of all the power I currently possess. I have naught but your word assuring me that you will abide by my wishes."

He frowned. "A man's word isna somethin' ta be scoffed at." Did she truly believe he would dupe her into marrying him with promises he had no intention of keeping?

"Except when it is," she said. "I mean you no offense with what I am saying. It is only that experience has taught me to be wary."

"I understand," he said. Whatever vows Gordon MacKinnon had made upon their marriage, he had certainly broken them. Her skepticism was not an insult to him but rather a manifestation of the character of her late husband. He had to remind himself of that.

"First, then," she said, "I would require a promise permitting me to provide for my siblings. I intend to send them money on a regular basis."

He frowned, deeply troubled. "Mrs. MacKinnon, did Gordon no' permit ye ta do such a thing?"

She didn't meet his eye, but there was no hint of a desire for pity in the way she held herself. "I was not permitted to make any purchases without his presence and explicit consent. It is why my sister and I were traveling to Craiglinne when the accident occurred—I was finally free to send money to my aunt for my brothers and sisters."

He didn't know why he was surprised to hear of Gordon exercising such control over his wife—the wife who had made it possible for him to keep Dunverlockie. A man who would leave marks on his wife's arm would certainly leave plenty of other scars. It made much sense why Mrs. MacKinnon would approach a second marriage the way she was now if she was accustomed to neglect and being deprived of the ability to care for those she loved.

He knew he shouldn't, but he couldn't help himself, and he turned toward her, gathering her hands in his. She looked up at him, a hint of alarm in her eyes—no doubt another relic of her marriage to Gordon. The man was fortunate he was already in the ground, for if he hadn't been, Lachlan would have put him there himself.

"Mrs. MacKinnon, I would *never* let yer family go wantin'. They'd be welcome to come live at Dunverlockie if ye wished for it."

He watched as her eyes watered and her throat bobbed.

"And your siblings?" she said. "What of them?"

He nodded. "'Tis somethin' we can discuss together."

She was looking at him with a strange, thoughtful expression. "I know so little of your family. How many siblings *do* you have?"

"Two sisters and a brother. My brother is studyin' ta become a doctor."

"I should like to meet them," she said.

"I hope ye shall. They'd like ye, all three of 'em. And now that we have that settled, what other stipulations do ye have?"

She gave a watery laugh and pulled one of her hands away to wipe away a tear. "I want to be more involved with the tenants—to make sure they are taken care of. Gordon was not a sympathetic landlord, and we lost good people as a result. I understand it is only thanks to your father that Glenna's family is still here."

"Aye," Lachlan said. "When he began ta suspect he'd been betrayed by yer father-in-law, he offered forty-year leases to the Douglases and two other families he respected greatly. He wanted ta be certain they were no' punished by havin' the rent raised on them."

"As Gordon did to most of the other tenants," she said with

a sigh. "I owe your father my gratitude, for I cannot say what I would have done without Glenna."

"She's a good-hearted lass—and a strong one. And, ta address yer point, I'd welcome yer help in seein' the tenants are taken care of. Now," he said. "What else is there?"

She hesitated, looking down at the hand he still held. Did she want him to release it?

She didn't look at him when she spoke. "I told you before that I mean you no offense by any of these stipulations, and I hope you will bear that in mind with what I say next."

He gave a shallow nod, trying to prepare himself for some sort of assault on his character or whatever she might say that would require such a preface.

"I do not wish to be touched," she said softly.

His heart stuttered, and he released her hand immediately, humiliation washing over him like a bucket of icy river water.

"No," she said hurriedly, reaching for his hand.

He allowed her to take it and hoped fervently that his emotions weren't apparent on his face.

"You misunderstand me." Her voice was soft, and there was something in it that he could only describe as embarrassment. "Perhaps I should have phrased that differently. I only meant that...that I do not wish to be intimate."

He blinked, again bereft of speech. She seemed to have that effect—among others—on him. And he had to admit to himself the disappointment he felt at her words. But he wouldn't allow her to see it. He had proposed the idea of a marriage between them as something purely functional in nature: a way to protect her, a way for him to recapture his heritage. What she was saying was in line with that.

But could he be satisfied with retaking the estate he was meant to inherit, even if it meant he would never have posterity to pass it on to? At least it would be their decision who *did* inherit.

"Can I ask ye a question?"

She nodded, her eyes searching his face as though to gauge his reaction to her last stipulation.

"Marryin' me may help keep Angus in his place—it may force him ta think twice about makin' any more attempts on yer life. But...." He exhaled through his nose, unsure how to say it. "Well, the fact is, if he managed ta take yer life afore we'd been married a year, the law ensures the estate would go ta him. I thought perhaps ye'd wish ta have a child ta prevent that."

She shut her eyes. "I know," she said softly. "But it would make little difference in practice, wouldn't it? If we married now, the soonest we could possibly have a child"—he thought he saw her cheeks redden—"would be just shy of a year of marriage. Besides"—she turned her head—"I am not even certain I can have children."

There was silence for a moment. He tried valiantly not to show how the condition she had put forward was affecting him. The last thing he wanted to do was give her reason for drawing back again—for believing that his purpose in marrying her was entirely selfish. His gaze went to the wound on her forehead that was now nothing but a small scab. It was a reminder, though, of just what was at stake. She needed someone to protect her from Angus.

And, as for him, could he be content with ensuring Dunverlockie never again belonged to a MacKinnon, even if he had no posterity of his own to inherit it?

"It is my understanding that, when we draw up the marriage agreement, we might specify that I wish for the estate to go to you, even if I were to die before the first anniversary of the marriage."

"Would it hold in a court of law?" he asked.

She lifted her shoulders. "With a skilled advocate, I hope so."

He set his jaw. "It doesna matter." He wouldn't let her come to harm.

She smiled sadly at him. "I understand if this stipulation is one you cannot agree to, or if the charge to protect me has become too burdensome." She gave a wry smile. "It is becoming a very consuming assignment, is it not?"

He couldn't resist a responsive smile of his own. He was glad to hear her using humor.

"Och," he said. "Yer brother and I were charged with soldiers who seemed intent upon bein' killed at least once a week in one way or another. In comparison, protectin' ye is child's play." He winked at her, and she laughed with a shake of the head.

"Is there aught else?" he asked.

"Surely that is plenty to ask," she said with a rueful smile. "But no. That concludes my list. And I am prepared to hear yours—whenever you have it."

He frowned in thought for a moment. "I have only one thing on my list."

She laughed lightly. "I seem like a tyrant in comparison. What is your stipulation?"

He interlocked his fingers in his lap and stared at them for a moment before responding. "I want ye ta be happy. If ye can be." He looked up at her.

She was staring at him, surprise in her eyes. Finally, he had managed to leave *her* speechless.

"I ken why ye're agreein' ta the marriage, Mrs. MacKinnon," he said, "and I agree ta everythin' ye've said—I'll sign my name under every one of the conditions ye've mentioned." He paused. "But I think we can do better than that. I mean ta show ye that I intend ta honor yer wishes, no matter whether they're written on a legal document, spoken through yer lips, or mere thoughts in yer head. I want Dunverlockie, aye. But I mean ta make ye happy, too."

He held her gaze, and what he saw there was fear. But he could have sworn that, behind it, there was a glimmer of hope.

"I will try," she said. "But *please*, Mr. Kincaid. You must not blame yourself if I seem to be unhappy."

"Lachlan," he said. "My name is Lachlan."

"Very well. Lachlan."

"Can I call ye by yer name as well?" His heart pattered. She nodded. "Christina."

"Christina." He said it slowly, letting his eyes take in her face as he did. "Ye willna regret marryin' me if I have anythin' ta say about it."

They sat on the bed in the charred room for a while longer, arranging the details of a wedding, and Lachlan could only hope that they might help each other salvage what had been taken from them—that together they could make something from the ashes.

19

Between the work expected of Lachlan at the inn and arranging things for the marriage, there were not only too few hours in the day but too few hours of sleep over the past two nights for the energy required of him. But he found that sleep was far from his thoughts as he performed his duties among the horses and saw to a few passing travelers in the morning hours.

Apprised of what Lachlan and Christina had decided together, Glenna had enthusiastically agreed to make excuses for him to Mr. Gibson later on when he needed time to pay a visit to the parish minister.

Miss Innes came to the stables to retrieve her sister's horse so they could make their way to Dunverlockie as Lachlan was preparing his own for a ride to the kirk.

He smiled at her and handed her Apollo's reins. "Is there anythin' else ye need?"

She returned the smile, but there was something in it that gave him pause. "Only a moment of your time, if you please."

"Aye, of course." He looped the reins of his horse on the nearest hook and turned to face Miss Innes.

She glanced behind her toward the inn, and seeming satisfied that they were alone, faced Lachlan. "You are to marry my sister, Mr. Kincaid."

She hadn't phrased it like a question, but he felt some response was called for. "Aye," he said slowly.

She gave him an evaluative look. He had faced all manner of threatening men over the course of his time in the army—officers, enemy soldiers, and the like—but somehow, the woman in front of him gave him more desire to squirm than any of them had.

"I want to make certain that we understand one another," Miss Innes said.

He waited for her to go on.

"I have watched my sister suffer at the hands of a husband, Mr. Kincaid. If Gordon had not died as quickly as he did, I would soon have killed him myself."

Lachlan's mouth tugged up in a smile, and Miss Innes's eyebrows shot up.

"You find what I am saying amusing?"

"Nay, 'tis just...I had the same thought just a few hours ago —that I would have put the coward in the ground if he was alive today."

She gave a nod. "I am relieved to hear that. You will understand, then, that I have no intention at all of standing by to watch Christina be hurt a second time. Gordon was, as you said, a coward. He was a brute. And, while you appear to be neither of those things, appearances can be deceptive, and I assure you that I *will* know if my sister is being mistreated."

"Miss Innes," he said. "I understand ye're worried for yer sister. And I'm glad for it. But I willna mistreat her. I give ye my word."

The first sign of emotion flashed across Miss Innes's face, and some of her sternness seemed to disintegrate, replaced with a pleading in her eyes.

"She has suffered much," she said, "and when I look at the way he changed her in the time they were married..." Her jaw tightened, and she looked away for a moment before meeting his gaze again. "She needs someone gentle, Mr. Kincaid. But more than anything—and she would never forgive me if she knew I said this—more than anything, she needs to be loved." She put up a hand to keep him from responding. "And I know that is not why you have decided to marry her, but"—she let out a frustrated breath. "Just be gentle with her, please."

Emotion rose in Lachlan's throat as the weight of the opportunity and responsibility before him settled on his shoulders and heart. "Ye have my word, Miss Innes." He cleared his throat. "I'll take care of yer sister."

She held his gaze, and the seconds stretched on in silence. "I believe you."

As she and Elizabeth made their way back to Dunverlockie late that morning, Christina knew a fear that they would arrive at the castle to the presence of Angus and his men. It was a baseless fear—they would have been aware if the men had returned early, as the route from Benleith required them to pass Glengour Inn. But, now that she had decided upon a course—now that a future promising lighter burdens was within reach—she couldn't help feeling anxious that it would somehow be frustrated.

But Angus was not at Dunverlockie, and she and Elizabeth were left to make preparations for the ceremony.

"Where is the ceremony to take place?" Elizabeth asked as she helped Christina into a fresh shift.

Christina had asked for her help with getting ready. She didn't want word spreading among the servants—it was possible one of them would find a way to alert Angus if it did.

She reached for her stays. "I do not know. Lachlan assured me he would arrange it all. I only requested that it not be held here inside the castle."

Elizabeth set to lacing up the stays in the back. "But it is not necessary, is it? A ceremony, I mean. You could simply proclaim in front of two or three of us that you agree to take one another as man and wife."

"Yes, we discussed that, but we were of the same mind that something more robust would serve best. Neither of us wish to give Angus reason to cast doubt upon the validity of the union."

Elizabeth sighed and helped Christina into her petticoats, tying them at the back. They were blue silk—the first time Christina had worn colors since Gordon's death. She hadn't realized how crushed she had felt by her black attire until now. They made the whole room feel lighter.

"I suppose you are right," Elizabeth said. "When do you expect Angus to return?"

Christina shrugged. "I believe he has gone to collect rents."

"Should his factor not be doing that?"

"Yes," Christina replied, "but you know Angus. He does not trust anyone fully enough to leave something so important entirely in their hands."

Elizabeth let out a scoffing sound. "Undoubtedly because, were he himself the factor, he would be an untrustworthy one." She came around to face Christina, putting a hand on both of Christina's shoulders. "You have made the right decision, Christina. I truly believe that."

"I hope so."

Elizabeth cocked an eyebrow. "You know I would not allow you to do this without speaking my mind if I disagreed."

Christina smiled and slid her stomacher into place. Her emotions were a disorganized, confusing jumble, but Elizabeth's words brought more calm to the forefront, at least temporarily. She could only pray that her sister was right and that she *was* making the right decision.

Once Christina was fully dressed and her hair coiffed, Elizabeth took a step back and surveyed her.

"You look beautiful," Elizabeth said.

Christina made an impatient noise, straightening her petticoats. "What has that to do with anything?"

Elizabeth gave a handheld mirror to Christina. "Nothing, I suppose. But Mr. Kincaid is bound to notice. He always does."

Christina willed herself not to blush, allowing herself only a brief glance at her reflection before setting the mirror down. What did it matter if Lachlan noticed her appearance or not? She couldn't afford to care about such things.

The reassurance she had felt from Lachlan that morning in the burned room was beginning to crack and splinter as fear pressed itself in on her again. There was fear everywhere, no matter what course she chose. This course seemed to hold the least.

But it was not without unease, and Elizabeth's words uncovered an anxiety that Christina had yet to confront: she knew the pain and misery of being tied to a cruel man. What of the pain of being tied to a kind and gentle one?

Lachlan was nothing like Gordon—she would not have agreed to any of this if he had been. But what if the mild nature which had made her agree to marry him proved to be more than she could resist? What if the inklings of attraction and connection she had felt grew?

There was something even more terrifying about the prospect of unrequited affection than there was in the mutual antipathy she had lived through for the last year and a half.

The clouds had diminished as the day warmed, and it was as the early summer afternoon light shone through the windows at Dunverlockie that Lachlan, the parish minister, and Glenna's father arrived to escort Christina and Elizabeth to the ceremony.

Christina's chest tightened at the first view of Lachlan standing outside the door.

Lachlan's gaze locked on her, and his mouth opened slightly —and wordlessly. His dark hair was pulled into a neat queue, and though the coat he wore was one she had seen before, the frills of the shirt underneath gave it a more refined appearance. The smell of bergamot lingered around him. The image was a sharp contrast to the man she had seen that morning: hair askew, wrinkled shirt open at the neck, and the smell of smoke overwhelming both of them.

She felt a slight nudge from Elizabeth and hurried to pull her eyes away from Lachlan to the other two men.

"Mr. Douglas is here to act as a witness to everything," Lachlan said. "And Mr. Geddes has kindly agreed to perform the ceremony."

"I am glad to hear that," Christina said. "Thank you both sincerely." She had had her doubts that Lachlan would manage to convince the minister to agree to such a haphazard ceremony.

"I kent Mr. Kincaid's father many years ago," the minister said, putting a hand on Lachlan's back and smiling fondly at him. "I would do anythin' for a Kincaid. Ye ken ye can call on us, my laird."

Lachlan gripped Mr. Geddes' shoulder, grimacing. "And I will do so if I see the need. 'Tis no' a small thing I've asked of ye both," he said in a somber voice. "'Twill make Angus angry with ye, and while I willna allow 'im ta do ye harm, I canna promise he'll no' make ye feel his displeasure in ways I canna prevent."

Both of the men nodded.

"We ken," Mr. Douglas said.

"Aye," said the minister. "We're well-accustomed ta his displeasure as is."

"Verra well," Lachlan replied, turning back to Christina and offering her his arm.

They began walking, and Elizabeth, Mr. Geddes, and Mr. Douglas fell behind.

"Ye ken that no one will face more of Angus's displeasure than ye?" he said to her. "Are ye certain this is what ye wish for?"

She took in a deep breath and nodded. The minister's words had given her an extra dose of strength. A marriage between Lachlan and herself would shift the balance of power in the district away from the MacKinnons—a shift sorely needed.

It was true Angus would be furious, but for once, Christina wouldn't have to face the anger of a MacKinnon alone.

"Ye're a brave woman," he said, helping her onto a path that led into the trees.

She shook her head. "You will face as much of his anger as I will, particularly when he discovers your true identity." She shot him a teasing look. "Besides, I have your solemn promise you will protect me. But who will protect *you*?"

He cocked an eyebrow. "You will, I hope."

She laughed and searched his face. "Are *you* having second thoughts?"

He looked down at her and smiled softly, giving her arm a gentle squeeze. "Nay, lass. I'm more certain than ever."

Her heart fluttered, and she hurried to look at the path ahead. His words only signified that he was determined to do whatever was necessary to take back Dunverlockie. He was leading them on a path Christina hadn't even known existed. It was thick with vegetation, and he walked slightly ahead of her in order to be able to push aside the branches protruding into their path.

"Where precisely are we going?" she asked.

He looked down at her with a half-smile. "Ye said ye didna wish for the ceremony ta be in the castle. I hope ye'll no' be upset with me if I chose somewhere on the grounds."

"Not at all." She loved the castle grounds—they had been one of few places of peace for her in what had come to feel much like a prison. She glanced behind her and noticed the others trailing behind them at a great distance.

Lachlan pushed aside a tree branch, and they emerged into a small grove.

Christina looked around in appreciation. It was an idyllic little spot, overgrown at the edges with trees and bushes, which clustered around a river, rushing high with May waters.

Lachlan watched her for a moment, seeming to appreciate her reaction. "Ye've never seen it afore, have ye?"

She shook her head. She wished she had. It was precisely the sort of place she would have loved to escape to.

"I discovered it when I was just a lad. My father found me here one day and scolded me. Told me 'twas too dangerous and no' ta return." He smiled nostalgically. "Said the river would carry me out ta sea. But I didna listen. I came here from time ta time, and I grew ta love it."

She tried to picture a young Lachlan sneaking into the grove alone. "Does it truly go out to the sea?"

He narrowed his eyes, staring at the water. "Och, perhaps. I was too afraid ta see. The waves frightened me. I wonder if 'twas just his way of gettin' me ta obey."

She laughed as Elizabeth and the others came up behind them. "It did not work very well, did it?"

"Nay," he said.

"Shall we begin?" the minister asked.

Christina felt her muscles tighten and tried to relax them as she nodded. She had made her choice; it was time to see it through. With the sound of chirping birds and rushing water filling the grove, she faced Lachlan.

His gaze rested on her, turning thoughtful again, as though he was still concerned she might be rethinking her decision. She offered a smile of reassurance, even though her heart was hammering inside her chest.

20

"Do ye have a ring?" Mr. Geddes asked Lachlan, opening the hefty book in his hands.

Lachlan looked an apology at Christina. There simply hadn't been enough time for all the arrangements he would have made if circumstances had been different.

"Of a sort, aye. 'Twill have ta do for now."

Mr. Geddes smiled sympathetically. "Verra good. Now, then."

Lachlan kept his gaze on Christina as Mr. Geddes began the ceremony, looking for any indication that she was regretting her choice. She looked paler than usual, and the smiles she offered up every now and again when she realized he was looking at her made his heart twinge. They were meant to reassure him, he assumed, but it was evident she was nervous. And little wonder, given what her sister had told him. In his urgency to secure his own future as well as hers, he hadn't truly stopped to consider what she might be feeling.

"I, Lachlann Muireach Kincaid, take thee"—he paused, realizing he didn't know Christina's full name.

She leaned in and said her name softly.

He smiled and repeated it after her, "Cairistìona Innes MacKinnon to my wedded wife, to have and to hold from this day forward..."

But he *wouldn't* hold her. He had promised her as much. And he would keep his promise, no matter how hard it might become.

Helped with Lachlan's full name, Christina said her part with poise and calm, and, when it was time to place the ring on her finger, Lachlan reached into the pocket of his coat for the little piece of twine he had cut from a spool in the stables before coming.

He looked an apology at Christina, but she seemed not to mind the humble nature of it, and he tied it loosely about her finger.

She fiddled with it for a moment then looked up at him as he retained her hand in his, her expression somber and intent.

"...I pronounce that they be man and wife together. In the name of the father, and of the son, and of the holy ghost. Amen."

Mr. Geddes looked on them benevolently, as he might a couple who was finally marrying after years of loving and waiting. He gave a coaxing nod, and Lachlan's heart pattered at the realization that the man was expecting a kiss. In all his haste to gain the minister's agreement to marry them, he had never fully explained what the situation was—that this wasn't a love match.

Lachlan looked to Christina, who seemed to understand as well that something was expected of them at this point. He tried to gauge what he was seeing in her eyes, but it was too difficult to tell. In any case, he had given her his assurance that intimacy would not be a part of their marriage, and he had privately promised himself that he would allow her to take the lead in determining what their interaction would look like.

Christina held his gaze, as if she, too, was trying to appraise

MARTHA KEYES

his feelings on the matter, and all the while, the minister, Mr. Douglas, and Miss Innes looked on. A flock of birds fluttered overhead, tree leaves rustled with the breeze, and the river rushed past the large stones in its path—inexorable movement urging them out of their paralysis.

He still held Christina's hand lightly in his, and in a decisive movement, he brought it to his lips and, shutting his eyes, placed a gentle kiss upon the knot of the twine ring. When their eyes met again, he saw relief reflected in hers—and gratitude. It was certainly humbling when a woman felt such sentiments after being spared the prospect of kissing him.

The minister and Mr. Douglas offered their congratulations to Lachlan and Christina and left shortly, both having matters to attend to before dark fell. Miss Innes turned to the couple with a satisfied smile and embraced them by turns.

"I instructed Cook to prepare something above the usual fare for dinner," she said. "I shall go see how she is getting along."

The rustling of her skirts was nearly drowned out by the sounds of the river, and Lachlan knew an extra dose of nerves as he found himself alone with his new wife.

"Well," Christina said, "it is done."

"Aye," he responded. "Though I fear that may have been the easy part of it."

She looked at him with a sympathetic grimace. "What will you say to Mr. Gibson? I cannot think he will be terribly pleased to discover he has lost you."

"Nay," he said. "I'll have ta do what I can ta find a replacement for 'im as quickly as possible." He offered her his arm, and they turned back toward the castle.

"I rather think you should take your time," she said. "It might be beneficial for Mr. Gibson to exert himself a bit."

"He's more likely ta make Glenna suffer by puttin' it all on her."

"Very true." She sighed. "Well, I can think of one or two people who might be willing to take on some duties at the inn. They will not be able to compare to *you*, of course, but I imagine their families would be grateful for the added income."

He glanced at her with a half-smile. "Willna be able ta compare ta me?" It was dangerous to tease her, but he couldn't help himself, and he so desperately wanted to set her at her ease after the step they had just taken.

She stopped, and he along with her as their arms broke apart, allowing them to face each other.

"What?" she asked.

He shrugged. "'Tis naught. It merely sounded like ye were offerin' me a compliment."

She averted her gaze for a moment, and seeing the genuine smile on her lips sent a thrill through him. When she brought her head back up to meet his eye, she tilted her head to the side in a curious gesture made all the more endearing for the little twinkle in her eye. "Do you always take it as a compliment when your skills as a grown man are pitted against those of twelve-year-old boys?"

His eyebrows shot up. "They're twelve?"

She nodded. "Or thereabouts."

"Och," he said, turning back to the castle and giving her his arm again. "A blow ta my pride."

She rubbed absently with a thumb at the twine on her finger.

"I'm sorry," he said. "I promise I'll find a more suitable one for ye."

She brought the ring up to look at it more closely. "And here I was just thinking I liked it."

"Ye like a piece of twine for a wedding ring?"

"You do not?"

He shrugged. "I've nothin' against twine. 'Tis only...well, it doesna precisely give the impression of strength or durability."

She toyed with the ring more. "You think it would give the wrong idea to Angus?"

"Perhaps. But I am more concerned with what 'twill make *you* think."

Her head whipped up to look at him, a question in her eyes.

"I mean ta be a good husband to ye, Christina. A proper one —no' one who gives ye a wee bit of rope for a ring." They emerged from the wooded path and stopped.

She smiled wryly and looked at it again. "My last husband gave me a proper ring, as you call it."

He said nothing, wishing he could put a hand on her cheek and reassure her that he would be nothing like Gordon, no matter what ring he gave her. But he resisted the urge.

Instead he took up her hand, staring at the thin, coiled thread. "The twine stays, then. Even if I have ta replace it every month." He gave her a teasing smile then sighed. "And now, I must go face Mr. Gibson."

"Do you wish me to come with you?"

He managed to suppress any indication of his surprise. He *did* want her to come with him. But only because he enjoyed her company, not because there was anything in particular she could do to make his errand easier. "Nay, I'll no' make ye do such a thing."

He wished he could decipher her reaction. When had it come to be so difficult—or important—to decipher another person's emotions?

"I wish you luck, then," she said, and he walked her to the castle door before they parted ways.

L achlan had the ride to Glengour to consider what to tell Mr. Gibson. In the end, he merely informed the innkeeper that he could no longer work at the inn, having found new employment that was better suited to him. The truth would keep. If Mr. Gibson was aware that Lachlan had just married the lady of Dunverlockie, Lachlan had no doubt at all that he would send a message to Angus at Benleith. They would have Angus at Dunverlockie in no time at all, and that wasn't what Lachlan wanted.

That encounter was an inevitable one, but he was selfish enough to want a bit of time with Christina before the confrontation occurred. Besides, the longer they had been married before having to face Angus, the more real the marriage would feel. He hoped.

When he arrived back at Dunverlockie with his small sack of belongings hanging from the saddle, it was growing dark, and he allowed himself a moment's pause on the path in front of the castle to admire his new—and old—home. By law, it now belonged to him. He could explore it, change it, even dispose of it as he pleased.

The agreement with Christina would mean little if he had a mind to discredit it or do anything counter to it. But he had no such desire. She had given him his home again—something he had only hoped to accomplish in his dreams—and he would never forget that or take it for granted.

Upon Lachlan's arrival at the stables, Kemp looked at him strangely, no doubt wondering what business the servant from Glengour Inn had at Dunverlockie when Angus wasn't present. Lachlan provided an evasive explanation for his presence there. If he could have just one night at Dunverlockie before having to face Angus, he would be content. He and Christina still needed to discuss how they would handle the conversation with him when it occurred.

He took his sack of belongings inside, smiling a bit as he thought on the irony of it—the new master of Dunverlockie entering through the grand front doors with every single item in his possession contained in the small sack slung over his shoulder.

He made his way up the stairs and paused at the top, looking down the length of the corridor. Outside the laird's bedchamber sat a pile of things, mostly clothing from what Lachlan could see. The door was closed.

Did this mean Christina had decided to take the bedchamber after all? He knew a small sense of disappointment at the thought—he had always assumed he would inhabit that room the day he became laird of Dunverlockie. He brushed away the feeling. He was glad to be here at all, to say nothing of what bedchamber he would be sleeping in. He applauded Christina for garnering the courage to make it hers. She deserved it.

For a moment, he considered setting his things down in his old bedchamber, but he decided against it. Christina was undoubtedly still in the process of moving her things. Instead, he opened the doors of a few of the other bedchambers until he found one that showed no sign of being inhabited by one of the MacKinnon men. Putting his sack beside the bed, he began dressing for dinner.

Miss Innes was already in the drawing room when he arrived there, but there was no sign of Christina yet.

"How did Mr. Gibson take the news?" Miss Innes asked.

"Och," he replied, "I didna tell him. 'Twas selfish of me—or cowardly, perhaps—but I thought he might send word ta Angus right away, and I dinna wish ta have him at our door just yet."

She nodded. "I think you are right to wait. He is bound to be in a terrible rage when he discovers what has happened."

Lachlan chuckled, resting an arm on the mantel above the fireplace. "Aye, especially when he sees he's been ousted from the laird's bedchamber without ceremony."

"I hope I shall be there to witness it, for a more satisfying sight, I can hardly imagine. It was the first thing Christina did when she returned today."

Lachlan prodded the logs in the fireplace with the poker. "I confess I was surprised ta see it. I thought she had no likin' for the room."

Miss Innes didn't respond, and he glanced at her. She wore a confused expression.

"She detests it," she said. "But she did not do it for herself. She did it for you—so that you had a place for your things when you returned."

Lachlan's mouth opened wordlessly, and Miss Innes laughed, though the sound held little humor. "Not for all the world would Christina sleep in that bedchamber." She glanced at the door. "I shall see what keeps her."

She left in a rustling of petticoats, and Lachlan stared after her, still unsure what to say. Whether Christina's gesture had been motivated by an intense dislike of Angus or by concern for Lachlan, he didn't know. He shouldn't wish for it to be the latter. But he did. He was a fool.

Miss Innes returned shortly, exasperation written on her face. "She is not coming down to dinner."

"Oh."

There was a pause.

"Is she unwell?" Lachlan asked.

"She claims she is not hungry."

Lachlan narrowed his eyes, reading into Miss Innes's words. *She claims.* "Ye dinna believe her?"

She pinched her lips together as if trying to keep herself from talking. "I told Cook to make roast goose. It is Christina's favorite."

Lachlan said nothing. It was difficult not to assume that Christina had decided that hunger would suit her better than dining with her new husband.

Lachlan did his best not to betray his disappointment as he

and Miss Innes went in to dinner together. She was an easy companion, though, and kept the conversation flowing between them, primarily asking questions about her brother.

"Perhaps one of us should take my sister a tray," Miss Innes said as they finished eating. Lachlan found he had less of an appetite than usual, and a great deal of food remained on the table.

"Aye, I dinna wish for her ta go ta bed hungry."

"No, certainly not." She dabbed at her mouth with the napkin and rose. "Would you mind taking it to her? I have a few things to see to."

Lachlan opened his mouth then shut it as Miss Innes disappeared from the room.

He set down his utensils and laughed softly at the orchestration on Miss Innes's part.

In theory, he could have a servant take Christina a tray. There was no reason *he* needed to personally see to it. But he did want to see her. If she was still feeling the effects of the suspected poison, she should be seen by a doctor. If that was not the case, and she was regretting her decision to marry him, he should know. Perhaps he could set her mind at ease. Or perhaps his interference would only solidify whatever doubts she had.

There was plenty he could do around the castle instead— things he had been wishing to do for years. And yet...

He rose from his place and took the clean plate at the other end of the table, setting a generous helping of roast goose on it as well as a few other things he hoped Christina would like.

He would take the opportunity that giving her the tray would afford him to evaluate what was ailing her. And then he would leave her be if that was what she truly wanted.

21

Christina lay on her bed, fully clothed and shod, staring up at the hangings. She had felt unexpectedly composed during the wedding, but since leaving Lachlan outside the castle earlier, she had begun to...unravel.

To quell her nerves and the unsettled feeling in her stomach, she had taken to removing everything from the laird's bedchamber, refusing help when it was offered by one of the maids. She needed something to occupy her thoughts and to keep her hands busy. She had no conceivable reason to doubt Lachlan's decency. This persistent sensation that she might lose the contents of her stomach was nothing but Gordon's specter rearing its head, and removing both his and Angus's things from the laird's bedchamber made her feel as if she was doing her utmost to rid herself of his pernicious influence.

She had long since finished the task of removing the MacKinnons' belongings, though, and her stomach was no less settled. When Elizabeth had come up to ask her whether she intended to join them for dinner, she hadn't been able to stomach the thought of putting anything in her tumultuous stomach, nor did she feel up to the task of appearing confident and unaffected as she would like—this had been her idea, after all.

She raised her hand, staring at the twine on her finger—her wedding ring. The one Gordon had given her, she had slipped into Angus's belongings. She wanted nothing to do with it.

There was a soft knock on the door, and she shot up to a sitting position.

"Christina?" Lachlan's voice met her ears, and her heart thundered in her chest. A memory flashed across her mind of Gordon coming to her room the night of their wedding. It was the first time she had begun to sense that the man she had married was not the man she had believed she was marrying. But Gordon had never troubled himself with knocking, despite his insistence that she do so on the rare occasions when she had been obliged to go to *his* bedchamber.

She glanced at the candlestick she had threatened Lachlan with once before. He had not hurt her then, but he was her husband now. In the eyes of the Kirk and the law, she belonged to him, and intimacy with his wife was his right.

She shut her eyes and took a deep breath, but her hands were shaking.

"He promised," she said to herself.

She walked to the door and lifted the latch, opening it a few mere inches. She blinked.

Lachlan was holding a tray of food, and as his dark eyes searched her face, his brow knit together in a concern so genuine that all her fear of him—however silly it had been in the first place—fled in an instant.

"Ye're no' feelin' well," he said. It wasn't a question but a statement.

"Did Elizabeth not tell you?"

"Aye, she did, but...well"—he gave a crooked, self-mocking

smile that tugged on Christina's heart—"I thought perhaps ye simply didna wish ta see me."

She couldn't exactly refute what he said—there was some truth in it—but neither did she feel she could confirm it. There was so much uncertainty in the gaze that met hers, and guilt added to the swathe of emotions churning inside her. She was so focused on herself. What did Lachlan feel through all of this? Yes, he was returning to the home he had grown up in, but that was hardly the extent of it. This couldn't all be easy for him. It was unlikely that life with a woman widowed less than a month—and one who refused to give him an heir—was what he had envisioned for himself.

"I thought ye might be regrettin' things," he continued, and he attempted a smile that only heightened the compassion Christina felt. On no account would she let him think she was ruing her decision to marry him. She wasn't. She was merely... scared was the only word for it.

"No." She opened the door wider, offering a little smile. "I am not regretting things. I haven't felt well since the ceremony—a combination of things, I think."

"Ye think it's the poison?" he asked.

"Perhaps," she said, opening the door wide enough that he could enter. "You can set the tray down on the table by the bed. It was very kind of you to bring it."

He hesitated a moment. "Will it make ye feel worse ta look at it? And smell it?"

She shook her head with a glance at the tray then, as her stomach spasm'd, covered her mouth with a hand.

His eyes widened, and he hurried to set the tray on the floor outside the room before rushing over to the window and opening it. A breeze blew in, fresh and strong, and he came to her side, guiding her to the window.

She would have laughed if she hadn't felt so ill. "You wish me to expel the contents of my stomach out the window?"

"Nay," he said. "Rest yer hands here"—he indicated the stone ledge beneath the window—"and breathe. Fresh air always helps me when my stomach is unsettled."

She rested her hands on the ledge as Lachlan rubbed her back with a gentle hand.

She shut her eyes and breathed in the cool air, noting how cold the stone felt on her fingers. "You experience this often?"

"I did. Particularly when I first saw battle. I've a stronger stomach now."

"Stronger than a twelve-year-old?" she said.

He chuckled. "There now. Look at that. Makin' wee jokes is a good sign."

She took in another deep breath and felt the edge of the nausea dull a bit more. The fresh air was good. So was the distraction. "Tell me about it," she said. "The army. How old were you when you joined?"

His hand slowed on her back for a moment then resumed at its original speed. "I was eleven."

She whipped her head around to look at him. "Eleven? Is that not very young? I was only teasing when I said what I did about the stomach of a twelve-year-old."

"'Tis younger than most, though there were lads naught but two or three years older than me. I was an assistant of sorts when I started."

She frowned, staring down at the dark and obscure view of the stables below and taking steady breaths inward. There was a question she had been wanting to ask him for some time now. "Why *did* you join the army? After what happened with your father, I mean. I would not have thought...."

"I didna have much of a choice," he said. "My brothers and sisters were left without a home or parents ta care for them. The captain was impressed with my passionate—and foolish—attempt at stoppin' them when they came ta take my father." He shrugged. "The army was the best way for me ta earn some money ta send ta my family."

She searched his face again, but his gaze was directed outside at nothing in particular, his hand still making a light, calming path around her back. She doubted he was even aware he was still doing it. Her fears about him suddenly disregarding his promises to her seemed even more unjust.

From the time they had met, she had wondered why he had been so willing to help her, and suddenly it made sense. He had spent his entire life taking on the responsibility for others. It was ingrained in him.

He glanced down at her. "I didna want my aunt and uncle ta bear the burden of all four of us."

"I understand," she said. That was precisely why she had made the decision to marry Lachlan—she knew what it felt like to be the oldest child, to feel the weight of responsibility with both parents gone. Lachlan had borne that responsibility for years and years now, since he was just a boy. Christina had only shouldered the burden for a short time in comparison, and even then, sometimes she thought it would crush her. It was comforting to know that the man beside her not only understood what she felt but knew how to bear it better than she.

"How do ye feel?" he asked.

"Better," she said truthfully. "Thank you."

He let his hand drop from her back and smiled. "I understand 'twas you who removed everythin' from the laird's bedchamber."

She sighed in satisfaction, stepping away from the window. "I was more than happy to do it myself—and it was a good distraction."

"I can imagine," he said. He looked at her through narrowed eyes. "'Tis yers if ye want it, Christina. The bedchamber, I mean."

She shook her head emphatically.

He smiled slightly. "Yer sister said ye'd never sleep there."

Christina knew a moment of curiosity. "Did she? What else did she say?"

"At dinner?"

She laughed. "As opposed to...?"

He raised his brows significantly and folded his arms across his broad chest, leaning against the stone window casement. "The stables at Glengour. She ambushed me there, ye ken."

"Oh dear," she said, smiling through clenched teeth. "For what reason?"

His eyes smiled back at her with something she could only describe as fondness. "Ta threaten me, of course."

Christina stared. "You jest."

He shook his head once, amusement twinkling in his eyes. "She wanted me ta ken she'd kill me herself if I hurt ye."

Christina broke eye contact, letting out a small, uncomfortable laugh. It was very much like Elizabeth to do such a thing, and Christina felt a mixture of affection and embarrassment to learn of it.

"She's a good lass," he said.

"She is. And a headstrong one. I wish I could reassure you that her bark was stronger than her bite, but I'm afraid she is entirely in earnest."

"I dinna fear yer sister, Christina," he said.

She looked at him, raising a brow. "Perhaps you *should*."

"Nay." He pushed off the wall with a shoulder and looked at her intently, though there was still a softness in his eyes. "She promised she'd kill me if I hurt ye, and I'll no' hurt ye. I swore it."

Her heartbeat quickened, and her gaze fixed on him, unwilling to break away despite her wishes.

She managed to speak before she managed to pull her gaze away. "I imagine you are impatient to see the letters and documents. I can show you where they are."

"It can wait. Ye're still unwell."

"Your trick worked," she said with a shrug of the shoulders. "Besides, the distraction helps keep the sickness at bay."

He frowned again. "Poison can be slow ta leave the body, from what I understand. I'm sorry ye're no' better already."

"Soon, I am sure," she said, taking up the nearest candlestick. "Come. I will show you to your new bedchamber."

He put out a hand to stop her. "Wait a moment."

She stopped, puzzled, and he strode from the room, reappearing less than a minute later with a nod of the head, inviting her to proceed him.

She looked at him in bemusement but asked no questions, leading the way from the room. Only when she stepped into the corridor did she realize that the food tray on the floor was gone.

"What did you do with the tray?" He hadn't had time to take it all the way downstairs, nor to call for a servant to come take it.

"I put it in that room." He indicated the room two doors away from hers. "I'll take it down with me later." He glanced to the room at their side, saying, "One more moment while I get my things." He disappeared into the room, emerging a moment later with a brown sack slung over his shoulder.

She stared at it for a moment. She hadn't considered the fact that he could fit everything he owned in such a small sack. The servants at Dunverlockie had more to their names than the new laird. What a different life he had lived from the one he was born into.

They reached the door to the laird's bedchamber, and despite having spent a fair amount of time there earlier in the day, Christina felt her muscles stiffen involuntarily. She had avoided the room as much as possible since taking up residence at Dunverlockie—indeed, she had chosen the bedchamber farthest from it for her own—and she had to remind herself that neither Gordon nor Angus was inside.

She took a steadying breath as inconspicuously as she could and opened the door, waiting for Lachlan to follow. How differently he regarded this room than she did, and how strange it must be for him to enter after all these years, knowing it was his now.

He walked in slowly, deliberately, gaze roving around the room, bathed in the shadows from the candle Christina held.

She said nothing for a moment, allowing him time to take it all in. It wasn't his first time there since returning from the war, though. "You came in here that night looking for the letters, did you not?"

He nodded, gaze still sweeping the room.

"It is different tonight, though," she said.

"Aye." His voice sounded strange, and he cleared his throat.

It occurred to her that perhaps she should leave him alone with his thoughts and feelings.

"Would you like a moment to settle in?" She used the candle she held to light the one by the door.

He let out a breathy laugh through his nose, setting his sack of belongings on the bed. "There's no' much ta settle."

"I know. I only meant...this is a notable moment for you, and"—she shrugged a shoulder—"I am an intruder."

"In yer own house?"

She was struck with how charming his slanted smile made him look. "It was yours before it was mine."

"Aye, but I wouldna be here at all if 'twere no' fer *you*."

She had no response to such a comment and stood uncertainly in the doorway.

He looked toward the tapestry on the far wall and walked toward it. "'Twas here ye found the letters?"

"Yes. There is a stone that sticks out a bit—it was just out of place enough to catch my eye, though it is so dark, I imagine you will need a candle to see it now." She took one over. "Here, I will show you."

He pulled the tapestry away from the wall, allowing her to go before him.

When she had come by herself, the need to hold back the tapestry had limited her movement. Now, though, Lachlan held it at bay with a hand, keeping it far enough away from the candle to prevent its catching fire.

"Here," she said, pointing to the stone in question.

He came up right beside her, letting the tapestry rest on his broad back as he turned toward the wall and pulled the stone out. She watched him, and even in the flickering candlelight, she could see the hunger in his eyes. He pulled out the tied scroll.

"Those are the letters." Her words sounded flat and deadened in the small space. There was an entire room behind them, she knew, but with the tapestry draping so heavily around them, it was hard to remember that. Their arms rested against each other, and her skin prickled at their proximity. She and Gordon had never been this close unless he wanted—or expected, rather—something from her. Lachlan, on the other hand, seemed not to even notice, so focused was he on the papers in his hands.

He removed the strings from the scroll and unfurled it, squinting at the ink on the paper. What precisely did he hope to find?

Realizing she had the means of making his task easier, Christina moved the candle closer, and the action seemed to pull him from his focus.

"Forgive me," he said. "I'll no' make ye stand here while I search. I ken where they are now—I can look later."

"I understand, Lachlan," she said. "You have been waiting years for this."

He rolled the papers up and slipped the strings back on.

"Aye, and it will keep a while longer." He pushed the tapestry back with an arm to make a path out for her, and, not wanting to argue with him, she walked back out into the open room, guarding the candle flame with her hand.

"Is it very different?" she asked as he emerged behind her. "This bedchamber?"

He took in a large breath and let it out in a gush as he looked around. "Aye. And nay. Much is unchanged, though the hangings are no' the same." He walked over to the mantel and ran a hand along it. "My father always had a carvin' of the Kincaid coat of arms here. Verra protective of it he was." He smiled slightly. "I remember when he first brought it home. I slipped in one day ta take a closer look—I was fascinated by it —but I could barely reach, and when I tried ta touch it, it clattered ta the floor—almost fell in the fire. My father came in ta find me holdin' it guiltily in my hands. I thought he'd be furious with me, and I was shakin' in my wee breeks. Without a word, he took the coat of arms and set it back in its place. And then he crouched down in front of me and told me he'd have a smaller one made just for me. 'Twas as though he was pleased at the interest I was showin' in somethin' so important ta the clan."

The thought of a young, guilty Lachlan being surprised by his father's kindness made Christina smile. "And did he have one made for you?"

Lachlan's nostalgic smile faded. "Nay. He was taken shortly after that." He sighed and looked around again. "More than anythin', the room *feels* different." He looked at her and laughed. "A silly thing ta say."

She shook her head. "I understand. Rooms take on a distinctive feel—a life of their own almost." She suppressed a shudder, keeping her gaze from the bed.

"Aye," he said softly, and she could feel his eyes on her. "Ye

dinna have the fond memories of this castle—or this room—
that I have, do ye?"

She met his gaze. "No, I do not."

There was a moment of silence.

"Was it terrible?" he asked gently. "Bein' married ta
Gordon?"

She didn't respond immediately, directing her gaze at the
mantel, thinking of what Lachlan had said—of the promise
that remained unkept because his father had been taken from
him at such a young age. He had shown little emotion when he
spoke of his father's untimely and gruesome ending, but such
an experience had undoubtedly left pain and scars in its wake.

"I am far from being the only person to have suffered
through something terrible," she finally said. "We each have
our trials to bear."

"Aye," he said, "but that doesna change the pain of livin'
through the trial."

She couldn't deny that. Others had undoubtedly lived
things far worse than she had, but her own adversity had been
real enough to her.

"If ye dinna wish ta speak of yer marriage ta Gordon, I'll no'
ask ye again. 'Tis no' my affair, and I understand if ye wish ta
guard yer privacy."

She let out a breath. "It is not that. I just…I do not want you
to pity me, Lachlan."

His eyebrows shot up. "Pity ye?"

"Yes. Pity me. And that is just what you would do if I told
you about the last two years."

He stared at her for a moment. "Is it wrong for me to wish
ye hadna gone through what ye did?"

"No, but wishing changes nothing, and it leads you to see
me as…"—she lifted her shoulders—"as weak. I see how you
treat me. As though I might fall apart at the least touch."

His thick brows contracted so sharply, they met above his nose. "Ye think I believe ye ta be *weak*?"

"From the beginning—almost as soon as we met—you have offered me your protection."

"Aye, but no' because I thought ye weak, Christina."

His baffled reaction gave her a hope she knew she didn't deserve to feel, and she set the candle down next to the one she had just lit, crossing her arms. "Then why?"

For some reason—reasons she didn't care to inspect more closely—she couldn't bear for Lachlan to see her as a weak creature—as a victim.

He pursed his lips, seeming to struggle for words. "Because ye deserve better than ye've had. And because I willna stand back and watch while the MacKinnons ruin more lives than they already have." He took a few steps toward her, the frustration he was feeling evident in his creased forehead, and he put a hand firmly on both of her arms. "I dinna think ye weak, Christina. Far from it. But I *do* think ye deserve a bit of a respite from bein' strong."

To her embarrassment, she felt her throat thicken and her eyes burn. She had often cursed Dunverlockie for what seemed like its impenetrable darkness, no matter how many candles were lit, but just now she was grateful for the lack of light and that Lachlan cast a shadow over her. For a woman maintaining she wasn't weak, crying was not the most convincing argument.

"Do ye believe me?" he asked.

She couldn't speak, but she nodded.

He looked at her another moment then dropped his hands. "Good. I'm sorry ye're no' comfortable at Dunverlockie—in yer own home. I wish I could change that for ye."

She lifted a shoulder. "It feels less awful knowing of the happy times you had here, at least. Perhaps the more I know of them, the less I will feel as I do." It was true. She had been in this room just two hours ago, and what she felt now in Lachlan's presence was already different.

He nodded. "Perhaps we can oust the bad memories. No' only with those from my childhood, but with new ones, as well —happier ones."

Was it possible? Part of her couldn't imagine it—how did one scrub clean the pervasive dirt that enveloped every part of this castle in her memory?

But another part of her wanted to believe Lachlan—and *did* believe him. It was difficult not to. Much as she might accuse him of treating her with too much caution and trying to shoulder the burdens of a woman he thought weak, she couldn't deny that the weight of her troubles felt much lighter and much more manageable since he had appeared in her life. She craved his gentleness, but she feared what it said about how he regarded her.

"I cannot imagine forming happy memories here until Angus is finally gone," she admitted. His return cast a dark shadow over the future—an inevitable reckoning to be had. If she hadn't known she would face it with Lachlan, the prospect would have made her sick again.

"Ye think he'll return tomorrow?"

"I do. I suppose it is too much to hope that he will do so without his entourage."

"Men like Angus MacKinnon surround themselves for a reason."

"Unlike you," she said. "A lone wolf."

"I'm no' a lone wolf," he said. "No' anymore, at least. I run in a pack of two now."

"A pitiful pack," she said with a wry smile.

"Nay," he said with feigned offense. "A fearful one. In many wolf packs, 'tis the dominant female who leads."

She narrowed her eyes at him. "Is this your way of telling me that you mean to leave the task of informing Angus to me?"

"Och," he said. "I couldna. No' because I dinna think ye capable"—he looked at her significantly, an implied reference to their recent conversation in his gaze—"but because I wouldna wish ta miss his reaction when he discovers the truth." A ruthless satisfaction entered his eyes at the prospect. It might have concerned Christina if she hadn't been so well-acquainted with the MacKinnons and just how much they deserved to lose Dunverlockie.

"You mean to tell him the full truth, then? Your name and all?"

He nodded. "I considered lettin' 'im believe ye'd married Mr. Murray from the stables of Glengour, but"—he grimaced—"he'll no' take the news of the marriage well, and I reckon his first thought will be ta kill me. If he kens I'm a Kincaid, though, well...he'll be forced ta think a bit if he doesna wish ta provoke a battle."

She raised her brows. "A battle between whom? The MacKinnons and our pack of two?"

He smiled. "Nay, lass. I may appear ta be a lone wolf, like ye said, but that doesna mean no one will come if I howl. It will just take a bit of time ta find them—they scattered far and wide after my father's death."

She could believe they would come. A man like Lachlan Kincaid would certainly inspire loyalty. Not by force or by threat as Gordon or Angus MacKinnon did, but by a devotion born of affection and trust. There was no doubt in her mind that the Douglases would take Lachlan's side over that of the MacKinnons if given the opportunity. Mr. Geddes had done so today, as well. There were surely others in the vicinity who remembered the Kincaids, and few enough people had love for the MacKinnons that even those who *hadn't* known the prior laird of Dunverlockie might be eager to be rid of Angus.

"Ye're tired, no doubt," he said. "Get some rest. We can discuss it more in the mornin'."

She nodded. She *was* tired. It had been a long day—a long two years, in truth. And the morrow was likely to be unpleasant.

As she picked up the candlestick and waited for Lachlan to open the door for her, she glanced one more time around the laird's bedchamber. It felt decidedly less unpleasant than it had. Perhaps there *was* a possibility of changing how she felt about Dunverlockie.

22

Lachlan closed the door behind Christina and stood with his hand on the latch for a moment, thoughtful. She had let him see more of her—both her humor and her depth—than she usually did. Whether it was simply due to his coming upon her while she had been too ill to bother with staying guarded, he wasn't certain. But he was grateful for it. She would never feel like Dunverlockie was her home if she had to restrain herself in his presence.

He turned back toward the bed, where the leather folio and the scroll of letters sat beside his sack of belongings. Taking the candle Christina had lit, he walked toward the bed. He was exhausted, but he could take half an hour or so to peruse the letters before going to sleep.

He pushed aside one of the curtains that hung from the bed poster and stopped to look at it. He hadn't missed the way Christina kept her eyes away from the centerpiece of the room.

He shut his eyes, trying not to explore what the past held for her that would inspire her with such an intense dislike of this room and the bed inside it. Whenever he thought on the cur she had been married to, his blood ran hot.

He stared at the hangings another moment then put down the candle decisively and set to pulling them down. The MacKinnons had changed them from what they had been during the Kincaids' ownership of the castle; Lachlan would do the same. It was unlikely Christina would reenter his bedchamber again, but if she did, he had no desire for her to be assaulted with unpleasant memories—or to associate them with him.

Within a few minutes, there was a pile of bed curtains at the foot and on both sides of the bed. He thrust them all into the corner of the room. He would have one of the servants take them tomorrow to be cleaned and sold—it was warm enough at night now not to require hangings. The bedcovers could be changed as well as soon as could be arranged. He didn't particularly care to sleep in the same ones Gordon and Angus MacKinnon had slept in.

Having removed everything but his shirtsleeves, Lachlan settled into the bed with his back against the headboard and the candle on the bedside table. He took up the scroll and unfurled it again. It was strange to see his father's handwriting after so much time. It was still so familiar, evoking memories of the piles of parchment on his father's desk in the library so many years ago.

The letters he perused contained information that primarily incriminated his father. The implication in them all was, of course, that Harold MacKinnon was complicit—and he *had* been. But when Bonnie Prince Charlie's rebellion had frayed and failed, the man had managed to make out as if he had merely been playing a part in order to expose Lachlan's father—a selfless act in the service of his king and country as opposed to the opportunistic betrayal it had truly been.

Lachlan's father, however, had clearly trusted MacKinnon until the end. And it was that unwavering trust which had proven his downfall when he provided aid to Prince Charlie's men after the Battle of Culloden.

As Lachlan read the letters dated April 1746, his fingers went white, and the parchment crinkled under their grip.

"I have room for a dozen or so men at Dunverlockie, and I imagine you could find space for a few more at least at Benleith. It would only be for a night—until they can take the path to the Wash and set sail Wednesday."

Lachlan clenched his eyes shut. He knew the story of what had happened that fateful morning—for days, discussion of it had been rife amongst the soldiers when Lachlan had accompanied them after his father's capture.

Some of Prince Charlie's men had managed to escape and set sail, but others had not—none of the ones hiding at Benleith. Early in the morning, the men at Dunverlockie had made their way to the designated area, and though a few managed to row themselves out to the ship, the rest had been ambushed while awaiting their turn—the indisputable work of Harold MacKinnon. It was later that morning that Lachlan's father had been taken.

Lachlan put aside the letters, too angry to read more, and took up the folio. He shuffled through a few of the less interesting documents, stopping on the first that stood out. It seemed to be an account or log of some sort. Perhaps servant wages?

There were four columns: a list in the left-hand column, sums of money in the left-center column, dates in the column right of center, and another list on the far right. The more he inspected it, the less certain he was what he was looking at. The amounts were too much to represent servant wages, and the dates wrong—none of them corresponded with quarter days, as might be expected. None of them had years, either. Just a month and a day, and none of them in the winter.

His eyes swept the list on the left.

The final names—*G Douglas* and *C Turner*—were written in different handwriting than the rest of them. There was no amount beside the names, but the date notated was June 4th, and the word *Falcon* was written in the final column.

Perhaps Gordon had written them before he died and never had the opportunity to fill in the other columns. Lachlan narrowed his eyes at the Douglas name. The first initial was G. It could be Gillies or Glenna Douglas—or a different Douglas entirely. The name wasn't exactly uncommon, unlike Tulloch or MacVaxter, which appeared there as well.

Was Angus aware of these papers? There was no real way of knowing without asking him, and Lachlan had no intent of doing such a thing.

He rubbed at his eyes and slipped the paper back into the folio, setting it on the bedside table. He would have plenty of time to pour over things later. For now, his body desperately needed sleep.

He moved himself to a lying position, unable to suppress a smile at the comfort of the bed. It was a far cry from the thin, lumpy mattress at the inn, and even that had been better than what he'd slept on during most of his time in the war. It was safe to say he had never slept on such a fine bed in his life.

His thoughts went to Christina, just a few rooms away. If Lachlan's life had gone according to plan, he would certainly not have been sleeping alone on his wedding night. What might it feel like to have her beside him and to hold her as he had done at the inn after the fire?

He forced the thoughts away. Exploring that would lead to nothing but disappointment. Besides, nothing in his life had gone according to plan.

He blew out the candle beside him and, within moments, he was asleep.

W ithout his regular duties at the inn to require his rising with the dawn, Lachlan slept later than he had in recent memory. There was no clock in the laird's bedchamber —undoubtedly Gordon MacKinnon had refused to be dictated to by a mechanical device—but based on the way the light filtered through the small gap in the curtains, he judged it to be well past seven.

He threw back the covers and swung his legs over the side of the bed. He could hear steps in the corridor and muffled voices, and he hurried to put on one of his two pairs of breeches, stuffing his shirt into them and trying to listen as the voices drew nearer.

The door latch jiggled, and Lachlan's head whipped toward it.

"You cannot go in there, Angus." Christina's voice reached Lachlan through the shut door, and he stilled. They hadn't anticipated Angus would return first thing in the morning.

"And why is that?" Angus asked aggressively.

Lachlan hurried to do the buttons on his breeches. There wasn't time to attend to his hair or any of his other clothing. He hadn't imagined he would be confronting Angus bleary-eyed and in unbuttoned shirtsleeves, but there was no helping it. He couldn't leave Christina to handle the encounter alone.

As he walked to the door, he ran a hand through his hair, well aware that nearly half of it had come free of the queue he had never untied the night before.

He opened the door abruptly, and Angus, whose hand had still been on the latch, stumbled forward a bit, nearly knocking into Lachlan. He took two steps back and looked at Lachlan, utterly baffled.

"Who the devil are you?" he asked. His eyes narrowed, as if trying to place Lachlan. "You are the servant from the inn, aren't you?"

Lachlan felt a flash of satisfaction. He had doubted whether Angus would recognize him at all. Somehow, though, this would be better—more gratifying—knowing he *did* remember him.

"Murray, was it?"

Lachlan glanced at Christina. Her body was still, eyes alert as she waited to see how Lachlan would respond. He shot her a quick smile to reassure her.

"I *did* work at the inn, aye," he said. "But my name is no' Murray."

A glint of anger ignited in Angus's eyes. "And just what do you think you are doing in my bedchamber, whoever you are?"

"It is *not* your bedchamber," Christina said.

Angus whirled around and took two steps toward her. "Perhaps *you* can tell me why this upstart is here—with the door locked, damn him."

She took a moment before responding. Lachlan almost chimed in—he would rather Angus's attention be directed at him than at Christina at this critical point. But just last night, he had assured her he didn't think her weak, and he had no wish to do anything that would make her believe he hadn't been in earnest.

"He is my husband," she finally said.

Angus laughed and threw a glance over his shoulder at Lachlan, who flashed a smile at him. He couldn't help himself —the knowledge that the laughter on Angus's face would soon turn to dismay made Lachlan feel a strange giddiness. He faintly recognized it from the times when his company had emerged from a battle victorious.

Angus's laughing expression wavered slightly, and his eyes searched his face, attempting to comprehend Lachlan's reaction to Christina's words.

"Good morning to ye, Mr. MacKinnon," Lachlan said.

Angus turned back toward Christina, the smile wiped from his face. "You are lying."

She shook her head. "I assure you I am not. We were married yesterday."

There was silence, and Angus's chest rose and fell deeply as he glanced between Christina and Lachlan. Suddenly, Angus lunged at Christina, uttering an obscenity as his hand struck her across the face.

Lachlan sprang to action, wrestling Angus away from Christina and turning the man toward him, where he cocked back an arm and threw his fist into Angus's face.

Angus stumbled backward, reaching a hand to the wall to stabilize himself and covering his nose with the other. His eyes were clenched shut in pain, and crimson seeped through his fingers.

Chest heaving and knuckles stinging, Lachlan hurried to Christina. An angry red mark marred her right cheek, which she was holding a hand to. He covered her hand with his and clenched both his jaw and eyes shut, reminding himself that it was caring for Christina that mattered right now, even if he wanted nothing more than to see Angus pay for what he'd done.

"I'm sorry," he said to her, bending to better see the injury. "I thought he'd take 'is anger out on me. I shoulda kend a MacKinnon would choose the coward's way."

A sheen of tears covered Christina's eyes, but there was no hurt there—only shock and anger. She shook her head and dropped her hand from her face. "I am well."

"You married a *stable hand*?" Angus sputtered.

Lachlan turned toward him. He seemed to have recovered his composure, and he wiped the blood dripping from his nose with the back of a hand, smearing it above his lip and onto one cheek.

"Stay away from my wife," Lachlan growled through his teeth as he came between Angus and Christina.

"Your wife!" Angus spat mockingly.

"Aye, *my wife*. And I swear to ye, if ye lay a hand on her again, 'twill be the last thing ye do. I give ye my word as a Kincaid of Dunverlockie."

"What is this nonsense?"

"'Tis no nonsense," Lachlan said.

Angus looked to Christina. Lachlan was struck by how beautiful she looked, staring at Angus with eyes alight, the red fading on her right cheek, her nostrils flared.

"He speaks the truth," she said. "This is Lachlan Kincaid. Perhaps you remember him or his father, Donald Kincaid."

An arrested expression entered Angus's eyes, and he searched Lachlan's face frantically, as if for evidence that Christina told the truth. He seemed to find the evidence he was looking for, for his eyes widened, and the dismay Lachlan had been waiting for began to appear.

"You should leave, Angus," Christina said. "Immediately. You have maintained that you remained here on my account— to help me. As you can see, that help is no longer needed. You are free to return to Benleith. Your belongings are in that room." She indicated one of the doors down the corridor.

Angus was still staring at Lachlan. "You have no right to be here. The Kincaids are traitors to the Crown."

"The same Crown I spent the last sixteen years servin'? My father served the cause and the Crown he believed in—he died for it. The MacKinnons have no cause or loyalty but ta their own self-interest. I'd rather die a Kincaid than live a MacKinnon."

"Perhaps that can be arranged." Angus's face was growing redder by the second.

Lachlan strode toward him, but a hand on his arm pulled

him back, and he halted reluctantly, glancing at Christina. There was both warning and pleading in her eyes.

"Ye heard her," Lachlan said. "Now go. And dinna return. Ye're no' welcome here, nor any of yer kin."

Angus's gaze shifted back and forth between them, his jaw clenching and unclenching. Finally, he gave an exaggerated bow. "I offer the two of you my felicitations. May your life together be as long and as joyful as you deserve it should be. I will send a servant to collect my belongings."

He shot one final sardonic glance at Christina then turned on his heel and left.

Lachlan turned to her. Where Angus had struck her, her cheek was still pink, and shame filled him at the sight.

"I'm sorry, Christina." He suppressed the impulse to take her hand.

"You have nothing to be sorry for," she said.

He shook his head. "I should 'ave been there when he came. I overslept and—"

"Yes, I noticed." She glanced at his open shirt with a slight smile then averted her eyes. "It is no matter. Neither of us anticipated he would return so early in the day. I am only glad he did so without the rest of his men. Besides, you needed the sleep."

He couldn't deny that. "Where *were* the rest of the MacKinnons?"

"Recovering from their revelries, I imagine. Collecting the rents is always a time of plenty."

He frowned at that. "And what of Dunverlockie's rents?"

She grimaced. "With the funeral, I think the tenants understand that everything is delayed. Gordon never involved me in such affairs, though, so I am afraid I am rather ignorant. I would like to learn, though."

He nodded. "We will learn together, then. I reckon Mr.

Douglas and some of the other tenants would be happy ta help us with what they ken."

"Certainly. They will need to show us some longsuffering, and I hope we can extend the same to them. They did not see much of that under the MacKinnons."

"Better times ahead for all of us, then," he replied with a smile.

She brushed at her cheek with a hand and looked toward the stairs. "Not if Angus has anything to say to it. For all their politeness, his last words sounded very much like a threat."

Lachlan touched the pink spot on her cheek with the back of a finger. It was warm to the touch. "Dinna fash yerself over Angus. I'll no' let 'im hurt ye again."

She swallowed then offered a little smile, though he couldn't tell whether it mocked him or herself. "Still protecting the weak?"

Lachlan dropped his hand from her cheek and opened his mouth to respond, but she cut him off.

"I am only teasing. I am grateful you intervened. Though, I must say, it was a bit selfish of you. I would dearly have loved to strike him myself."

He smiled down at her. "If I'd kend ye wished ta deal him a blow, I'd have held him in place meself while ye did it."

She chuckled. "Very obliging of you. But it is for the best, I think. There is no telling how far Angus will go when he is angry. He has a better hold on his temper than Gordon did, but of the two of them, I have always believed him capable of worse, for he is more calculated in what he does than Gordon could ever manage to be."

"I think ye're right. I intend ta keep a close eye on 'im."

"And the other eye on me?"

He laughed and lifted his shoulders. "I canna help it, lass. And, truthfully, I'd rather have both on you. I dinna particularly care for the sight of Angus. And, whatever ye say, yer brother would wish for me ta watch over ye. Besides, I'm yer husband now. 'Tis my duty. And my pleasure." He hadn't meant to say those last words, and he watched with a stir of nerves for her reaction. But those eyes that were often so expressive also managed to conceal a great deal at times.

Her eyes flitted to his open shirt and away again. "I should see to a few things."

He put a hand to his shirt, pulling one side of it as far as he could to meet the other side. In the excitement, he had forgotten how disheveled he was. "Aye, I should dress for the day."

She gave a perfunctory smile and turned, but she stopped in place. The door to Lachlan's bedchamber was still open, and her gaze was directed there.

"You removed the hangings."

"Aye," he responded. Should he tell her that it was largely out of respect to her that he had done so? "I didna care much for 'em."

"Nor I." She looked at the bed one more time then strode to her door, disappearing through it.

He passed through the doorway to his own bedchamber with a frown on his face. Somehow, up until yesterday, he had managed to convince himself that his reasons for marrying Christina were two-fold: to gain back Dunverlockie and to protect the sister of his comrade in arms. One was selfish; the other was not.

But it was clear to him now that there was a third reason. And that reason tipped the scales decidedly toward selfishness —selfishness and foolishness. Perhaps if he and Christina had met years ago, before her marriage to Gordon, there might have been the possibility for something to grow between them.

But her experience of marriage had not been kind to her. And she had made it clear that she wished for no real intimacy in her second marriage. Not in any sense of the word. And he had agreed to her terms.

Lachlan had always considered himself a man of his word —it was his greatest pride. But for the first time in his life, he was beginning to wonder whether he would be capable of keeping it when every moment with Christina left him wanting more.

23

Christina returned to her bedchamber, putting a hand to her cheek once the door was closed. The sting of Angus's blow had dissipated, but she could still feel the ghost of Lachlan's touch there. For some reason, the realization brought her heart into her throat.

Was it possible that such force and pain could be eclipsed by tenderness?

She dropped her hand from her cheek and sighed. It was becoming so easy to share her burdens with Lachlan, and that frightened her. It had been a long time since she had allowed herself to need anyone. Did needing someone always feel like anticipation at the thought of seeing them? Looking for reasons to seek out their company? Twice that morning, she had found herself near to instructing that Lachlan be woken so that she could speak with him on one matter or another.

There were few similarities between Lachlan and Gordon, but there *was* one Christina couldn't allow herself to forget: they had both married her for strategic reasons. They had both married her for Dunverlockie. And she had married Lachlan for deliberate reasons, as well. She lost sight of that at her own peril.

A knock sounded on the door, and her heart jumped at the thought that it might be him, soon as it was after seeing him. But, like everything else about him, Lachlan's knock was gentle, not imperative like this one.

"Come in," Christina said.

Elizabeth appeared, dressed for riding. Her cheeks were lightly flushed and her eyes bright. "I missed it! He came while I was out!" The disappointment and sense of treachery was heavy in her voice. "How disobliging of him." She shut the door behind her with more force than was warranted.

Christina looked at her sister with amusement. "When has Angus ever been anything *but* disobliging?"

"Very true. I saw him riding down the lane just as I was approaching the stables from the other direction, and I could hardly believe my eyes. What happened? Spare no detail!"

Christina sat down on the bed. "I think it is likely for the best that you were not present. I only just managed to prevent a war between the clans as it was. For now, at least. There is no telling what the future will hold."

"They didn't come to blows, then?" There was disappointment in Elizabeth's voice again.

Christina hesitated. If Elizabeth knew Angus had struck her, she would be livid. But they had promised not to keep things from one another.

"He hit me," Christina said.

"He *what*?"

"Angus did. He slapped me."

Elizabeth stared at her, aghast. "And Lachlan allowed it?"

"It was very sudden. Neither of us anticipated what he meant to do, though Lachlan blames himself, so please say nothing to him about it. I am well, as you can see. Angus, however, may well have a broken nose from Lachlan's retaliation."

"Is that all?" Elizabeth said, still wide-eyed. "I confess I am surprised the man is still alive."

"He might not be had I not prevented Lachlan from reacting as he intended to Angus's various provocations."

Elizabeth let out a sound of disgust and plopped down on the bed next to Christina. "Why in heaven's name *did* you stop him? If I had been there, I would have helped him put an end to that blackguard—it would only make the world a better place. I have a mind to see to it myself."

"Please, Elizabeth," Christina said, taking her sister's hand. "You mustn't do anything rash or try to take revenge upon Angus. You needn't worry for me."

"I am not worried, my dear," Elizabeth said pleasantly, squeezing her hand. "You have no need of my protection anymore."

Christina raised her brows, and Elizabeth tilted her head to the side thoughtfully as she looked to the windows. "Something about Lachlan tells me he would do anything for you. Angus would be a fool to cross him."

Despite her best efforts, Christina found that her days began to center around her encounters with Lachlan, whether it was a simple passing in the corridor, being the first down for dinner together, or going over estate business with him in the study. One of the first orders of business he insisted upon was questioning the servants. He was suspicious of anyone who had been serving Gordon MacKinnon. Christina was able to allay some suspicions and confirm others, having become familiar enough with Dunverlockie's servants over the course of the last two years to feel confident about where their loyalties lay. Those who had to be dismissed simply made room for new servants from families Lachlan felt he could trust and wished to reward for their loyalty.

Lachlan was unlike any man of Christina's acquaintance, and she was struggling to understand what it was about him that made her grateful for any reason to seek out his company.

Perhaps it was simply the calm he exuded. There had been so little calm in her life at Dunverlockie. Surely, it was natural for her to wish for it after so much time in the company of someone as quick to anger as Gordon had been. Lachlan was capable of anger—she knew that from seeing him with Angus —but as she observed him in their interactions, it took a great deal to ruffle him.

There was no word from Benleith, aside from the servant Angus had sent, as promised, to retrieve his belongings. The castle was, for the first time in a great while, serene and quiet.

A week after the wedding, Christina set herself to the task of the correspondence she had been putting off for too long. First on the list of people she needed to write to were her aunt, her younger siblings, and Alistair. None of them knew she had remarried, and she took up the quill, only to put it back in the inkstand four times before settling on a way to communicate the news.

She had yet to send money to her aunt, and guilt mingled with urgency when she thought on the oversight. She had been so distracted by everything that had happened since the accident, she hadn't managed to make the journey into Craiglinne. Despite the fact that it had been well over a week since the last time she had partaken of the tea, nausea was her frequent companion, and she had wondered more than once if perhaps Angus had managed to persuade one of the servants to assist him in his goal. How to discover whether or not this was the truth was a dilemma she had yet to puzzle out.

When she had finished writing the three letters, she

donned something more suitable for a ride. Elizabeth had offered to accompany her into the toun, despite the fact that she was in the throes of a summer cold. Christina had refused to hear more of the idea.

"Stay abed," Christina insisted. "And I shall have Cook make you some soup."

In the corridor, Christina came upon Lachlan, emerging from his room. His mouth drew into a smile at the sight of her, his gaze sweeping over her clothing and the letters in her hand. One had been left unsealed in preparation for the money she would include within.

"Ye're goin' someplace," he said.

"Yes. To Craiglinne. I never managed to get there after the accident, and my aunt requested I send money the last time she wrote." It occurred to her that she should have perhaps discussed this with Lachlan before. It was *their* money now. But she had specified in the marriage arrangements that she expected to be free to give financial help to her family.

"I was wonderin' about that only this mornin'," he said. He hesitated a moment. "Can I accompany ye?"

She gave him a teasing look. "You are concerned for my safety?"

"Aye," he said unapologetically. "'Tis part of it. There's room for me in the carriage, is there no'?"

"I thought to ride, in fact."

"Oh," Lachlan said.

She wet her lips indecisively. She was pushing back on his intention to accompany her, but the truth was, she welcomed his presence. Part of the reason she hadn't gone into the toun yet was that the idea of riding in a carriage held some fear for her after her previous experience. The thought of going with Lachlan lessened those fears considerably. He set her at her ease, made her feel safe.

"Perhaps you are right, though," she said. "It might be

better to take the carriage. I have a few things I wish to purchase while there, and I will manage it all more easily in the carriage."

Lachlan looked at her with the hint of a smile and slightly narrowed eyes.

"What?" she asked, hoping it wasn't obvious to him that she wished for his company.

"I canna tell if ye're invitin' me or merely informin' me that ye intend ta take the carriage alone."

She laughed and looked away. "If you are only coming because you believe I require your protection, you needn't trouble yourself. If you have another reason for coming, then by all means, join me."

She hoped she sounded nonchalant. But, if he chose not to come, she would likely ask one of the servants to drive her. She was not feeling brave enough to go alone in the carriage.

"Verra well," he said, reaching for the door to his bedchamber. "I'll just get my coat, and we can be on our way."

Lachlan made a close inspection of the carriage, a fact which Kemp clearly did not appreciate.

"Ye've found a reason ta doubt my work?" Kemp finally asked.

Lachlan was crouching to inspect the wheels, but he rose to a stand, looking at the groom. "Aye, Kemp. The last time Mrs. Kincaid took the carriage, she met with an accident."

"That was no' my fault," Kemp said.

Lachlan said nothing, helping Christina into the carriage, and they were soon on the road to Craiglinne.

"Poor Kemp," Christina said.

Lachlan scoffed. "I've a mind ta turn 'im off without a reference."

"Yes, I have been thinking it would be better for him to find work elsewhere."

"Or find a new profession," Lachlan retorted. "Either he

conspired with Angus ta put ye in danger or he doesna ken his work enough ta recognize what Angus did ta the equipment."

She looked at him, feeling secretly gratified that he was still so incensed at what had happened to Elizabeth and her. "You are so certain it was Angus behind it."

He turned his head to look at her. "There've been three attempts on yer life, lass. And Angus stands ta benefit the most from yer death. 'Tis logic, nothin' more. A man like him canna resist the opportunity ta expand his power and influence. Bringin' Dunverlockie and Benleith together would do that better than almost anythin' else."

She sighed. He was right. Dunverlockie and Benleith had been connected by their proximity and their ownership by brothers—and then cousins—of the MacKinnon clan. But combining their power under one MacKinnon was a goal that would have great appeal to a man like Angus.

"Perhaps seeing you and knowing your identity was enough," she said. "Perhaps he will leave us alone now. There has been no word from Benleith since he left Dunverlockie."

"Aye, perhaps." Lachlan didn't sound convinced.

The banker in Craiglinne offered Christina his condolences on the passing of Gordon. She found it painfully awkward to respond, given how little she required consolation and, perhaps even more so, given the fact that she stood beside her new husband. He still referred to her as Mrs. MacKinnon, and it was all she could do to maintain her dignity as she corrected him and watched his eyebrows raise with the knowledge of her new circumstances.

Lachlan chuckled softly on their way out of the bank.

"Yes," Christina said with a bite to her voice, "it is all very well for you, as you merely stood there and left all the awkwardness to *me*."

"Nay, then, lass. Ye canna be angry with me for that."

"Oh, can I not?" She looked up at him with a challenging expression. "And why is that?"

He shrugged. "Ye've accused me of protectin' ye too much—of thinkin' ye're weak. So ye canna blame me for lettin' ye handle a simple situation yerself."

She pursed her lips, partially in an effort to control the smile that threatened. He was right, of course. If he had insisted on handling everything, she would undoubtedly have been bothered.

He gave her a playful nudge, looking down at her with smiling eyes that made it suddenly feel difficult to breathe.

The next stops were the tailor's and the small shop where they could purchase some tea. Christina wanted to bring Elizabeth a blend that might make her illness a bit less uncomfortable. She had also intended to request that her special blend of tea leaves be made up, but she changed her mind at the last minute. This was an opportunity for a change, however small it might be, and she asked Lachlan for his help in choosing a new blend. He was no tea connoisseur, and his responses to her questions were obviously given with nothing more than a desire to make her laugh.

"Well," she said as they left the shop with the new blend, "it will certainly be an interesting experience to try this."

Lachlan put out an expectant hand toward the container. He insisted upon carrying everything they had acquired.

She shook her head, cocking an eyebrow at the load he already had. "I fully expect that you will join me in tasting the first pot of it. Though, it does seem a terrible waste to throw out the entire batch Angus bought."

"Aye," Lachlan said in a woeful voice. "A waste of perfectly good poison."

Christina couldn't stop a laugh. "I suppose you are right. There is nothing for it but to throw it out." She sighed. "And now that we have fulfilled all of *my* commissions, what do *you* need to accomplish while we are here?"

He shook his head and arranged the things in his arms so that he could help her over the puddle that stood between them and their carriage. "Nay, we can make our way back ta Dunverlockie now."

She shot him a funny look, but he gave it no heed, helping her up into the carriage then handing her the boxes to arrange at their feet.

He took the reins in hand and climbed in.

She narrowed her eyes at him. "I thought you had a reason for coming other than to protect me."

"And I did."

She let out a laugh. "And you apparently intend to keep it a secret?"

He glanced over at her briefly then returned his eyes to the road. "Do ye truly wish for me ta tell ye?"

"After whetting my curiosity in such a way? It would be unkind of you not to."

He didn't answer immediately, and the expression he wore made Christina doubt herself suddenly. Perhaps he *did* have a reason for coming which he wished to keep secret—some private matter she had no business inquiring into. Strangely, the thought ignited a flicker of jealousy within her.

"Forgive me," she said. "I had no intention of prying."

"Nay," he said. "'Tis no' that." Still, his gaze remained fixed ahead of them. Whether he was simply an especially attentive driver or was avoiding her eye, she couldn't tell. "I came because I enjoy bein' with ye."

The only sound was the creaking of the carriage and the clopping of the horse's hooves on the dirt.

"Oh." There were a number of questions she wished she could ask, but the single-word response was all she could manage to say. The tenderness she had been seeing in his eyes, his kindness toward her—were they the marks of the sort of affection a man held for a friend or perhaps a sister? Or was there something more there?

To assume the latter seemed like folly—and conceit. Lachlan had spent the last sixteen years of his life surrounded by soldiers. It was little wonder he was enjoying new company. Though, she couldn't be the only woman he had spent time with in the last few years. She knew enough about the life of a soldier to understand that they found plenty of opportunity for entertainment and fraternizing with the opposite sex.

She doused the absurd jealousy the thought triggered with the reminder that, not only did it make no difference at all what Lachlan's history with women was, Christina herself had been married to another man just a few short weeks ago.

She was spared the necessity of responding any further by the questions Lachlan asked of her. It was as if he knew his remark had unsettled her and was attempting to reassure her with mundane talk of affairs at Dunverlockie. He was ever thoughtful.

After an assurance that it was *not* the same blend Christina had been partaking of, Elizabeth showed genuine gratitude for the tea Christina had brought back for her.

"Now I can be as grand as you, with my very own blend," she said in the most refined voice she could manage, given how congested she was.

"Good heavens," Christina said as she poured the steaming liquid into Elizabeth's cup. "Is that how I sound?"

Elizabeth sighed. "No. It is very hard to sound refined when one has a cold, isn't it?"

"Impossible."

Christina made a point of locating what was left of her own blend to dispose of herself. She had swiftly rejected the idea of asking one of the servants to do it. She could hardly have explained her reasoning to them, and there was a high probability that, whoever was charged with the task would see no harm in taking the expensive leaves for themselves instead of discarding them.

She made a point of wearing gloves as the took the box outside—she had no idea what sort of poison Angus had used and whether it might be able to affect her by simply touching it —and made her way down the same path Lachlan had led her down for the ceremony.

Summer was coming on in full force at Dunverlockie, and she couldn't help smiling at the idyllic sounds that enveloped her there. Dunverlockie felt less like a prison each day. Lachlan had been making changes there, always after consulting with Christina, who was more than happy to agree to anything he saw fit to alter. The changes at the castle were each small and subtle on their own—rugs, portraits, hangings—but the overall effect was to change the atmosphere in a way Christina hadn't expected.

Crouching down on the mossy bank of the river, she opened the lid of the box and sighed as she stared at what was within. As if on cue, she felt a rush of nausea and shut her eyes, breathing in the fresh air to quell it. The worst seemed to pass within a few minutes, and she immediately dumped the contents of the tea box into the water.

"Good riddance." She watched the leaves float lazily. Some of them bunched around the large rocks in their way until the force of the water urged them around and downstream where she lost track of them.

She looked around the small grove, remembering what it had been like the day of the wedding. It was still hard to believe she was married—again. This marriage was nothing like the last one, and she felt a rush of gratitude for that.

Why was everything so much more beautiful and enjoyable when life was less tumultuous? Her gaze landed on a large, fallen branch. On the end that had broken away from the tree, it was thick, with a dozen or so rings inside. She stared at it for a moment then stood and walked toward it, an idea forming.

She set the empty tea box on the ground and picked up the thinner end, snapping as much off as she could so that only the most substantial part remained. She cradled what remained under her arm and set the tea box on top of it then slowly made her way back to the castle.

By the time she reached her bedchamber, the nausea had returned again, and she hurriedly set down the log and box, rushing to the window and opening it just as Lachlan had done.

"Christina?"

Christina didn't turn toward Elizabeth, worried that the movement might be what finally caused her to retch.

"I was only wondering," Elizabeth said in her congested voice, "if you remembered what it was that Glenna used to make for you when you were sick—" She stopped talking as she reached Christina's side. "My dear, are you ill?"

Christina took in a deep breath of the fresh air. "It is only the poison. I have just come from dumping out the tea leaves."

"And you believe they are taking their revenge on you now?" There was humor in Elizabeth's voice, but Christina had no desire to laugh. "You have not drunk it recently, have you?" There was condemnation in her voice.

"Of course not," Christina answered, sucking in another breath, as deep as she could manage.

"Then it has been nearly two weeks, has it not? You should be getting better by now, not worse."

Christina felt a flash of annoyance at Elizabeth as she tried to keep down what seemed determined to come up. What did it matter what Elizabeth thought? The fact was that Christina *was* getting worse.

"Christina," Elizabeth said gently. "Could it be something else?"

There was a pause.

"Might it be that you are with child?"

Christina shook her head hurriedly, feeling the heat bloom in her cheeks. It seemed to occur with increasing frequency of late. "Lachlan and I have not...We are not..." She didn't bother finishing. Elizabeth was intelligent enough not to require her to. "Could you rub my back?"

Elizabeth set to the task immediately, and Christina kept her head turned just enough that it would be impossible for her sister to see her expression. She shut her eyes tightly, unable to clear her mind to think—unsure she wanted to.

She had been married to Gordon for nearly two years, and, in all that time, she had never become pregnant. Her courses had always been consistent before her marriage, and the first time they had been delayed, she had felt certain it was because she was pregnant. But, with time, it had become clear she was not, and from then on, she never knew when to expect her courses. They came and went with no regularity at all.

Her inability to become pregnant had added significantly to Gordon's disdain for and dislike of her. She was well-aware that he had sought consolation elsewhere, and it was generally accepted that he had fathered two children with other women in the short time she had been married to him. She had seen the pity in people's eyes when news had spread of the birth of the second child, but, the truth was, she had been grateful for the other women. They had granted her a reprieve from Gordon's unwanted attentions.

"Perhaps a cup of tea would help," she managed to say, eager to be alone.

Elizabeth nodded and left the room.

Christina *couldn't* be pregnant with Gordon's child—she refused to contemplate the possibility any further. Fate could not be so unkind.

24

Lachlan sat on the edge of the bed, pulling on his boots. The room looked bare with the bed lacking hangings, and he still wasn't used to seeing the mantel empty. It had always been the first thing to draw his eye when he entered his father's bedchamber.

There was a knock on the door, and he gave his boot a final tug before striding over to open it. One of the maids—Lachlan was still coming to know the Dunverlockie staff—stood in the corridor, holding a heap of fabric in her arms.

"Good morning, sir," she said. "Mrs. Mac"—she stopped, coloring up slightly—"Mrs. Kincaid said ta bring these ta ye in case ye wanted them for the bed."

His gaze moved to the fabric, and his brows came together. He looked back at the maid. "Where did ye find these?"

"Oh, 'twas no' me that found 'em, sir. 'Twas the mistress." She waited a moment. "Would ye like me ta put them up?"

He reached a finger to the neatly folded pile, running it along the familiar pattern. "Aye," he said slowly. "Thank ye."

He moved to allow her to pass by then glanced down the corridor, hoping to see Christina, but she wasn't there. It took a quarter of an hour to get the hangings up, threading the wooden rod through the loops of fabric and arranging the heavy cloth so that it fell evenly.

The maid returned to her other duties once the task was complete, and Lachlan stood by the door, twisting his beard in his fingers as he stared at the bed. He swallowed the lump that rose in his throat. Just a few weeks ago, the most he had been able to hope for was that he might live to see the MacKinnons known for what they were. Now, he stood in the bedchamber his father and grandfather and generations of Kincaids before them had slept in; he stood there as laird of Dunverlockie.

He turned around and opened the door, making his way to Christina's bedchamber and knocking softly.

"Come in."

He opened the door with a bit of hesitation, wondering if perhaps she was expecting her sister or one of the maids. She had a hand on her stomach and was standing by the window, looking at her other hand—at the knotted twine ring on her finger.

He frowned in concern. "Are ye still feelin' unwell?"

She immediately dropped both hands, clasping her fingers together in front of her and smiling at him. "I am well enough. And how are you today?"

Of course she would diminish her discomfort. She didn't want to be coddled, and he resisted the impulse to pursue the subject. "Better than ever," he said. "I've just come from helpin' one of the maids with the hangin's for the bed. How did ye ever find them?"

"*Are* they the ones your father used, then?"

He nodded. "The very same."

She smiled. "I am so pleased to know that. When I considered what other hangings we had, I remembered seeing a set somewhere in the castle—not with the rest of the linens. It struck me as strange at the time, and when you mentioned that the hangings on your bed were not the ones that had been there during your time here as a child, I thought perhaps the old ones were still in the castle somewhere. It took me a few days—and a stroll around the servant quarters—to remember where I had seen them."

"A great deal of trouble, then," he said wryly.

"Oh, it was no trouble at all. I wish we still had the bedcovers as well, but it seems they must have been sold or given away."

"Nay bother," he said. "I didna expect for any of it ta remain here. And I didna expect how much 'twould mean ta me ta see the hangin's on the bed again. I just..." He clamped his mouth shut, uncertain how to say what he had come to say.

She was looking at him intently, waiting for him to continue.

"I suppose I just wanted ta thank ye." He felt the lump rise in his throat again and forced it down determinedly. "I canna believe I'm here again." He looked around. "Home."

"As you should be."

"'Tis only because of *you* that I am. And I want ye ta ken how grateful I am ta ye. I always will be."

She shook her head. "You deserve it." She smiled ruefully. "Certainly more than any MacKinnon does."

"Och, but life has little care for what is deserved and no' deserved, Christina. If it did, perhaps my father would no' have died, and my family would have remained at Dunverlockie. And certainly *you* would no' have been married ta Gordon MacKinnon." He hesitated, heart thudding against his chest as his mind told him to keep the next words to himself. "But perhaps then I'd no' have met ye. And I confess, I dinna much care for the thought of that life, either."

She stared at him for a moment with an expression he couldn't identify. It looked almost...stricken.

"Well," he said, immediately regretting his moment of bravery, as he turned toward the door. "Forgive me for disturbin' ye." He had promised himself to make Dunverlockie a place where Christina could feel comfortable, and here he was, saying things that went in direct opposition to that goal.

"It was no disturbance," she said quickly.

He stopped with his hand on the door latch and turned toward her. He didn't respond, attempting to gauge whether she was in earnest or simply trying to make him feel better. She smiled at him reassuringly, but there was a trace of sadness in it, and it troubled him. He wanted more than anything to change that sadness to joy, but he didn't know how.

"Truly," she said. "I welcome the distraction."

No matter how much he tried, he found it impossible not to read more into her words than she meant—what he wanted to hear. He would gladly have stayed, but with his hand already on the door latch and the uncertainty of whether she wished for *more* distraction, he didn't dare.

"Can I have somethin' brought for ye?" he asked. "A cup of tea?"

She smiled but shook her head. "Thank you, but I have some already."

Sure enough, there was a cup on the table beside her bed.

"Have you found anything interesting in the correspondence in your bedchamber?" she asked

"No' yet. But there's still a fair amount ta go through. 'Tis what I intend ta do right now."

"Would you care for any help?"

He stared at her thoughtfully. "Ye must be verra bored ta offer such a thing." It was a silly thing to say—a childish way to obtain the reassurance he sought.

She lifted a shoulder. "As I said, distraction is welcome to me."

Distraction. That was what she was seeking. Distraction from the illness she wouldn't even admit to? Distraction from what? And yet, he would gladly accept an offer of her company, whatever her reasons.

"Come, then," he said.

C hristina looked at the letter in her hands, with its faded, sloping script and the Kincaid crest adorning the top. She had taken it while helping Lachlan look through the letters and documents yesterday.

They had both sat on the bed, one pile of correspondence and one of other documents spread out over the bedcovers. When she had first seen the crest atop one of the letters, she had stared at it for some time then glanced over at the mantel, where Lachlan had said the clan crest had sat for so long. No doubt it had been destroyed after the forfeiture of the estate, whether by agents of the Crown or by the MacKinnon clan once they had purchased Dunverlockie, Christina couldn't say. She had never seen any sign of it in the castle, and she knew Gordon well enough to know he wouldn't have allowed such a thing to remain on MacKinnon property.

She had never before seen the Kincaid crest, though, and looking at it had sparked an idea in her mind. She might have simply told Lachlan what the idea was, but she wasn't certain she could execute it properly, so she had taken one of the many letters, slipping it into her pocket unnoticed.

Lachlan had instructed her what to look for in the letters. He was trying to piece together any compelling evidence of Harold MacKinnon's duplicity. The more time she spent with Lachlan, the more evident it was to her that, while the soul behind his dark eyes and scarred face was gentler than one might at first assume, there was a determination about him that would make him a formidable foe. It seemed to her that he would give his all to those with whom his loyalties lay—his protection, his kindness, his love—but one betrayed him at their own peril. Hence the intense, focused way he read through the letters addressed by his father to the man who had brought about his downfall.

She set down the letter on her desk and went over to the wall where the block of wood she had taken from the grove a few days ago leaned below the window. She picked it up and set it on the desk, narrowing her eyes as she surveyed it.

Over the past few days, she had whittled away the rough bark anytime she needed to focus her mind and keep it from going places that frightened her. She knew what she wanted to carve now—it was only a matter of whether she had the skill for it.

She sat in the desk chair and took out the small sack of tools in the drawer, shutting her eyes for a moment as a swell of nausea gathered within her.

She had been paying better attention to her symptoms—fatigue, nausea, and something she couldn't put into words. It was simply the sense that something was different. She *felt* different. How had she not noticed it before? It seemed so obvious now. But there had been so much going on since Gordon's death. Everything had been changing.

There was very little doubt remaining that she was indeed pregnant, and the knowledge left her feeling an array of emotions that only added to the exhaustion she felt.

Her conscience convicted her as the worst of traitors for keeping it from Lachlan—she was an undeniable coward, just as she had told him. She couldn't keep it from him forever, but she was terrified of telling him. It felt like she had emerged from one nightmare only to enter into another. In the last nightmare, she herself had been miserable; in this new one, she was going to make someone else miserable—someone who deserved nothing but happiness. How could she tell him that he would be raising Gordon MacKinnon's child?

Her most selfish thoughts insisted on intruding, adding to her fears. What would he think of her? Would he think she had purposely chosen to dupe him?

The truth was, she should have considered the possibility before asking him to marry her. It had only been a few days before Gordon had passed that he had called her to his bedchamber for the last time. But pregnancy had never resulted from such encounters before. Why would she assume anything would be different that time? The timing could hardly have been worse, particularly as the affinity she felt for Lachlan grew with each encounter.

She had hoped that keeping herself occupied would help her avoid both her guilt and the suspicion she had been managing to keep at bay that a shift in her feelings toward Lachlan was occurring. Her success in those things had been questionable. At best, the carving helped distract her from the nausea.

There were occasions, though, when the roiling in her stomach was too strong to be ignored in favor of anything, be it perusing the decades-old correspondence of Lachlan's father or whittling away wood. It pressed itself in upon her, demanding her attention, reminding her that it was only a matter of time before everyone knew the secret.

E ach morning after breakfast, Lachlan invited Christina to continue perusing his father's correspondence with him. Each morning, Christina resolved anew to tell him.

Each morning, her courage failed her.

Every moment she spent with him made it harder rather than easier to complete her task, but she found herself incapable of refusing his invitations. Little though the act of reading through documents might accomplish, she felt as though she was helping him in some small way, and for a short time every day, they were taken up together by the ghosts of the past. It was a respite from the lonely challenges of the present.

In the afternoons, she spent much of her time carving in her room. With all the time she had spent on it this week, the crest was nearing completion, though Christina couldn't say she was fully satisfied with it. Her competence at carving didn't match her vision. But it had familiarized her intimately with the Kincaid crest and kept her mind and fingers occupied while she hadn't had her sister to keep her company.

But Elizabeth's health returned, and her familiar knock soon sounded on Christina's door.

Christina hurried to set the piece of wood on the side of the desk where it would be somewhat hidden. She took in a deep breath. "Come in."

True to form, Elizabeth hadn't waited for the invitation, and her curious gaze was on the side of the desk as she entered and closed the door behind her.

An intrigued smile grew on her face. "What was that?"

"Nothing," Christina said, rising from her chair. "Just something to keep me occupied while you have been sleeping your life away. How are you feeling?"

Elizabeth put her hands out to the side and shrugged playfully. "As good as ever. Only a slight cough remains." She peered around Christina at the place where she had set the crest, and her eyebrows went up. "You are carving again?"

Christina surrendered to the inevitable and stepped aside so her sister could pass, which she did, picking up the carving.

"I am out of practice, as you can see," Christina said, wondering what conclusions Elizabeth might be forming at the subject she had chosen for her first foray back into carving.

"I see nothing of the sort," Elizabeth responded, tilting the crest in her hands to admire the work. "It is exquisite. Did Lachlan ask you to do it?"

"No. It was just a silly idea I had and wanted to test my hand at."

"He will love it."

Christina said nothing, and Elizabeth's eyes shifted to her as she continued to hold up the carving in front of her. "You *do* intend to give it to him, do you not?"

Christina took the wood from her sister and set it back down on the floor. "It is a crude attempt. It could be taken as an affront to the Kincaid clan."

Elizabeth let out a laugh. "You are ridiculous."

Christina swallowed uncomfortably as her nausea surged, and Elizabeth's smile disappeared entirely.

"Still unwell?" Elizabeth made her way to the bell pull. "You *must* see a doctor."

"Stop."

Elizabeth's hand hovered on the pull, an exasperated expression on her face. "Whether you are still experiencing effects of poison or it is some other malady, you really must be seen."

"I am pregnant," Christina blurted out.

Elizabeth stared, and her eyebrows knit together. "But you said—"

"It is Gordon's child." Christina turned her head, unwilling to watch her sister's expression.

"Good heavens," Elizabeth said softly.

Good was not the word Christina would have used to describe the situation the heavens had put her in.

"What does Lachlan say?" Elizabeth asked.

"Nothing."

Christina could feel Elizabeth's eyes on her, and she wished she could disappear.

"You haven't told him," Elizabeth said. "Oh, Christina. You cannot keep it from him. You—"

"I know." The words came out harsh, and she tempered them as she repeated, "I know. I just...."

Elizabeth took two steps toward her and put a hand on her arm. "He is a good man, Elizabeth. He will understand."

He *was* a good man. And it was precisely that which gave Christina pause. He deserved so much better.

25

After speaking with Elizabeth, Christina promised herself she would tell Lachlan the next day. She wanted a final evening where things could be normal, for she had no idea what her relationship with Lachlan would be like once he knew the truth.

It made for a painfully bittersweet meal. Every smile Lachlan sent her way, every interaction they had was saturated for her with what might have been if things had been different —if Gordon had not summoned her to his bedchamber that awful evening.

Lachlan was not one to linger over drink on his own after the meal, and as the three of them rose from the table, he called her name.

Elizabeth gave her a short but significant look, as though to say, *here is your chance.* Christina ignored it and turned toward Lachlan. He looked particularly handsome this evening, and she recognized at once the tender gleam his eyes took on whenever they were fixed on her. She had taken it for granted until now. She wanted so much to be worthy of that affection—to embrace it and return it.

"I reckon we've made it through most of the letters by now," he said. "Just a few more left if ye wish ta help me tomorrow after ye've breakfasted. And then I thought we might take a ride, perhaps, ta see if we can discover what it is we keep comin' across in the letters—the Wash. I thought perhaps Glenna might ken what it means."

Christina swallowed, feeling that familiar impulse to put off the difficult task before her so that she could finish what she had begun with Lachlan. Well, she would join him tomorrow if he had any desire for her company after what she told him in the morning.

"I would like that," she said.

He smiled, and she found herself wishing for an excuse to spend more of this last evening with him—the last evening where he held her in affection rather than aversion. Perhaps he was feeling a similar desire, since he lingered another moment before wishing her good evening and making his way out of the dining room.

She stood where she was for a moment, putting a hand on her belly. She didn't wish the child away—it was an innocent. But she *did* wish that it was Lachlan's child. She sighed and went to her bedchamber, taking out the letter, the crest, and the carving tools. She could finish it tonight. And then tomorrow, she would toss it in the fire and watch it go up in flames, along with the future she had begun to envision.

She would have a true craftsman carve the crest to display in Lachlan's bedchamber—something he could be proud of instead of her own amateur attempt.

She didn't allow herself any tears as she took out her tools. What was the purpose? There was no changing reality. She had borne a marriage with a man who despised her before—she could do it again.

A knock on the door made her jump, pulling her out of her melancholy thoughts.

"Who is it?" she asked.

"'Tis I," Lachlan said.

Her breath caught, and she hurried up out of her seat and to the door, opening it enough not to give offense while ensuring he couldn't see past her into the bedchamber.

"I dinna mean ta disturb ye," he said, "but I was goin' through the letters, and I canna find one of 'em. It mentions the Wash, and I was rereadin' 'em all ta see if there's somethin' I missed. Ye dinna remember seein' one layin' about, do ye?"

Her heart sputtered. "Oh," she said guiltily. "I do, in fact. I am terribly sorry—I didn't know you would need it. Just a moment." She turned around and hastened to the desk, picking up the letter in question and taking it back to him.

He looked bemused as he took it from her. Some explanation was warranted, and only for a moment did she try to think up an alternative to the real one. No more prevaricating. No more avoiding the truth.

"It is silly," she said, "but I saw the Kincaid crest on some of the letters, and I had never seen it before. It gave me an idea, and so I brought it here with me."

He gave her a quizzical look. "An idea?"

She gave something between a smile and grimace. "I wanted to use it for a carving."

"A carvin'?"

"Yes. As I said—a silly idea, and I should have told you, but I wasn't certain I could manage to do it justice. And I was, unfortunately, correct."

An arrested expression entered his eyes. "Ye mean ta say ye carved it?"

She pursed her lips in response.

"Can I see it?"

She gave a rueful smile. "I have no desire to offend you, Lachlan."

He chuckled. "I've seen yer carvin's, Christina. Ye'll no' offend me."

He took a step forward, making clear his intention to see it, and the step brought him right before her, close enough that impulse told her to step back. But she didn't move.

"'Tis a Kincaid crest," he said with an irresistible smile and a teasing challenge in his eye. "I believe I've a right ta see it."

She had a hand on the door, and he covered it with his as he craned his neck to see behind her. She tried to block his vision by rising up on her toes, but he was too tall, and it only brought them into closer proximity, making her heart hammer.

She hesitated another moment. But what was she trying to do in keeping it from him? Tomorrow morning, there would be nothing left to salvage of whatever it was they now had between them.

She backed down with a sigh and opened the door.

"Bully," she said, but he only smiled and stepped into the room. She followed for a moment behind him then stopped, folding her arms and remaining in place, a few steps short of the desk.

There were small wood chips and slivers scattered across the desk, and the three tools she used lay haphazardly around the crest. Lachlan stared down at it for a moment then, in a slow movement, reached to pick it up.

His gaze took it in for a moment, then he looked at her. "Ye did this yerself?"

She couldn't judge from his expression whether his reaction was a positive or negative one, but she nodded. "I wish I could blame the inadequacy of it on the fact that the crest on the letter is a bit faded or that the wood is difficult to work with, but"—she shrugged—"the responsibility is mine alone."

He ran a finger along it. "Where did ye find the wood?"

"In the grove. Where we were married."

He glanced up at her, eyes searching her face. For what, though? He ran a finger along one of the ridges. "'Tis perfect."

She stepped beside him, frowning deeply as she looked at the crest. "It has too many blemishes to count. Besides, it is not even finished." She took it from him and pointed to the area she hadn't managed to finish the detail on. "I was too intimidated to do more here."

"Och," he said. "I never cared much for that part of it anyway."

She looked up at him, and he winked, though as their eyes held, his smile faded, and his expression became more intent. "I love it, Christina. And I'll treasure it."

He meant it. She could see it in his eyes. He would treasure the thing she had been on the verge of using as fuel for the fire in the grate—something full of deficiencies and blemishes. He looked at it with the same appreciative gaze he looked at her with. They saw things so differently. How did he manage to see beauty where she saw only flaws and faults?

She broke her gaze away, afraid if she kept it on him any longer, she might not be able to look away. The more he regarded in her that way, the more she needed it. It was dangerous.

"I think the Kincaid name would be better served if we commissioned someone with real skill to make a carving." She moved to put the carving back on the desk, but he stopped her, putting a hand over hers.

"I dinna want another carvin', Christina. I want this one."

She scoffed lightly. "You cannot truly prefer a thing so crude and imperfect when you might have something superior."

He shook his head. "Ye dinna see it clearly."

"Perhaps it is *you* who does not see it clearly."

"I'll tell ye what I see, then." He looked down at the crest. They held it together, his hand still covering hers, warm and steady.

"I see the symbols that have represented my kin for hundreds of years. I see the words—*This I'll defend*—that guided my father and have guided me my entire life. I see wood from a part of Dunverlockie that I love."

He directed his gaze at her rather than at the crest they held, and her heart began to thud.

"In it, I see bits and pieces of *you*, though, Christina, and 'tis what I love most about it. For that reason alone, 'tis more beautiful to me than the work of any stranger, whatever their skills."

Her hand gripped the crest more tightly, and the fire lighting and warming the room suddenly felt too hot.

Lachlan continued to look at her, but he seemed to be struggling with himself, and his hold on her hand tightened until he looked down at it and released it suddenly.

"Forgive me," he said. "I promised ye I'd no' touch ye.

"Lachlan," she said, shaking her head. "I told you I did not mean it in that way...."

"I ken, Christina. And I tried ta tell meself there was a difference—that the small touches between us were no' what ye meant when ye said ye didna wish ta be intimate. But...but that's just it. Ta me, 'tis all the same." His throat bobbed behind his cravat. "'Tis all intimate. And I find meself lookin' for reasons ta"—he shrugged in frustration—"stand near ye or ta brush yer hand or...anythin'."

Christina couldn't speak. Her body wouldn't allow it. Her heart was beating so fiercely that neither her voice nor her lungs would have obeyed her even if she had known what to say.

He took a step back. "I ken what I promised. And I swear ta ye, I'll keep that promise. I willna touch ye because I canna do so without wantin' more. But I canna keep meself from tellin' ye how I feel."

He stared at her for a moment then let out a gush of air through his nose, turning to the chair beside them, the top of which he clutched with both hands. "I admit when I proposed marriage ta ye, I had it in my mind that I would be passin' Dunverlockie ta a son—or a daughter—of my own. And when ye told me ye wished ta be married but had no wish ta be intimate, I was... well, I was crushed inside." His thick brows pressed together, and his bearded jaw clenched and unclenched for a moment. "But the more time passes—the more time I spend with ye—the more I feel I can be content with just us—you and me." He turned his head to look at her, lifting his shoulders in a helpless gesture completely at odds with the powerful man before her. "I've fallen in love with ye, Christina. I canna help meself."

She was rigid, her gaze fixed on Lachlan's face, where the guilt was written in the lines of his forehead and the somberness of his eyes, as though he was admitting to a crime rather than saying words she had never heard a man utter to her—words she hadn't realized how much she had needed until the tears came.

"Kiss me." Her voice came out scratchy.

Lachlan's eyes widened, staring at her in bemusement. "What?" The word croaked out. He let go of the chair and faced her. "Christina...I swore to ye."

"I know what I made you promise." She stepped toward him, her body trembling as she looked up to meet his eyes. "Kiss me, Lachlan," she repeated softly.

He stared down at her, eyes roving slowly over her face and down to her lips, where they lingered. She could see the desire there, and it kindled her own. He brought a hand up and set it on her cheek, closing his eyes as he brushed his thumb along it.

Christina took in a quivering breath and shut her own eyes. If she hadn't felt his hand on her face or his soft breath, she might have wondered whether he was even there still. Without her vision, the trembling in her body felt heightened, and she reached out for Lachlan's arm.

And then she waited.

The first touch of his lips on hers was so soft, she thought she was imagining it. Just the ghost of a kiss. She lifted her face, and their lips met more fully, sending a thrill down her neck, her back, and her arms. His hand moved from her cheek down under her chin, guiding her mouth closer to his as he put a hand to the small of her back. Its pressure invited her to move closer, and she submitted to its suggestion, responding by gripping his arm and pulling him toward her.

Lachlan's kiss was everything Christina had come to know about him: gentle but steady, deep and poignant. There was no hesitation in it now, only devotion and tenderness with a hint of desire. She hadn't known a kiss could tell a story, but Lachlan's kiss said without words everything he had admitted to her —he loved her.

She pulled away abruptly, turning aside and covering her mouth with a hand as she tried to catch her breath.

"Christina," Lachlan said, reaching a hand out and then dropping it. "Forgive me. I should no' have—"

"No," she said shakily. "It is not that. I...." Every part of her urged her to turn back to him, to continue the kiss and forget that there was anything in the world but the tenderness she had just felt and the words he had said.

But she couldn't. She couldn't let him love her in ignorance.

"Lachlan," she said. Her voice sounded strangled, as if it was trying to keep her from saying the words. "I need to tell you something."

"Aye, what is it?"

She couldn't see him, the way she was faced. She didn't want to, couldn't bear to. But she had to.

She forced herself to turn back toward him then forced her eyes up to his.

"I am with child."

26

Lachlan blinked. He couldn't have heard right. His heart was still thudding and his mind caught up in the kiss they had just shared. "Ye're...I dinna understand."

A tear slipped from Christina's eye and left a wet trail down her cheek. "My illness—I thought it was from the tea, but...I only realized this week what the cause was."

"But"—he shut his eyes and rubbed a hand across his forehead. It slowed as it reached his temple—as understanding began to dawn. "Ye mean ye're pregnant with...with *Gordon MacKinnon's* child?"

She didn't say a word, but her stricken expression was confirmation enough.

He shut his eyes and covered his face with his two hands, trying to focus his mind but afraid of truly thinking through the ramifications of what Christina was telling him.

"I am *truly* sorry, Lachlan. I swear to you, I had no notion, or I would never have agreed to this marriage."

He let his hands drop from his face and looked at her. Her fingers were clasped together, covering her mouth.

"Do ye ken what this means?"

He thought he saw the hint of her chin trembling behind her hands as she nodded her head.

"We are *married*, Christina." He kept his voice calm and soft, but it shook despite his best efforts. "Which means that it doesna matter that the father of the child in yer belly is Gordon MacKinnon. In the eyes of the law, the child will be *mine*—and the heir ta Dunverlockie."

Saying the words aloud made him physically ill in a way he hadn't felt since he first saw action—and death—in the war.

He put up a hand to stop the words Christina was about to say. "I canna—I must go."

He hurried from the room, running toward and then down the stairs, where he made his way outside, taking in a breath of fresh air, just as he had taught Christina to do when he had come upon her feeling unwell. Unwell because she was carrying Gordon MacKinnon's baby—Lachlan's legal child and future heir.

Dunverlockie *would* belong to a MacKinnon once again.

He let out something between a groan and a yell and hurried toward the stables. He needed to get away.

Christina listened for Lachlan's return until sleep finally overtook her. The crest still lay on the desk, forgotten with the kiss and its aftermath.

When she woke in the morning, she rang the bell for one of the maids.

"Is the master awake yet?" she asked, trying but unable to pretend indifference.

"He sent word last night for a few of his things to be brought to the inn this morning, mistress," said the maid.

Christina swallowed the lump in her throat. "Oh. I see. That will be all, Janet, thank you."

The maid curtsied and left Christina alone.

Her gaze went to the crest again, and the words he had used to describe what he saw when he looked at it came to her mind. *Bits and pieces of you*, he had said.

She shut her eyes, but having them closed only reminded her of the way Lachlan had kissed her, as though she was the most precious, desirable thing in the world to him.

That was all over now. She had seen it in his reaction—one that had hurt her more than any of Gordon's red-faced railing. The calm with which he had responded was more frightening somehow.

She never should have allowed him to kiss her. She had *asked* him to, cowardly and selfish woman that she was. She had wanted to know what it was like—just once—to be held and kissed by a man who truly cared for her, who believed her to be beautiful and worth loving. Gordon had rarely kissed her, and even when he had, they had been rough kisses, reeking of whisky and entirely indifferent to her wishes.

Lachlan's kiss—the care he had held her with—had been opposite in every way. Better than anything she could have imagined. Something she would never again experience.

She fiddled with the ring she wore. The twine had been a practical decision—hurried and spontaneous, just as their marriage had been. It was precisely the reminder she needed.

Her revelation had brought about a reaction from him which only confirmed to her what she had known from the start: he had married her for practical reasons, and, whatever he had convinced himself he felt for her, the revelation of her pregnancy had disabused him of that delusion.

Her inability to produce an heir had set Gordon unalterably against her; how ironic that the success Gordon had wanted so badly should prove the reason for her second marriage's failure.

The future she had envisioned with Lachlan had never

been anything but a fantasy, so divorced from reality as to be irrelevant, except for the way it made that hard reality feel so much more unbearable.

P erhaps Lachlan would have slept more if he had stayed at Dunverlockie. He woke wondering when he had fallen asleep and feeling refreshed not at all.

Glenna had asked him no questions upon his arrival at Glengour, but in the short time he had spent outside of his room, he had seen her eyes on him, curious and concerned. She knew him well enough to recognize the signs that all was not well.

Mr. Gibson had looked on him with disfavor when he expressed his intention to stay the night, but Lachlan had no energy to care for the innkeeper's opinion.

The depression that had come over him upon leaving the castle had begun to give way to guilt. He had left Christina with tears on her face. He had vowed to protect her, to give her a life different from the one she had endured with Gordon MacKinnon, but when the repercussions of her miserable marriage became apparent, he had left her crying and alone.

And the blame for the situation lay just as much with him as it did with her. He should have considered the possibility that she might be with child. He had married her so soon after her husband's death, and he had gleaned enough about Gordon MacKinnon to know that the man had undoubtedly forced himself on Christina. It was why she had insisted upon the last term of their marriage.

But that didn't change the pain and the heaviness of the situation.

He dressed and shuffled down the stairs to the coffee room. There was one other man there, but he rose shortly after

Lachlan took a seat, tossing a coin on the table next to his cup. Glenna entered with a tray and, after a quick word with the traveler, came over to Lachlan.

"Ye're awake," she said, setting down a cup of coffee in front of him.

"Canna say I ever properly slept," he said.

She looked at him with an evaluative eye. "Somethin' troublin' ye?"

He didn't answer right away, and when he did, all he said was, "Aye."

She stood at the table for another moment, but when he kept silent, she said, "Verra well, then," and turned away with her tray.

He clenched his teeth. If he kept everything inside, he thought he might die. "Glenna, wait."

She stopped and turned toward him with a sad, little smile, as if she had never truly meant to leave. She came to sit at the other chair at his table, and Lachlan glanced at the doorway to the coffee room.

"I dinna wish ta bring Mr. Gibson's displeasure on ye," he said.

She waved a dismissive hand. "Dinna fash yerself. He's fair occupied with the shipment."

"If ye're certain," he said doubtfully. He wasn't even sure what he wished to say to her. He only knew that the burden he was carrying felt too large for him. He took in a deep breath. "Ye remember that Christina was unwell."

Glenna nodded, her eyes taking on a glint of concern again. "Has something happened ta her?"

He fiddled with his beard. "'Twas no' poison, Glenna."

Her eyebrows contracted. "What?"

"Nay." He knew a moment of misgiving. Would Christina be upset if he broke the news of her condition? But Christina and Glenna were devoted friends. "She is with child."

Glenna's eyebrows flew up, and her mouth broke into a smile. "What happy news! I offer ye my felicitations." She took his hand in hers and pressed it excitedly, but her smile began to waver when he didn't reflect her same enthusiasm. "Ye're no' happy."

He took up the coffee in hand and took a deliberate sip, not meeting her eye when he spoke. "'Tis Gordon MacKinnon's child."

She took in a quick breath and uttered something unintelligible behind the hand what went to her mouth. "Are ye certain?"

He grimaced and nodded, tapping a finger on the rim of the coffee cup. "When she told me, for a moment, I couldna help but wonder if she kent it when she came ta me, tellin' me she wished ta marry me. I thought perhaps 'twas *that* which changed her mind and made her accept the offer I'd made—that she didna wish ta raise the bairn on her own."

Glenna hurried to shake her head, and he put up a hand to stop her from whatever she was on the verge of saying.

"Nay, Glenna. I ken she'd no' do that. It only took a moment for me ta admit it ta myself. Och, it only took one look at her face ta see it—ta see how it hurt her ta tell me."

He leaned his forehead in his hands, and the rickety table shifted on its uneven legs as he stared down at the grains of wood. "But how, Glenna?" He swallowed with effort. "How can I raise the child of my enemy as if he were my own? How can I bear ta call a bairn by the Kincaid name when the blood that flows through those veins is the same blood that betrayed my father? How will I stomach givin' Dunverlockie back into the hands of a MacKinnon?" He spat the last word. He couldn't help it.

Glenna clasped her hands and set them on the table, her fingers gripped as tightly together as her brow. She took a moment before responding. "'Tis unjust. And the most unkind twist of fate. But ye *will* do it, Lachlan. Ye'll do it because ye're a good man—a better man than Gordon or Angus or any MacKinnon. And ye'll do it because the bairn is innocent. It may have MacKinnon blood, but it willna ken the MacKinnon ways. That wee lad—or lass—will grow up with *yer* example. Ye'll teach the bairn what ye've kend since ye were a bairn yerself: 'tis no' blood which makes kin, but loyalty.

"And ye'll do it all kennin' that 'tis just as heavy a burden for Christina as it is for *you*." She gave him a pained look. "She's bearin' the child of the man she despises more than anythin' in the world, Lachlan. The Kincaids have suffered grave injustices at the hands of the MacKinnons. There's no denyin' that. But the type of sufferin' my mistress endured"—she shook her head, and her lips turned down in a tremulous frown. "Well...I dinna ken if that pain *can* be healed."

He grimaced, feeling a familiar surge of protectiveness—accompanied by an equal measure of anger toward Gordon MacKinnon. "So, what, then? The innocent bairn is ta live its entire life remindin' both his parents of what they hate most?"

She shook her head.

He shrugged, nonplussed.

"I ken 'tis difficult ta imagine right now," Glenna said, "but, I dinna believe ye'll feel that way once the bairn is here." She gave a sad smile. "I think ye'll come ta love that lass—or lad—when ye hold her in yer arms and spend yer time carin' for her. Ye'll forget that she doesna have yer blood, and ye'll do anythin' ta keep her safe."

Lachlan cleared away the emotion that made his throat thick.

Glenna shrugged. "Perhaps ye'll have bairns of yer own and come ta see that there's no difference in the way ye feel for them and the way ye feel for this one. And who kens but that 'tis a lass ye'll welcome, and then all yer frettin' will be for naught when ye have a lad of yer own ta inherit Dunverlockie?"

Lachlan attempted a smile and looked away. Glenna didn't know the terms of his marriage to Christina. When he and Christina had kissed, it had only left him wanting more. But what had it meant to her? Had it left her feeling the same way? Or had it reconfirmed to her that she wanted no intimacy? She *had* pulled away, after all.

"My mistress is no' like anyone I've ever met, Lachlan," Glenna said. "She's special. When Rachel Tulloch disappeared, the mistress had only just arrived at Dunverlockie, but she tried to muster the MacKinnon forces ta search for the lass. Gordon put a stop ta that, though, claimin' he couldna spare the men. But the mistress went out with me and the Tulloch family herself for hours, searchin'."

Lachlan's eyebrows snapped together, a thread of a memory teasing him. He strained at it. "What was the lass's name ye said?"

"Rachel," she said. "Rachel Tulloch. She worked here at the time. I think I mentioned her afore."

His mind went to the list he had found amongst the documents hidden in his bedchamber. *R Tulloch.* Had that been one of the names on the list, or was he simply imagining it? No, he remembered that name specifically, as it was one he had never heard of before.

"When did she disappear?" he asked.

"Just after the mistress arrived at Dunverlockie, like I said. So that would have been, oh, perhaps July. Nearly two years ago now. I canna hardly believe it."

Lachlan stared at Glenna, thoughts running wild. Was it coincidence that *R Tulloch* had been on that list and had also disappeared? His mind went to the other names, and his heart beat more quickly as he stared at Glenna.

The date next to *G. Douglas*—he couldn't remember what it had been exactly, only that it was in June. He shut his eyes in an attempt to see if he could recapture the view of the document he had held in his hands, but it was no use.

"Why do ye ask?" Glenna said.

He opened his eyes, fixing his gaze on her. Was Glenna in danger? If so, what sort of danger, and how imminent was it?

He needed to see that document again. "I must go." He shot up from the table, taking long strides toward the door that led to the reception area and then outside.

Voices met his ears—one belonging to Mr. Gibson—coming from outside, and he stopped short, listening for a moment with his hand on the door latch.

"...at dawn or never, I'm afraid. The Falcon has already been moored for two days. The captain willna wait any longer, sir. He made that clear when I spoke with 'im."

"But the plan was for the 21st," came the voice of Angus, full of annoyance.

"Aye, sir. But the captain seemed anxious ta be on 'is way, what with the storm brewin' and the way things went last time. Whoever is to board the ship must be at the Wash before dawn."

Lachlan frowned at the mention of the Wash.

"Very well," Angus replied. He signaled his horse, and the dance of hoofbeats sounded, quickened, then grew more distant.

Lachlan lifted the latch and opened the door, nodding at Mr. Gibson, whose expression was one of chagrin at the sight of him.

"Are ye stayin' another night, sir?" Mr. Gibson called after him.

Lachlan thought a moment before responding. "Nay."

"But ye've no' got yer things," Mr. Gibson replied.

He turned back toward the innkeeper. "I'll send a servant for 'em."

Mr. Gibson nodded, and his shoulders relaxed a bit.

"Good day, Mr. Gibson," Lachlan said, making his way back to his horse.

He galloped all the way back to Dunverlockie, but the unsettled feeling in his stomach made the pace feel too slow. He didn't even wait for the horse to come to a stop before swinging his leg over the saddle and dismounting. He looped the reins over the post and strode through the door to the castle.

It was calm inside, and he strained his ears for any sign of the voice of Christina or Elizabeth. Footsteps on the stairs sounded, and he waited for the owner to appear at the bottom.

"Oh, 'tis you," Janet said. "Good day, sir."

"Where is Mrs. Kincaid?" he asked.

"She and Miss Innes went for a ride, oh, I'd say about an hour ago."

Lachlan sighed. It was undoubtedly for the best. He needed to speak with her—to set things to right, but that was a conversation that required more time than he had at the moment.

"Thank ye." He hurried past the maid and up the stairs to his bedchamber. The letters and documents were still scattered over his bed, unmoved from where he had left them before going to Christina's bedchamber the night before to ask her about the missing letter.

He shuffled through one of the stacks and pulled out the paper in question, his eyes sweeping over the top and down to the area in question.

His memory *had* served him. The entry for *R Tulloch* had July 15th in the date column. His gaze moved down to the entry for *G Douglas* and over to the final column: *Falcon*.

He stared. That had been the name of the ship Mr. Gibson and Angus had been discussing. What did it mean, though? Glenna had spent her entire life in Kildonnan. It was simply unbelievable that her very first time venturing out into the world would be on a ship—or that it would be of so little significance that she would have failed to mention it to him. And if the G was referring to her father, Gillies, the same still held true. An intended journey by ship would be the subject of discussion amongst the toun for some time, and Mr. Gibson had made it abundantly clear that the ship was meant to leave at dawn.

Lachlan pulled on his beard, glancing over the list of names again, then strode over to the bell pull and tugged it.

It was one of the footmen who appeared shortly after.

"Martin," Lachlan said. "How long have ye lived in Kildonnan?"

"Fifteen years, sir," he replied.

Lachlan nodded and raised the paper again, choosing a name. "Do ye ken anyone by the name MacVaxter?"

He nodded. "Aye, sir. Used ta live in the toun."

"Did any of the MacVaxters have a name startin' with the letter L?"

He frowned. "Aye. One of the lasses. Lily."

"What happened ta the family? They're no longer here, ye said?"

"Aye, they didna get along well with Mr. MacKinnon. And after Lily disappeared, they left—ta Perth, if I'm rememberin' right."

Lachlan's grip on the paper tightened. "Disappeared?"

He nodded. "People say she must've had a lover, though her father never would hear such talk—maintained she was a proper lass."

"Thank you, Martin."

He bowed and left the room.

Lachlan stared at the paper, at the date beside *G Douglas,* glaring back at him. It was two days from now.

27

As Christina and Elizabeth approached Dunverlockie, Christina tried to rein in her impatience. She hated that she was so anxious to know whether Lachlan had returned. It terrified her how much she felt a need for him now, how much she wished to be reconciled.

She couldn't allow herself to need or wish for such things. She had dealt him a blow that couldn't help but alter things between them forever. Inside her she carried the offspring of his mortal enemies—a child who would have had the MacKinnon name, might have led the MacKinnon clan and carried on the MacKinnon bloodline—a child who *did* have MacKinnon blood. And she had put Lachlan in a position where he had no choice but to be recognized as the child's father—and to recognize the child as his heir.

She needed to check her attachment—to stifle it before it gave her more pain than it already was. She needed to relearn how to survive on her own. This had been a strategic marriage from the beginning—she had been a means to an end for Lachlan, just as she had been for Gordon. And, to be fair, her reasons for marrying Lachlan had also been strategic.

Assuming that had changed because of a short kiss and a few words was her fault and hers alone. She knew better.

"Christina?"

She blinked, bringing her thoughts to the present. "Hm?"

Elizabeth raised a brow at her. "How much have you gathered?"

"What?"

Elizabeth shrugged a shoulder. "You have been wool-gathering for most of the ride. I was merely wondering whether you needed any help carrying the copious amounts of wool you have managed to gather by now."

Christina sent her an unamused glance. "I have not been wool-gathering."

Elizabeth looked forward toward the stables, which were coming into view over the hill. "So, the three questions of mine you failed to answer I must attribute merely to ill manners, then." She sent a teasing glance at Christina and reached for her hand. "Never fear, sister. It will all be well. What you told him would overset any man for a time."

Christina managed a smile and a nod, but she didn't share her sister's confidence. How could Lachlan ever come to accept the reality she had forced upon him? It was too much to ask of a man that he raise the grandchild of the person who forced his father to the scaffold, who took his birthright and his home—to say nothing of asking him to love the child.

They paused on the threshold of the stables, waiting for Kemp to appear. But it was a stable boy who appeared there instead—one unfamiliar to Christina. He couldn't have been more than nine or ten years old.

With his head down in a show of deference, he hurried to take the reins of both horses, guiding them to the mounting block.

Christina watched him as she dismounted. "What is your name?"

He looked at her uncomprehendingly, and she repeated herself, this time in Gaelic.

"Colum, miss."

"I have not seen you here before. Are you new?"

"Mr. Kemp told me ta come help today, miss."

"And he left you here all alone?" Elizabeth asked.

"I ken how ta take care of horses, miss," Colum replied.

"I do not doubt it," Elizabeth replied wryly. "But it is Mr. Kemp who is being paid for such work."

"He said he'd give me a dram for my trouble."

"Ah," Christina said, shooting her sister a glance that urged her to leave matters be. "You are duly recompensed, then. Though, here at Dunverlockie, we pride ourselves on taking good care of our servants, so I hope you intend to take your dinner with the others in the servant hall. Fresh bannocks and perhaps some mutton."

His hungry eyes grew wide, and he swallowed. "I couldna leave the horses, miss."

"Does Mr. Kemp not intend to return?"

"He said ta mind things till he come back, miss, and that it wouldna be long, but that he'd whip me if he found I'd done anythin' wrong or tried ta go explorin' the grounds." He looked up at her guiltily. "I've too curious a mind, my ma says."

Christina felt a flash of annoyance at the groom. "Well, I shall have one of the servants bring you something to eat while you wait for Mr. Kemp's return, then. And you can tell him I had it sent to you myself."

"Thank ye, miss," Colum said sincerely.

Christina smiled at him, and he excused himself to get the brushes.

"You were very kind to that boy," Elizabeth said softly.

Christina watched Colum disappear into one of the rooms at the end of the row of stables. "I doubt he has met with any kindness from Kemp, whatever the man has promised to give him."

"You are right, no doubt. And he does seem a good sort of boy. Perhaps you should give him Kemp's position; he seems to take it more seriously."

Christina laughed, and her gaze landed on the stall that normally contained Lachlan's horse. Her heart skittered at the sight of the animal there. He had returned. What did that mean?

They made their way to the castle entrance, and Christina found it hard to focus herself on providing appropriate responses to Elizabeth's conversation. If she was going to see Lachlan, she needed time to prepare herself.

But she was destined not to have such time, for Lachlan appeared on the stairs just as they reached the base of them.

All three of them paused, and after a brief and awkward silence, Elizabeth spoke. "Good afternoon, Lachlan. If you will excuse me, I wish to change out of these clothes before the stain on the hem sets."

He gave a curt nod, and, lifting her petticoats—which were free of any visible stain—Elizabeth hurried up the stairs. Christina watched her sister go, heart thudding against her chest, and when she looked back at Lachlan, his eyes were on her.

"I'm afraid I canna stay ta talk," he said, continuing down the stairs toward the landing. There was an air of urgency about him, and his brows were drawn together as though he was displeased.

Of course he was displeased. That was hardly news. And of course he had no desire to stay and talk. She was a reminder of painful things for him. What had she been expecting?

But his brusqueness still stung.

He seemed to recognize that she was dissatisfied with his words. "I *do* wish ta speak with ye, Christina, but this is a matter that canna wait. I need ye ta stay here. On no account must ye leave the castle."

She blinked at him. "What?"

Lachlan was already moving away toward the door. "I'll be sendin' Glenna here, ta keep her safe."

Christina took a few steps toward him as his hand reached for the door, feeling worry and frustration rise simultaneously.

"Keep her safe? From what?"

He grimaced and opened the door. "I canna explain it all right now. I'm sorry." He paused under the large, wooden door frame, looking at her, then took a few steps to bring him back before her. He reached for her hand. "I'll tell ye everythin' when I've returned. I promise. But ye *canna* leave the castle. Glenna either."

Christina struggled against the burning in her eyes. Part of her wanted to refuse what he was demanding of her—to show him that she and only she controlled her actions, that she didn't need him to protect her—that she didn't need him at all. She *couldn't* need him.

"I must go now. But *please*, Christina. *Stay here.*"

She gave a stiff nod, and he dropped her hand and left. The door shut with a thud that resounded through her body, and she stood in place, trying to sort through her feelings: worry for Glenna, frustration at not knowing what sort of danger her friend was in, disappointment at her interaction with Lachlan.

Somehow, so gradually that she had hardly noticed it happening, she had come to care profoundly for Lachlan Kincaid—to love him. He had come to care for her, too. She had seen it and felt it. And he had told her in no uncertain terms.

The question was whether his attachment to her—the love he had spoken of—had survived what he knew now. His need to see justice served to the MacKinnons had brought him here in the first place. It was a matter of honor for him, of honoring his father's memory and his clan's name.

How could she expect him to choose her over his own blood?

She set a hand on her stomach and shut her eyes. Glenna was in danger, and Lachlan was expecting Christina to help keep her safe. That was where her focus needed to be right now.

With the help of Janet, she changed her petticoats and tidied her appearance, keeping an eye on the view through the window and trying to settle her nerves as the time passed with the arrival of Kemp but no sign of Glenna. Christina wasn't certain how Glenna would arrive, but she intended to greet her as soon as she could—and ask her a number of questions.

With the view of the stables, the young boy Colum came to mind, and Christina dismissed Janet, instructing her to see that he was taken some food.

She stood by the open window, breathing in the air as nausea built inside her. Her eyes strayed to the crest sitting on the desk, still in the same place. Lachlan's reaction to it had been a testament to how he viewed the Kincaid name and legacy rather than an indication of her skill. The name was everything to him. And with her thoughtlessness in agreeing to marry him—in *asking* him to marry her when she was carrying a MacKinnon child—she had sullied the Kincaid name.

Approaching hoofbeats sounded, and Christina whipped her head around to see Glenna heading in the direction of the stables, alone.

Christina hurried from the room, and Elizabeth peeked her head out from her bedchamber, a question in her eyes, likely regarding how Christina's conversation with Lachlan had gone. Christina had nothing to say on the matter. Nothing had changed.

"Glenna just arrived," Christina said, pulling her door shut. "Lachlan believes her to be in danger."

Elizabeth's eyes widened. "Danger?"

"He had no time to expound. I am going to her now, though. I think I shall take her through the servant door. If anyone should come asking for me, inform them that I am unwell and not receiving callers."

Elizabeth nodded, and Christina hurried downstairs and through the heavy front door.

Glenna was still in the stables, and she turned when she heard Christina's footsteps.

"Glenna!" Christina put out her hands in an invitation and relief.

Glenna looked somewhat breathless and bright-eyed, despite having arrived on horseback. "Mistress," she said, coming over and giving her hands to Christina.

Colum was seeing to Glenna's horse, but he glanced at the half-eaten bannock that sat on the chair Mr. Kemp stood next to. A few telling crumbs hung on Kemp's brown coat, and he watched Glenna and Christina intently.

Glenna stepped back slightly, her gaze moving to Christina's stomach. "Ye're...with child?" The watchful glint in her eyes made it clear she wasn't certain how Christina felt about the fact.

Christina's eyes flitted to Mr. Kemp. She didn't particularly want to have this conversation here.

"We can talk about everything inside," Christina said. "All that matters is that you are safe."

"I am," Glenna said with a breath of relief, "though my mind is playin' tricks on me, for I thought I was surely bein' followed."

"Come," Christina said, linking their arms together. "Let us go inside."

"Oy!" Colum's surprised yell filled the stables as a *thunk* sounded and Glenna crumpled beside Christina.

Whipping around, Christina found herself facing Mr. Kemp, holding a club, which he began to raise, his malicious gaze intent on Christina.

She stumbled backward, tripping on her petticoats and trying to recover her balance as she looked around her for anything that might be used to protect herself. She reached for the only thing in sight—a fraying rope hanging from a hook—and swung it with all her might at Kemp.

He howled, and his hand flew to his arm where the rope had made contact. She gathered it up as quickly as she could, watching Mr. Kemp's face contort with rage. The last thing she saw was Colum's aghast expression staring at her from behind Kemp, then darkness.

28

Lachlan urged his horse on over the dry dirt, sending up an anxious look at the skies above, where rounded white clouds were beginning to submit to dark, angry gray ones, and the light of day was showing signs of giving way to evening.

Finally, the trees opened to reveal the crooked lane that led into Craiglinne. Grudgingly, Lachlan pulled up on the reins. No matter how much confidence he had in his abilities, it wouldn't do to gallop through the toun when there were so many people crossing the lane.

He came up beside a white-haired man with a large sack slung over his stooped shoulder.

"Good day, sir," Lachlan said. "Can ye tell me where I might find the justice of the peace?"

The man didn't even look up at him as he replied. "Down the lane, third door from the end."

"Thank ye, sir."

The man grunted, and continued to shuffle along as Lachlan urged his horse to move to a trot.

When he reached the door in question, he swung down and hurried to rap on it in a way that conveyed the urgency he felt.

Gibson had said the ship wouldn't depart until dawn, but the captain had already changed his mind once, and if the approaching storm looked to arrive sooner than anticipated, it was possible he would alter his plans again.

Glenna hadn't had any idea that she was in any sort of danger when Lachlan had spoken to her. She *had* known the destination of the ship, though: the Colonies. She had been so astounded, so incredulous at what he was saying that it had taken him precious minutes to convince her of the plot's reality.

He might have successfully prevented them from whisking Glenna away, but he couldn't stop thinking of the other name on the list that sat in his pocket: *C Turner.*

The sooner he could assure himself he had the help of the justice of the peace, the sooner he could set to discovering the identity of Turner. He only hoped he had enough time. And, while he didn't begrudge doing whatever was in his power to save Glenna and whatever other innocent young woman had been targeted by Gibson and Angus, he couldn't help lamenting the timing of it all. He longed to be back with Christina, doing what he should have done in the first place: comforting her and reassuring her of his love.

It wasn't that he was reconciled to the fact that he would be the father to a MacKinnon. He wasn't. Truthfully, he didn't know how he would be. But he had to find a way to resign himself to reality.

He knocked on the door a second time, this time with even more force. A few heads of passing tounspeople turned toward him, wearing expressions of disapproval. He didn't have the time or energy to care, though.

The door of the next house down opened, and a woman emerged, eyes on Lachlan. "Mr. Fleming isna home," she said in Gaelic, a broom in hand. "Left an hour ago."

"Do ye ken when he'll return? Or where I might find him?"

"I dinna when he'll return, but there was a fuss at the

market earlier, so I reckon ye'll find him there." She jerked her head in the direction of the market.

Lachlan thanked her and hastened back onto his horse. This was the sort of delay he couldn't afford if he had any hope of saving the Turner girl. He hadn't any idea where she even lived.

"Wait!" he called out to the woman just before her door shut entirely.

She opened it again, looking at him impatiently.

"Do ye ken any Turners, ma'am?"

She gave a crooked smile, displaying a few missing teeth, and chuckled. "Aye, of course. Everyone kens the Turners."

"Any with a given name startin' with the letter C?"

She gave him a quizzical look.

He grimaced. It was likely the woman was unable to write. He fumbled for a moment, trying to decide how to convey his question in a different manner.

"Try the green door down the road," she said.

"Thank ye, ma'am." He turned his horse back the way they had come. It would only take a minute or two to inquire at the Turner house, then he would make his way to the market.

He dismounted and knocked on the door, twisting at his beard and tapping his foot on the ground. A small girl with dark hair and soot on her face opened the door to him, looking up at him with large, curious brown eyes. He was distracted for a moment by her petite features and innocent gaze. Glenna's words resounded within him: *ye'll do it because the bairn is innocent.* Would the baby Christina was carrying look like this sweet child?

There was a clearing of the throat, and Lachlan blinked, looking up to meet the gaze of the young man standing behind the little girl. He must have been thirteen or fourteen years old. He wore an expression of mixed wariness and curiosity as his eyes took in Lachlan's clothing and the well-groomed horse behind him.

Lachlan greeted him with a nod. "Is Turner yer name?"

"Aye, sir. Arthur Turner."

Lachlan hesitated, realizing how strange it was to appear at someone's door and make the sort of inquiries he needed to make. But there was no helping it—not when a life was at stake. "Do ye ken yer letters, Arthur?"

He nodded. "I learned 'em at school afore Pa died."

Lachlan glanced at the state of the small home behind the boy and girl. It was dismal inside—dark and cramped. "Have ye any sisters whose names begin with the letter C?"

The boy thought for a moment and shook his head. "Nay, sir. Only a brother."

"A brother," Lachlan said thoughtfully. He had been assuming that all the names on the list belonged to young women. Perhaps he had been wrong. "Where is he? And what's his name?"

Arthur shrugged. "Colum. But I've no' seen 'im since this mornin'. He's always off gettin' inta mischief."

Lachlan frowned. Perhaps the boys' tendency to explore would keep him safe. Or perhaps he was already gone. "Thank ye, lad." He took two coins from his pocket and gave them to the boy, whose eyes widened as he accepted them in a hand covered in dirt and calluses.

Again, Lachlan got up onto his horse, guiding it around in the direction of the market. He stopped short as he saw a man approach the door belonging to the justice of the peace.

"Sir!" he called before the man could disappear into the house.

The man stopped. His clothing was neat, and he held himself with a confidence that spoke of someone accustomed to speaking with authority.

"Are you the justice of the peace?" Lachlan asked.

"Aye, sir. I am. And who might ye be?"

Lachlan breathed a sigh of relief and hurried down from his horse, extending a hand. "The name is Lachlan Kincaid of Dunverlockie. Can I have a word with ye?"

C hristina leaned her head back on the tree she was propped against, wincing as her head made contact. She wiggled to shift her body so that she could sit more upright—a difficult task when her hands were tied behind her. Kemp must have carried her here.

She looked around at the tall trees and dense vegetation surrounding her. There was little light in the woods, and at first, she thought it was twilight. But a look up through the few patches free of branches above revealed storm clouds, roiling and moving at a rapid pace. The forest looked vaguely like the area surrounding Dunverlockie, but there was no way to know for certain. Thunder rumbled in the distance, and when it faded, she noticed the sound of a nearby river. Kemp could not have carried them far. They must be in the woods of Dunverlockie.

There was no sign of Kemp, but the boy Colum was sitting on a nearby stump, picking at the petals of a small flower. Where was Glenna? The question filled Christina's mind and heart with dread.

"Colum," she said.

His head whipped up, and he rose from the stump, flower petals sprinkled from his breeches to the forest floor as he came toward her. "Shh. Ye canna talk," he said in Gaelic.

"What do you mean?"

He sent a nervous glance around. "Mr. Kemp doesna wish for ye ta talk."

Christina pursed her lips, watching Colum with an evaluative glance. "What does he intend to do with me?"

Colum shrugged his shoulders. "He didna tell me. Just said I'd get another dram for 'elpin' 'im."

She raised a brow, but it tugged at the tender skin on her scalp, causing her to flinch. "And you believe he shall give it to you? He ate your bannock, did he not?"

Colum's brows knitted together in a sulky expression that accentuated his youth, and he nodded.

"He should not have done so," she said. "Help me out of these ropes, and I promise you as much food as you could hope for—ale, bannocks, potatoes. For you *and* your family."

She watched the debate in his eyes, and she knew a hint of guilt for urging him to go against Kemp when the prospect of disobeying him so clearly frightened the boy.

Leaves rustled, the crunching of footsteps approached, and Colum whirled around toward the source of the sounds.

Christina's heart picked up speed. Lachlan would surely come. He had promised to return.

But it was Mr. Kemp who appeared with Glenna in his arms, her head lolling back.

"Glenna!" Christina cried out.

"Quiet!" Mr. Kemp said, setting Glenna down in front of another tree. He stood and directed a menacing look at Colum. "Ye've no' been talkin' ta her, have ye?"

Colum sent a wide-eyed look at Christina and shook his head rapidly.

Glenna's head lolled a bit then came up, her closed lids fluttering then shutting hard again. No doubt her head felt like Christina's did. Christina had seen the force with which Kemp had hit Glenna, and her blood ran hot at the memory. She had thought Lachlan overly suspicious when he had cast doubt upon Kemp's character.

She had been wrong.

"What are you doing, Kemp?" Christina asked.

Her voice seemed to rouse Glenna more, and she managed to open her eyes, though they narrowed in discomfort.

"Quiet!" Kemp said again. Beads of sweat glistened on his forehead, and his actions had a jitteriness to them that brought up a host of questions in Christina's mind.

More footsteps approached, and Kemp swung around this way and that, holding a knife threateningly in his hand.

Mr. Gibson's form soon appeared, and Kemp lowered the knife.

"Gibson," he said. "'Tis you."

"Of course 'tis I," Gibson said snappishly. He looked at Glenna then Christina, and his eyes widened as they rested on her.

"I never meant to take her." Kemp's voice was full of apology but also fear. "But she was with the lass when she arrived, and she put up a fight. I didna have a choice."

Gibson shook his head, gaze fixed on Christina, excitement in his eyes. "Nay, 'tis better than I had hoped. MacKinnon wants 'er on that ship—'tis why he was so put out when he discovered the timeline had been put forward. He'll pay well when he finds we've managed it."

Christina stilled then looked at Glenna. Ship? What were they talking about?

"Where are you taking us?" she asked.

Gibson looked at her, a little sneer growing on his lips. "Come, Kemp, Turner." He pulled up Glenna by the arm. "Let's get 'em aboard afore this storm makes it impossible. I dinna wish ta be caught out on the seas. Not for what 'e's payin' us."

Kemp came over to Christina and tugged her up by the arm. Once on her feet, she yanked her arm from his grip. He took it back in hand, pulling her toward him so that her face was inches from his. "Ye'll no' give me trouble, wench!"

"Will I not?" She stared him in the eyes, nostrils flaring.

Kemp's sneer grew, and he held up his knife, bringing it closer to her neck. "Nay. Ye'll no'. No' if ye wish ta spare that bonnie throat of yers."

She raised her chin, swallowing, and the cool metal of the blade touched her neck. Colum came up beside them, watching with large, panicked eyes.

Kemp gave a kick at the boy, and Colum scurried out of the way.

"Make haste, Kemp," Gibson called back at them.

Kemp stared Christina in the eye for another moment then dropped his knife and pulled her forward roughly. She allowed him to guide her along, still able to feel where the blade had touched her neck.

They walked through the trees, climbing over fallen branches and skirting bushes. The sound of the river grew louder all the while, and Christina thought on what Lachlan had said on the day of their wedding. His father had forbidden him from following the river, saying it would take him out to sea. Apparently he had not been lying. The sea must be their destination if she and Glenna were fated to board a ship.

Her eyes searched her surroundings for something—anything—that could assist her in escaping. Would Lachlan come for them? Or would he find himself well rid of the tangled marriage Christina had forced him into?

The mere thought brought tears to her eyes, and she blinked quickly. She wouldn't show Kemp or Gibson weakness.

29

Finally, they reached the mouth of the river, which spilled into the dark sea. In the distance, a lightning strike lit the darkening horizon.

Christina glanced around the small cove they were emerging into. Three men stood waiting, with two small boats on the sand behind them. With their arrival on the coast, the protection the trees had offered was gone, and a little gust of wind blew at Christina's hair.

The three men approached, one walking in front of the other two and wearing clothing that proclaimed him the leader among them. He was frowning as he looked at Christina.

"What is it?" Gibson asked.

"These are the three?"

Christina followed his gaze from her to Glenna to Colum. The boy looked confused, eyes flitting back and forth between the shipman and Kemp. He couldn't understand what any of them were saying.

"Ye're sendin' the lad too?" Glenna asked, aghast.

"'Tis for 'is own good," Kemp said. He turned to Colum and addressed him in Gaelic. "Ye'll do well in the Colonies, Colum.

And ye'll no' be a drain on yer family there. One less mouth ta feed for yer mother."

Colum's eyes widened, and Christina's did the same.

The Colonies. They were to sail to the Colonies.

"This one"—the shipman indicated Christina—"willna fetch as much as the others. She looks soft. Unused ta work. The lad will fetch more than her."

"Perhaps ye can find another use for her than hard labor," Kemp said suggestively, chuckling as he put a hand to the curl that hung at her neck and stroked it.

She spat in his face, and Gibson stopped Kemp's retaliation with a hand.

"MacKinnon isna concerned with how much she fetches," Gibson said clearly.

The shipman shrugged. "Verra well. I can give ye eleven for the lad, nine for the short lass, and seven for the tall one."

Christina yanked her arm away from Kemp as the shipman paid Gibson in coins. "We are not for sale! You cannot take us against our wills."

"Captain's orders, miss." The shipman glanced up at the sky. "We had best be settin' off. The captain plans ta set off as soon as we're aboard."

Panic bloomed inside Christina. They were to sail for the Colonies, where they would be sold into indentured servitude. But what could she possibly do? They were woefully outnumbered and deprived of the use of their hands. Christina could only hope they would untie them once they had boarded the ship. But, even if they did, what could be done? Would they dock somewhere to replenish their supplies before setting sail for the Colonies? Someplace where she, Glenna, and Colum might escape? Or had they done that already before anchoring here?

The thought of being separated from Elizabeth and her

siblings, of being separated from Lachlan sent her heart into a frenzy. She had never even told Lachlan she loved him.

If she was to end up in the Colonies, her one hope was to find Alistair there.

The shipman put out a hand for her, but Kemp pulled her away from his reach. "MacKinnons orders is ta see them aboard ourselves."

The shipman paused then looked over his shoulder at the rough waters and shrugged.

Kemp held her arm tightly and guided her toward one of the large rowboats that sat on the sand, leaning to one side with water lapping against it as the waves rolled in and then back out. The wind was beginning to pick up and the waters becoming more choppy.

"You cannot force us aboard that ship," Christina said as they approached the boat. "And you cannot sell us into servitude." Kemp offered no response. "I am with child!" she said.

"No' my problem." He roughly handed her into the boat, pushing her down onto one of the wooden slats and following after her as the boat tipped precariously from side to side. Glenna and Colum were being helped in by Gibson.

Christina looked at Colum, whose eyes were as full of fear as of tears.

The shipman came over and stepped into the boat.

"What are ye doin'?" Gibson asked.

The shipman looked at him, raising a skeptical brow. "Do either of ye ken how to row a boat in waters like this?"

"Aye," Kemp said, while Gibson remained silent.

The shipman nodded and went to the head of the boat. "Help me push it out," he said to Gibson.

The two of them waited for a wave to roll in then heaved. The boat slid in the sand until it was deep enough for the water to buoy it up, and the two men clambered in, causing the boat to rock from side to side.

Without her hands to stabilize her, Christina kept her balance with difficulty, and the movement stirred her stomach. She tried to breathe deeply, but the memory of Lachlan rubbing her back as she leaned out of the window in her bedchamber brought her heart into her throat as the first raindrops began to fall.

She found Glenna's gaze on her, solemn and apologetic.

"I'm so sorry, mistress." Her voice was nearly drowned by the sound of the waves.

Christina shook her head and mustered a smile she was certain fell far short of convincing. She couldn't maintain eye contact with Glenna, but looking at Colum only heightened her emotions. Her own fears and regrets were eclipsed at the sight of him, and she promised herself to protect him as best as she could, whatever happened.

She set her gaze on the shore, watching as it grew more distant—a reminder of everything she was leaving behind. Lachlan would ensure Elizabeth was taken care of, at least. And her family too.

She shut her eyes, focusing on the movement of the boat and the rhythmic sound of the oars splashing as they went in and out of the water, hoping it would help to alleviate the nausea. But the motion only aggravated it.

"I feel unwell," she said, eyes still closed.

"Sure ye do!" Kemp said with an amused snort.

"I truly—" Her body heaved forward of its own accord, expelling its contents onto Kemp beside her.

Lachlan frowned at the sweat glistening on his horse's neck and the froth at its mouth. They were nearing Dunverlockie, though, where the horse could finally rest. Lachlan, however, could not. His work was only just beginning.

Once Mr. Fleming, the justice, had been informed of the situation, it took some time for them to find him a horse so that he could accompany Lachlan back to Dunverlockie. There were still a few pieces of information Lachlan was missing in order to put a stop to whatever Angus and Gibson had planned, and without a way to know where the Turner boy had gone, there was no way to prevent his being taken. He needed to find out what the Wash was.

"Ye set a fine pace, sir," said Mr. Fleming, breathing as quickly as though he had been the one galloping to Dunverlockie instead of the horse he rode.

Lachlan didn't respond. There was no sign of Kemp—or indeed anyone—in the stables, but there was no time to properly tend to the horses himself. He would have to send a servant out to look for Kemp or attend to the duties, if needed.

"Come," Lachlan said, and they made their way to the castle.

They opened the door and stepped inside to the sight of Elizabeth speaking in an urgent voice with three of the servants in the entry hall. Her gaze immediately flitted to the door at the arrival of Lachlan and Mr. Fleming, though, and she stopped speaking, rushing over to him.

Elizabeth reached out and grabbed hold of his arm. "Have you seen them?"

"Seen whom?" The exigency in her tone unsettled him even more than he already was.

"Christina and Glenna," Elizabeth said, and the worry deepened on her pale brow. "I cannot find them anywhere, and none of the servants have seen them."

Lachlan stared at her, trying to understand.

"But Glenna did come?"

She nodded. "Christina said she was going out to greet her. She meant to take her through the servant entrance and told me to deny any visitors. But I've asked all the servants. None of them ever saw Christina *or* Glenna, and they're nowhere in the castle."

Lachlan looked to where the servants stood, looking nervous, waiting to be instructed. Christina was universally liked amongst the staff—it was natural that they would be concerned at her sudden disappearance.

Lachlan tried to focus his mind, to keep it from venturing into the dangerous territory it insisted upon visiting: imagining the very worst reasons Christina and Glenna might have vanished at the same time.

"She went ta greet Glenna at the stables, ye said?" Lachlan asked.

Elizabeth nodded hurriedly.

Lachlan thought on the empty stables he and Mr. Fleming had just come from, and he turned to the servants. "Has anyone seen Kemp? He wasna in the stables when we arrived."

All three servants shook their heads, but one of the maids spoke. "I've no' seen 'im since midday, sir, but the lad in the stables might ken where he is?"

Lachlan frowned. "What lad?"

She shrugged a shoulder. "The mistress asked me ta take a bit of food to 'im. Just a wee lad, he was. Colum was 'is name. I've seen 'im a time or two in the toun afore."

Lachlan's focus riveted on the maid. "Colum?"

She nodded.

"Do ye ken his family's name?"

Her eyes looked blank, but she nudged the footman beside her. "Do ye remember 'is last name? 'Tis the family as lost their father a year or so ago."

"Turner?" Lachlan supplied.

They both looked at him.

"Aye, Turner. That's it," said the maid.

Lachlan swore under his breath.

"What?" Elizabeth asked, gripping his arm again. "What is

it? Tell me, Lachlan. Christina told me nothing except that Glenna was in danger. What sort of danger?"

Lachlan balled his hands into fists to stop their trembling. He had never considered that Christina might be in the same danger as Glenna. Surely Angus and Gibson—and Kemp, apparently—wouldn't take someone like Christina? It was madness.

"'Tis Angus," he said to Elizabeth. "We believe he means ta put them on a ship bound for the Colonies."

Elizabeth's grip on his arm tightened, and he could feel her fingernails through his coat and shirtsleeves.

Lachlan turned back to the servants. "Do any of ye ken what the Wash is? 'Tis a place—a location somewhere near."

Janet's head came up. "Aye, sir. 'Tis the wee cove nearby where the river flows inta the sea. I heard it spoken of by Mr. Kemp and Mr. MacKinnon once."

Lachlan looked at Mr. Fleming, mutual understanding dawning in their eyes simultaneously. So, that was where the boats would depart from to make their way to the Falcon. It all made sense now—it was the same place the Jacobite soldiers had been meant to meet on the morning of their failed escape.

"Come," he said to Mr. Fleming, and without waiting, he strode to the door.

The clacking of heels on stone followed him, and he looked around to see Elizabeth following.

"I am coming with you," she said.

"Nay."

"You cannot stop me." Her chin was lifted, her eyes alight.

"Ye're right," he said. "But I ask ye ta stay all the same."

She shook her head and moved to open the door herself.

"Stubborn Innes women," Lachlan said under his breath. But he secretly admired her refusal to submit to his request. If it had been Elizabeth in danger, he knew Christina would have done the same.

The sun had not yet dipped below the horizon, but it might as well have, given how dark the landscape was, enveloped in threatening storm clouds. It might start raining at any time, making their task even more difficult to carry out.

What if they were too late? What if the captain had decided to set sail tonight instead of in the morning to outrun the storm?

All of his preoccupation with Gordon MacKinnon's child seemed so trivial now, in the face of losing Christina.

All that mattered was saving her and the others.

R ain had begun to fall, hitting the dirt path and eliciting the fresh scent Lachlan normally relished. But all he could think now was what it meant for the ship. No sane captain would choose to sail in a storm he could avoid. It might well be too late.

He refused to let his mind dwell on such a thought, focusing instead on the path as it sloped downward and the sound of Mr. Fleming's footsteps following closely behind. He had never been this far down the path, and it felt interminable. It had to end sometime. Dunverlockie was not so very far from the coast.

Finally, the trees began to grow more sparse, and the ominous view of the sea spread before them. Heart hammering louder than the waves and rain, Lachlan's eyes searched the scene frantically. The rain acted like a wall of mist, but his sights landed on two boats, rowing out toward the foggy beyond. None of the occupants seemed to have noted Lachlan, Elizabeth, or Mr. Fleming's presence. The men were intent on the task of rowing, while the others had their backs turned toward the shore.

Lachlan's gaze scoured the cove for another boat, but there

was nothing but sand and moss-covered rocks. He had no way to go after them.

He looked at the boats again. They were only a few fathoms from shore, but they had the advantage of oars. And yet, he couldn't stand and watch as the woman he loved was rowed beyond his reach.

Running toward the water, he pulled off his boots and stripped off his jacket and hat, letting them fall forgotten to the ground.

"Sir!" called Mr. Fleming. "Ye canna...."

But Lachlan paid him no heed, hastening into the water as fast as the waves would allow then diving into one that built and crested before him.

And then he swam. He swam as fast as his arms would take him, controlling his breathing as water—both rain and sea—pelted his face. Slowly but steadily, the boats drew closer and his view of them became clearer, more distinct. His arms ached from exertion, and his chest screamed at him to stop swimming, to allow the waves to consume him, if only for a moment of rest.

But he could see the forms of Christina and Glenna in the nearest boat, and, with a silent plea to God, he increased his efforts once more. Whether it was the view of Christina or the prayer he had offered, a burst of energy filled him, as if his arms were moving of their own volition.

But the sensation did not last, and it was just as he thought he might expire that his outstretched hand grasped the back edge of the boat. The feel of something solid—something other than fluid water—filled him with a sense of victory, and he savored the opportunity to hang upon the boat for a moment.

But his presence was remarked, and he heard the chaotic fuss it created.

He swung himself toward the long side of the boat and hoisted himself up, only to be met with the side of an oar to the jaw. Stunned, he staggered and fell back into the water, taking in a gulp of the salty fluid.

He grabbed for the edge of the boat again in time to see Christina send a foot into Kemp's stomach. Gibson rose to his feet, but Glenna hurled her shoulder into his gut, and the young boy behind pulled Gibson back by his arm.

With every ounce of strength he could muster, Lachlan pulled himself up and into the boat, tumbling onto the boards. He hurried up, scrambling to his feet in time to deflect the fist thrown at him by a man he didn't recognize. He returned the gesture, and his hand made contact with the man's cheek, sending him overboard.

Boat rocking beneath him and panting like a dog, Lachlan readied himself for Kemp and Gibson, both of whom had recovered from the assaults upon them and had their eyes on him, full of menace.

Kemp was closest to him, and Lachlan turned his attention on the portly man, clenching his fists in preparation. But before Kemp could step over to him, Christina had leaned back on her seat and sent another heeled shoe into the man's chest. He toppled backwards and into the water.

"Look out!" Glenna's urgent cry brought Lachlan around in time to see Gibsons' form descending upon him.

He threw a hasty, clumsy punch, and Gibson ducked before sending his own punch into Lachlan's shoulder. Lachlan stumbled back and onto Christina. He pushed himself up, feeling as though he might fall right back over, so little control did he have over his weak limbs. His injured leg, more than anything else, demanded attention. He sent another exhausted punch at Gibson, and the man faltered backward. The young boy clambered over the wood board and, with all his might, shoved Gibson, whose leg hit the side of the boat, causing him to fall over its edge and into the water.

Lachlan dropped onto the wooden seat behind him, spent.

Gibson's hands appeared on the rim of the boat, but Colum stamped on one and then the other, yelling in Gaelic, "Ye'll no' come back in here!"

Gibson fell back with a cry. The other two men seemed to have thought better of attempting a return and were instead swimming toward the other boat.

"Colum! Untie me!" Glenna spoke to Colum in Gaelic. "Hurry! We need ta get ashore. They'll be comin' for us."

Colum nodded and set to the bulky knot at the small of her back.

Lachlan turned to Christina. She was soaked and her cheeks covered in raindrops. She turned her back to him, and with fumbling, weak fingers, he untied the knot around her wrists.

She rubbed at them then sat on the board behind her, taking the oars in hand. She and Glenna shared a glance and began rowing.

"Nay," Lachlan said, moving to take Christina's place.

She shook her head and continued rowing. "Rest. If they follow us ashore, we will need whatever strength you can muster to fight them off again."

"But"—he looked to her stomach.

She put a hand on his and looked at him intently. "You have protected me for so long, Lachlan. Let me protect you for once."

He swallowed and nodded.

The wind was blowing against them, and the roughness of the water made the task even more difficult. Lachlan watched with guilt and pride as Christina and Glenna rowed them toward shore, Colum attempting to handle the third set of oars with questionable success. So mesmerized was Lachlan by the determination in Christina's eyes, it was only when the boat skidded into the sand and Mr. Fleming and Elizabeth pulled it to shore that Lachlan saw the way she shook from fatigue as her hands dropped from the oars.

The four of them clambered out of the boat with the help of Elizabeth and Mr. Fleming.

"Go!" said Mr. Fleming, pointing them in the direction of the woods.

Elizabeth had one arm protectively around Colum and the other linked with Glenna's. Lachlan grabbed for his boots, pulling them on and looking at Mr. Fleming. Exhausted as Lachlan was, how could he leave the justice to handle the three men on his own?

Mr. Fleming pulled his pistol from its place at his side, readying it as the boat approached the shore. "Go." His voice was firm. "See ta yer wife and the others." His gaze moved to Colum, and his face screwed up. "He's the same age as my own son."

The boat slid onto shore.

"Hurry!" Mr. Fleming called.

Lachlan nodded and turned to Christina, taking her hand in his, and together they ran toward the trees, their feet sinking into the wet sand with each step.

30

The cover of the trees sheltered the four of them from the rain that pelted towards earth from the abyss above, but in the dark, they tripped over stray rocks and slid in the quickly forming mud. Only the frequent lightning in the distance provided light for the path.

Lachlan kept a firm hold on Christina's arm, steadying her at need, while the other extended out into the dark before them, searching for any obstruction on their path.

A particularly bright strike of lightning illuminated their surroundings, revealing the small grove the path passed through—the place Lachlan and Christina had been married— just as they stepped out of it and into the black of the woods. Rain pattered on the leaves and thunder rumbled in the distance, but none of them spoke, too focused on their goal.

Finally, the path came to an end, and the indistinct form of the castle loomed before them, the glow from its windows providing a welcome and consistent source of light after so long spent in a darkness punctuated only by brief flashes.

They hurried into the entry hall, and Lachlan shut the door with a thud behind them, turning to Christina. His hair was matted to his head and dripped onto his sodden coat as he searched her face, his breath coming as quickly as hers.

"I saw ye, sir," Colum said breathlessly. His eyes were alight with excitement. "Saw ye swimming up ta the boat, and I kent that the others were no match for ye!"

Christina couldn't stop a breathless smile, and Lachlan held her gaze for another moment, reluctant to redirect his attention.

He finally turned his head to Colum. "Even after swimmin' such a distance?"

The boy nodded emphatically. "Aye, sir!"

Elizabeth smiled and put her arm about him. "Come, child. Let us get you before a fire and send a message to your mother. You, too, Glenna. Both of you are soaked to the bone."

Colum allowed himself to be shepherded, and the last thing Christina heard was him asking, "Are there any bannocks left?"

Glenna lingered and approached Christina and Lachlan, her hands clasped at her chest and tears in her eyes. "Thank ye. Thank ye for savin' us." She swallowed then turned and followed after Elizabeth and Colum.

They both watched her disappear down the corridor, and with every step she took, the air in the entry hall grew thicker.

"We should get ye warm and dry," Lachlan finally said. "Ye'll catch a cold."

She gave him a quizzical look but followed him to the stairs. "I appreciate your concern for me, but what of yourself? Do you intend to simply defy the threat of illness?"

He smiled down at her in a way that made her heart flutter and hope. "Nay, lass. But I'm only one man, and there are two of ye ta consider now."

He nodded at her stomach, which lurched at the reference to the thing that had come between them—the subject that hovered over them like the storm outside. It couldn't be avoided; it had to be weathered. And only once it was would she know what, if anything, was left between them.

They reached the door to her bedchamber first, and Lachlan opened it for her, making room for her to pass through. She did so slowly, hesitantly. A trail of water and dirt had followed her from the entry hall. Every article of clothing she wore was soaked through. But more than she wanted to shed her water-laden garments, she wished to speak with Lachlan.

She was being unreasonable, though. It was only natural that they should change their clothing before having such a conversation.

Once she was in the room, she turned to him. "Thank you for coming for me—for us."

He gave a slow nod, a hint of confusion in his eyes.

With a small smile of thanks, she began to slowly shut the door.

He stopped it with a hand. "Christina, wait." His frown deepened. "Did ye think I'd no' come?"

She stared at him, uncertain how to respond. She lifted a shoulder, afraid to voice what she had thought. "I feared you might be relieved—as I was after Gordon's death."

Her words were soft and quiet, but Lachlan looked as though she had struck him.

"Christina," he said. "I'd have followed ye ta the Colonies if 'twas what was necessary."

She swallowed the growing lump in her throat, but it stuck there stubbornly.

He stepped into the room and put his hands on her arms, pinning her in place with the intensity in his eyes. "I love ye, Christina. That has never been in any doubt. And I dinna care that the bairn has MacKinnon blood. No' anymore, at least. My love for ye runs stronger and deeper than my hatred of the MacKinnons." He looked down at her stomach, taking a hand from her arm and placing it there. "The bairn is a part of ye, and for that alone, I'll love the child as if 'twas my own flesh and blood. The past doesna matter—only the future, and that bairn *is* the future. Our future."

Christina covered his hand with hers, unable to speak for a moment. "I hope there will be others, too, after this one." She looked up at him, and watched his throat bob and a quivering smile grow on his lips.

"I hope so, too." His smile faded slightly, and his brows drew together again. "Can ye forgive me?"

"Forgive you?"

He lowered his gaze. "For leavin' ye. When ye needed me most."

She put her hand on his whiskered cheek and guided his face up so she could look him in the eye. "You returned when I needed you most."

He shut his eyes and set his forehead on hers.

"When I was on that boat," she said, "I thought I would never see you again. That I would never be able to tell you that I love you." She pulled back enough to look at him again. "Whatever the past, I will always need you most in the present."

He pushed aside one of the locks of hair that the rain had matted to her forehead. "I *am* here in the present, lass." He wrapped an arm about her waist. "And I dinna think ye'll ever succeed in forcin' me ta leave."

"I would never attempt it," she said.

He leaned his head in, capturing her lips with his. They were warm and soft and wet with rainwater. But she wanted more—she wanted him to hold her so that nothing could take her away from him again. Grasping his wet shirt, she pulled him toward her, and he seemed to understand. He moved his hand up from the small of her back, and she trembled under its touch as it became more firm, binding her to him.

He pulled away, catching his breath and looking at her with

concern. "Ye're shiverin'." He chafed her arms. "I meant ta get ye warm and dry, and here I am, keepin' ye in these garments, drenched in water."

"I don't want to be protected right now. I want to be held."

One of his brows shot up, and he smiled mischievously then scooped her into his arms. "And if I can do both?"

He shut the door with a kick of the foot and walked over to the fire that blazed in the grate

She laughed, but the sound was soon cut off by the lips that pressed to hers.

She gladly surrendered.

EPILOGUE

With Elizabeth and Glenna in their wake, Lachlan and Christina stepped down from the carriage onto the streets of Fort William. They had left Dunverlockie safe in the hands of Lachlan's kinsmen—five Kincaids had arrived so far, bringing a level of security to the castle that relieved much of the burden Lachlan had been feeling as laird. It would be foolish of Angus to attempt to harm Christina again, but a man who would kidnap another man's wife right under his nose could not be trusted to stop at anything. He hoped today would be a reckoning for Angus and the MacKinnons.

Young Colum Turner stood at the horses' heads, looking proud.

Lachlan gave Christina his arm and walked over to the boy. He was taking well to his position in the stables at Dunverlockie. He reminded Lachlan a bit of himself at that age.

"Are ye ready?" Lachlan asked him.

Colum nodded, and looked to the new Dunverlockie groom, Mr. Bannerman, who smiled and took the boy's place holding the reins.

Lachlan surveyed Colum. He looked much more

presentable than when Lachlan had first seen him, and his eyes were almost worshipful as they looked on his master.

Christina smoothed the small jacket Colum wore and looked at him with concern in her eyes. "Both Mr. Kemp and Mr. Gibson will be there," she said in Gaelic. "You understand that?"

He nodded. "Aye, miss. And I'm no' afeared of them."

Lachlan smiled, gripping Colum's shoulder. "That's right, lad. Ye need no' fear them anymore. Just tell yer story and dinna let Kemp or Gibson or any lawyer frighten ye. Come. We should be on our way."

They began the short walk to the courthouse, and Colum fell in behind them with Glenna and Elizabeth.

"You have the documents?" Christina asked Lachlan anxiously.

He smiled down at her and patted the pocket of his coat. "Aye, my love. And when ye ask me a fourth time, the answer will be the same."

She sent him a sheepish look. "Have I truly asked three times? Surely it has only been two."

He shook his head with a laugh and bent to kiss her forehead as they approached the small building that housed the courts.

"Dinna fash yerself," he said, pressing her hand on his arm. "We've a strong case against Angus. And all that matters is that both you and the bairn are safe."

As if on cue, the door of the carriage that had come to a stop in front of them opened, and Angus stepped down, followed by Malcolm MacKinnon and another kinsman.

It was the first time they had seen any of the MacKinnons since the abduction, and, despite promising himself that he would allow the court of law to see justice served, all Lachlan's muscles went rigid, his grip on Christina's hand tightening involuntarily.

Angus allowed his gaze to travel over the group of them slowly and deliberately. There was no air of fear or doubt about him. He looked, as ever, self-assured, even at the prospect of his own criminal trial.

"Good day to all of you," Angus said. His gaze lingered on Christina and Glenna. "I had understood that Miss Douglas and Mrs. Kincaid were set to take a journey to the Colonies. What a pleasant surprise to see you here."

Lachlan pulled his arm free of Christina's, intent on replacing the sneer on Angus's face with something more fitting, but Christina held him back, sending her own smile at Angus.

"I hope you still find it pleasant at the end of the trial," she said.

"I see you've brought your minions to protect you," Elizabeth chimed in, looking at Malcolm and the other MacKinnon. "How very inspiring is their loyalty. Do you feed them scraps of food from the table as a trophy for their dog-like devotion?"

Malcolm MacKinnon's brows snapped together, but he said nothing.

Elizabeth tilted her head to the side with a faux smile. "And look how you've trained them to not even bark without your command. It is terribly endearing." She put out a hesitant hand. "Will they bite if I attempt to pet them?"

Angus's smile flickered. "How unbridled is your tongue, Miss Innes. You could do with a bit of training yourself. The right man could break you to bridle."

Before Lachlan knew what was happening, Christina had stepped forward and slapped Angus across the face. She lingered in front of him for a moment, chest rising and falling rapidly, then moved back beside Lachlan. She took in a deep breath and displayed a satisfied smile. Unable to understand the conversation that had been taking place around him, Colum stared wide-eyed at the turn of events.

Angus blinked with surprise, and his cheek was taking on a red hue.

"I believe I owed you at least one of those," Christina said.

Pride flared up inside Lachlan—along with a desire to laugh. Somehow, there was just as much satisfaction in watching Christina strike Angus as if he had done it himself. It was a far cry from what the man deserved, but he trusted the court would remedy that as much as it could. He had promised Angus that, if he hurt Christina again, it would be the last thing he did, and he had been intent on seeing that through once Christina and the others were safe and well. But Christina had convinced him against it. Her desire to see Angus brought to account was no match for her desire to keep her husband out of trouble and by her side.

She looked up at him. "Shall we go inside, my love? We wouldn't want to miss the spectacle that awaits us."

With great effort, Lachlan suppressed a smile and nodded. "Aye."

He inclined his head at Angus and his kinsmen, and the five of them scaled the stairs to the courthouse. Once they had passed into the antechamber, Lachlan looked down at his wife, a teasing smile on his lips.

"I must confess," he said, "I'm feelin' a bit threatened."

Christina raised her brows and stopped walking, allowing Elizabeth and Glenna to pass them by and into the next room. "Threatened?"

"Aye. It seems ye dinna need me. 'Tis obvious ye're capable of protectin' yerself."

"Have I not always said so?"

He chuckled. "I suppose ye have."

She reached up a hand to his face, smiling at his exaggerated disappointment. "Would you rather be needed or wanted?"

He considered her question. "Both?"

She laughed and went up on her tiptoes. "And both you are."

He dipped his head and kissed her, savoring her words and the feeling of his lips on hers. Christina had given him so much more than he had ever dared hope for: the home of his forebears, a wife he loved more than himself, and a future full of hope, now drained of the desire for vengeance Lachlan had been so set upon when he had first arrived in Kildonnan. The bairn she carried inside her was a perfect embodiment of the decision they had made together: to fill their life and home with love, to leave the past behind and focus on the beauty of the present and a future more promising than they ever could have imagined.

"Come," Christina said as the door opened to admit Angus and his men. "Let us see justice carried out."

THE END

R ead the next book in the series, *The Enemy and Miss Innes,* to find out what happens next in the Tales from the Highlands series.

All that stands between him and freedom? Turning her hatred to love.

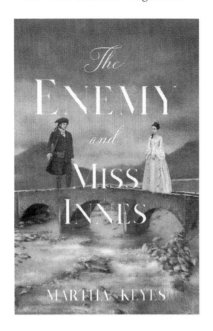

AUTHOR'S NOTE

I believe in the power of history, I am fascinated by it, and I read history books regularly, but I am not a historian; I am a storyteller. As such, there are undoubtedly flaws in my work. But I have done my best to ground the story in history while expanding upon it and, in some cases, taking a bit of license as I felt it merited.

The middle of the 18th century was an incredibly tumultuous time in the Scottish Highlands. The influence and the balance of power was shifting away from the clan system, which had held both for so long, to the Crown in London, which was trying valiantly to make order out of what it viewed as the chaos and fractured loyalties in the rugged Highlands.

The state of language in mid-1700s Scotland was complex. Depending upon location and social class, a person might speak English, Scots, Gaelic, or a combination of the three. After debating on the subject, I attempted to give a flavor to the dialogue to help ground it in the Highlands while avoiding anything I thought might detract from the story too much for readers. I have used that "flavor" to help demonstrate the background of characters.

Lachlan, though initially raised in an environment where he was likely taught English and Gaelic, has spent the majority of his life in the army, surrounded by Highlanders of varying classes, hence his accent, which is similar to Glenna's. Christina, Elizabeth, and Angus would all have been fluent in both English (spoken with a Scottish accent, of course) and Gaelic.

This story was born in my mind as I read about the Jacobite leaders whose estates were forfeited after the failed rebellion of 1745-1746. The majority of these estates were auctioned off, as is the case with the fictional Dunverlockie. Other Jacobite estates were taken over by the Crown and managed by a committee in an attempt to modernize the Highlands.

While the Kincaids had been in existence for hundreds of years, they were not a recognized clan during the 18th century. Their coat of arms was not registered until in 1808, and no one was referred to as Chief of the Name of Kincaid until the mid-1900s. I chose to use the name in my story despite this.

The part of the story which deals with abduction is an expansion upon the historical record. Up until the end of the 1700s, there was a large servant trade between Scotland and the Colonies, supplied primarily by the transportation of convicted felons but supplemented by those escaping religious or political persecution and poverty. While many—even a majority—of those who sailed to the Colonies as indentured servants seem to have agreed to the terms of their voyage and sale, contemporary reports and court cases detail the use of coercion in many cases and suggest more forceful means in others. Kidnapping was only a misdemeanor at the time. It did not become a felony until 1814. Other manipulative methods like outright lies, deceptive promises, and impairing the victim's judgment with alcohol were not against the law.

Marriage laws in Scotland differed significantly from those in England. There were a number of ways and methods whereby a marriage could be recognized as legally binding, including a declaration by the couple in front of witnesses that they agreed to take one another as man and wife. Once married, nearly everything belonging to the wife became the husband's (the exceptions being things like clothing and other feminine articles). The wife could not act for herself legally. If the death of one of the spouses preceded a year of marriage, and if no child had been born within that year, the marriage was essentially dissolved, and things returned to the state they were in prior to the marriage. In Christina's case, this meant that Dunverlockie would fall to Angus. Scottish inheritance law also dictated that a child born within the bonds of marriage was the legal child of the parents, regardless of the child's true paternity, unless it could be proved otherwise.

Thank you so much for reading *The Widow and the Highlander*. I hope you enjoyed Lachlan and Christina's story.

OTHER TITLES BY MARTHA KEYES

If you enjoyed this book, make sure to check out my other books:

Tales from the Highlands

The Widow and the Highlander (Book One)

The Enemy and Miss Innes (Book Two)

The Innkeeper and the Fugitive (Book Three)

The Gentleman and the Maid (Book Four)

Families of Dorset

Wyndcross: A Regency Romance (Book One)

Isabel: A Regency Romance (Book Two)

Cecilia: A Regency Romance (Book Three)

Hazelhurst: A Regency Romance (Book Four)

Phoebe: A Regency Romance (Series Novelette)

Regency Shakespeare

A Foolish Heart (Book One)

My Wild Heart (Book Two)

True of Heart (Book Three)

Other Titles

Of Lands High and Low

The Highwayman's Letter (Sons of Somerset Book 5)

A Seaside Summer (Timeless Regency Romance Book 17)

The Christmas Foundling (Belles of Christmas: Frost Fair Book Five)

Goodwill for the Gentleman (Belles of Christmas Book Two)

The Road through Rushbury (Seasons of Change Book One)

Eleanor: A Regency Romance

Join my Newsletter to keep in touch and learn more about British history! I try to keep it fun and interesting.

OR follow me on BookBub to see my recommendations and get alerts about my new releases.

ACKNOWLEDGMENTS

There are always so many people to thank with any given book! First and foremost, my husband deserves those thanks. He makes everything possible and never complains about the strangeness that is life married to an author.

Thank you to my critique group partners and dear friends, Kasey, Deborah, and Jess. I count myself so fortunate to associate with you and to receive your input every week.

Thanks to my editor, Jenny, and to all those who provided beta feedback.

Thank you to Nancy Mayer for her willingness to share her wealth of knowledge and to point me to valuable resources.

Thank you to my mom, who cheers me on every step of the way and drops everything to read my first drafts.

This book wouldn't be here without any of these people and many others.

ABOUT THE AUTHOR

Martha Keyes was born, raised, and educated in Utah—a home she loves dearly but also dearly loves to escape whenever she can travel the world. She received a BA in French Studies and a Master of Public Health, both from Brigham Young University.

Word crafting has always fascinated and motivated her, but it wasn't until a few years ago that she considered writing her own stories. When she isn't writing, she is honing her photography skills, looking for travel deals, and spending time with her husband and children. She lives with her husband and twin boys in Vineyard, Utah.

Printed in Great Britain
by Amazon

82987755R00171